MISTER CREECHER

A NOVEL
IN THREE PARTS

BY
CHRIS PRIESTLEY

B L O O M S B U R Y

LONDON   BERLIN   NEW YORK   SYDNEY

Bloomsbury Publishing, London, Berlin, New York and Sydney

First published in Great Britain in October 2011 by
Bloomsbury Publishing Plc
50 Bedford Square, London, WC1B 3DP

This edition published in March 2012

A CIP catalogue record for this book is available from the British Library

ISBN 978 1 4088 1105 4

Typeset by Hewer Text UK Ltd, Edinburgh
Printed in Great Britain by Clays Ltd, St Ives Plc, Bungay, Suffolk

1 3 5 7 9 10 8 6 4 2

www.bloomsbury.com
www.chrispriestley.blogspot.com

CIRCLE LINE

AROUND LONDON IN A SMALL BOAT

CIRCLE LINE

Summersdale Publishers Ltd
46 West Street
Chichester
West Sussex
PO19 1RP
UK

www.summersdale.com

Printed and bound in the UK by CPI Group (UK) Ltd, Croydon, CR0 4YY

ISBN: 978-1-84953-293-8

THE TALES OF TERROR COLLECTION

'Wonderfully macabre and beautifully
crafted horror stories'
Chris Riddell

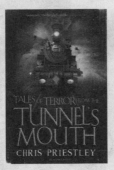

'Guaranteed to give you nightmares'
Observer

HAUNTING BOOKSHOPS NOW

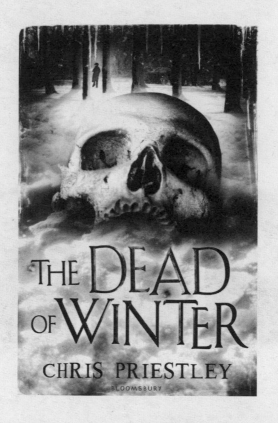

ABOUT THE AUTHOR

Chris Priestley has found great success with his beautifully judged and macabre stories for younger readers. He is the author of the chilling and brilliant *Tales of Terror* series, nominated for many awards, and *The Dead of Winter*, nominated for the 2011 Carnegie Medal, and *Death and the Arrow* (2004), nominated for an Edgar Award. He has published thirteen books to date. He is also a talented artist and illustrator. His cartoons have been published in the *Independent* and other national newspapers. Chris lives in Cambridge, where he continues to write his seriously scary stories.

MISTER CREECHER

Also by Chris Priestley

The Tales of Terror Collection:

Uncle Montague's Tales of Terror
Tales of Terror from the Black Ship
Tales of Terror from the Tunnel's Mouth

———◆———

The Dead of Winter

For my father, Tom Priestley

PART I.

CHAPTER I.

Billy pulled his clammy coat collar tightly to his throat. It was damp with the fog and felt like the tongue of a dead animal lolling against his neck. His thin body shivered and trembled. He was fifteen but looked eight. A fever sweat glistened on his forehead. His breaths were short; they puffed from his mouth in feeble wisps.

He walked warily out into Finsbury Square. The fog gathered here, undisturbed, ominous. Billy carried a small cocoon of visibility with him, so that, as he walked, it was as if the world outside this bubble were as yet unformed and he invented his part of it at every step.

It was late and the owners of the pocket watches and handkerchiefs that Billy predated were safely home and happy by their firesides, sipping brandy, counting their blessings and their money.

Amber light seeped like honey from upstairs windows, glowing between the heavy curtains and solid shutters that formed a barrier to the cold and to the fear-filled world beyond.

Voices likewise seeped out into the dank night air: the happy hubbub of laughter and good cheer. Then the giddy tumble of church bells rang out across the city and Billy heard the sound of toasts and singing, and the cold gnawed more deeply into his bones. It was January 1st: New Year's Day, 1818.

Billy was sick. He had been sick before, but this was different. He grabbed the nearby metal railing for support. It burned his hand with its fierce chill. Tiny forests of white crystals were sprouting over metal and wood, over bricks and cobbles. Minute thorns of ice prickled over every surface. The fog seemed to close in around Billy. Soon it would simply erase him and everything he had been. All would dissolve into that desolate nothingness.

The gilding at the edge of the wooden sign overhead flickered with the light from a nearby lamp. The painted letters spelled out *Lackington, Hughes, Harding, Mavor & Jones – Publishers*. Billy had worked the customers at this bookshop. They were easy targets as they left, their faces fixed on the pages of their new books, their minds elsewhere.

The shadow of the sign fell across a body lying against the wall beside the publisher's doorway, face down and motionless. Billy knew a dead body when he saw one. The hands were as colourless as rancid meat. There was no sound, no movement.

He looked at it with the cynical detachment that years on the street had gifted him. He did not know this man and did not care how he had lived or how he came to die. Only the rich could afford to be sentimental. He cared for no one but himself. He was alone. Everyone was.

As ill as he felt, Billy could not bring himself to ignore a possible treasure. This body was a resource to be made the most of. This was a tree that might have fruit to be picked.

Billy had already gathered from the briefest of glances that the clothes would be of no use to him at all. The man was huge. Even though he made his coat look small, Billy could see that it would smother him. Time to see what the pockets of that coat concealed.

He looked about him. He had a feeling there was someone watching, but then he always had that. It was what made him sharp, what gave him his edge. He lived his life on the balls of his feet, always ready to run. But he didn't have the strength to run tonight. Perhaps it was Death waiting in the fog.

As he bent down to the corpse, his eyelids became heavy, his vision blurred. He was shaking now more than shivering. Billy had seen more bodies than he could remember: who could live on the streets of London and not? The dead were just another waste product of this great machine of a city – like smoke and sewage.

Old age did not seem to be the cause of death: Billy could not see his face clearly, but his hair was long and raven black. Chances were he had been murdered or had died of some disease or other. *Perhaps*, thought Billy, *he simply died of want*. Hunger could kill you stone-cold dead without any hue and cry. Want was a murderer who never swung.

The world seemed momentarily to slither to one side and Billy almost fell, face first, on to the corpse at his feet. He steadied himself, blinking his eyes back into focus.

There were no obvious signs that the man had been attacked: no blood on the ground or on his clothes, no cuts, no gashes. But a cudgel was as deadly as a knife in the right hands. Billy had seen it done. More than once.

He touched the body's blue-white hand. It was as cold as a hangman's heart. He'd probably been dead for hours. A rime of frost was forming on his clothes like a white mould. He had more than likely been robbed already, but Billy owed it to himself to check.

'So,' said a voice behind him. 'What have we here?'

Billy's heart skipped a beat. He knew that voice anywhere. It was Fletcher. Immediately he looked right and left, trying to size up which gave him the best route for escape, but he could already see the shadowy figures in the mist.

'I never had you down as a killer, Billy,' said Fletcher, walking slowly forward out of the fog, so that he seemed to materialise out of the blankness like a thought: a nasty, vicious thought.

'I didn't kill him, Fletcher. He was dead when I got here. Honest.'

Out of the corner of his eye, Billy saw the arrival of Skinner and Tyke, two of Fletcher's toughest cronies.

'Honest?' said Fletcher. 'You? I'm surprised you've got the nerve to even use the word. Why don't we call for a constable and see what he thinks?'

Fletcher's boys chortled at this idea, but Billy knew that Fletcher was never going to call a constable.

'You cheated me, Billy,' said Fletcher. 'And I don't take kindly to being cheated.'

'I'll pay you back,' said Billy. 'You know I will.'

'I don't know nothing of the sort!' shouted Fletcher.

His voice cut its way through the fog and skittered across the icy cobbles like a dropped knife. Billy noticed that he had moved a little closer.

'That's what I was doing, just now,' said Billy. 'I thought the stiff might have some goods on him. I was going to bring them straight to you, I swear.'

'Billy, Billy, Billy,' said Fletcher with a sigh. 'The time for paying back has gone. Tyke – check the pockets.'

Fletcher smiled briefly and clicked his neck.

'Truth is,' he continued in a soft, conspiratorial tone, putting his arm round Billy's shivering shoulders. 'Truth is, I'm going to have to hurt you.'

Billy whimpered and tried to pull away. Fletcher's grip tightened. Billy could smell the gin on his breath.

'I don't want to hurt you,' Fletcher murmured. 'I like you, Billy. I've always liked you. Weren't

it me who looked after you when you run away?
But what would it look like if I was to let you
show that kind of disrespect?'

Billy knew Fletcher was blind in one eye, but
he could not for the life of him recall which. He
was sure it might be some kind of advantage
to him if he could just remember, but both eyes
looked equally dead and Fletcher seemed to read
his mind.

'You looking at my eye?'

Billy knew that no reply was necessary, so
made none. He just wanted Fletcher to get on
with whatever beating he was going to hand out.
He had been beaten before. As long as nothing
broke you were all right. Billy sometimes felt he
was one big scar. He was suddenly so very tired.

'I was born with only the one eye working,'
Fletcher went on. 'Probably on account of my
mother being blind drunk when she had me.' He
chuckled throatily at this joke, but no one else
was foolish enough to join him.

'You'd think that would have held me back, but
no – it's made me what I am. You see the world
clearer with one eye. I'm going to give you that
gift, Billy.'

With one deft movement, Fletcher brought
out a huge clasp knife and flicked the blade out

in front of Billy, his ashen face reflecting in the pitted steel. But before he could make another move there was a screech of such animal wildness from Tyke that Fletcher, Billy, the whole of London and Time itself seemed to freeze in wonder at it.

All eyes – including Fletcher's blank left eye – turned to the sound. The corpse that Tyke had been in the course of searching was now standing up and had him gripped by the arm.

'It's alive!' shouted Skinner. 'It's alive!'

If that had not been enough, the reanimated corpse was easily the tallest man Billy had ever seen and certainly the ugliest. This giant must have been nigh on seven feet tall – maybe even eight. His lank black hair fell across his face like trickles of ink, partly, but not wholly, obscuring a face that looked as though it had been hanging at Execution Dock for many days and had had the Thames washing over it, tide after tide.

His eyes were limpid and, though shadowed by his furrowed brow, still managed to catch what little light there was. They seemed so alive compared to the rest of him.

'Libberrrrerrrr legarrrrrsssonnnn!' growled the giant, pointing at Billy.

This gravelly, guttural outburst was greeted by a few moments of astonished, uncomprehending silence.

'What the hell . . . ?' said Fletcher, his voice sounding thin.

The giant tightened his hold on Tyke's forearm, turning it as he did so. Tyke's scream died in a gurgling croak and the relative silence allowed for a sound like a chicken leg being twisted apart. He dropped to the cobbles and screamed again.

'Layliberrrrrerrrrr!' growled the giant, without once looking at the writhing Tyke at his feet. Billy felt another wave of weakness wash the life from his limbs and his eyes drifted out of focus. Had Fletcher not still had hold of him, he would have dropped to the ground like Tyke.

Fletcher seemed uncertain as to what to do next. The first to react was Skinner, who had already pulled a knife from his coat pocket and now lunged at the giant.

The giant barely seemed to move, but Billy saw the knife fall to the ground as the stranger grabbed Skinner by the throat and, holding him at arm's length, began to lift him slowly into the air.

Skinner enjoyed his pies. He was not your normal skin-and-bones street urchin. He was big.

He was heavy. Billy stared in disbelief. What kind of man was this?

The stranger flung Skinner away as though he were nothing but the stinking clothes he was wearing. The boy landed with a sickening clang against the nearby railings and lay in a motionless heap.

Billy could sense the conflicting emotions in Fletcher: should he leap to attack this giant while he had the chance, should he run – or should he carve a piece out of Billy before he went?

Billy felt sure he had decided on the latter and shut his eyes, waiting for the cold kiss of the knife blade, but opened them immediately as he heard the giant, with a speed and agility that belied his size, come rushing forward.

Before Fletcher had time to move or cry out, the giant grabbed his right arm. Billy heard the wrist bone snap and Fletcher's knife fell to the pavement.

Fletcher was tough if nothing else and, broken wrist or not, he fought back. He kicked and lashed out with his good arm, but it was to no avail. The giant struck him with a fearsome blow to the side of the head and he dropped like a sack of flour. He did not stir.

When Billy turned away from Fletcher, he found himself staring straight at the giant's chest. He looked up. The giant looked down. His skin had the almost translucent look of a drowned man Billy had once seen by London Bridge. *Perhaps this is what Death looks like*, thought Billy. Or *his* death, at any rate.

The giant leaned forward, staring at Billy with the bemused look of a snake about to strike. The fog seemed to rush forward suddenly, and then there was nothing.

CHAPTER II.

Billy was flying, floating a few feet off the ground. His head lolled back and forth. When he opened his eyes, the world lolled queasily along with him, as if he were bobbing on a boat adrift on ocean waves.

The scene was blurred, as though viewed through greasy glass. His eyelids flickered, never fully open, never fully closed. Everything he saw seemed determined to slide away and out of sight; all solid objects had lost their moorings.

Noises washed across his ears but Billy could not identify them. They merged and surged, sometimes echoing loudly inside his head, other times faint and barely audible.

He felt chilled to the marrow. The air was cold on his clammy face and he became aware of being pressed up against something even colder.

'Where now?' came a voice near his ear.

Billy lifted his head and peered into the distance. He was dreaming. He must be. He could see features he recognised – a shop sign, a crooked railing, a shabby courtyard with an alleyway beyond.

'That way,' said a voice so faint and far away that it took him a few moments to realise it was his own.

———◆———

Billy was inside now – he was sure of it. Warmer: the air was warmer, but he still felt cold. He shivered and found that once he started he could not stop.

The shivering rattled his jaw and joints and seemed set on dislocating every bone in his body. His teeth chattered and the harsh noise clattered horribly in his head.

Billy blinked, and blinked again, screwing up his eyes, trying to focus on something, anything. But the world seemed resistant to all his attempts to make it solid.

Maybe I've died, he thought. *Maybe this is what the world looks like when you die.* But if he was dead, then where was this? He was fairly sure that he wouldn't gain entry through heaven's pearly gates, but it didn't look much like hell either.

Maybe he was in that other place: the place where you waited to have your fate decided. He tried to remember its name but could not recall it. Perhaps this was all there was.

Billy now became aware that there was a large shadow some feet away. Or at least it seemed as dark and formless as a shadow. He strained his eyes, trying to will some clarity into the black smudge in front of him, but instead of becoming clearer, it merely grew and shifted its shape.

The shadow grew and seemed to flood the room with darkness, swirling like a cloud of smoke, and then, out of this inky vagueness, a terrible face loomed towards him. Billy cried out and covered his face with his arms, cowering on the floor, not daring to look back and see if it had gone.

Sleep overtook him. It was a chill, comfortless sleep, but still it came, pulling him down into oblivion. He opened his eyes but the darkness remained. He could taste the soot in his mouth and knew that he was a climbing boy once more, wedged inside a chimney.

The sweep was barking orders into the fireplace below. His sharp tone carried the threat of a beating to come. Billy took a deep, gasping breath and gagged on the soot as it rushed into his nostrils and throat.

The chimney was narrow, but Billy was skinny – deliberately starved by the sweep. 'It's for your own good,' he'd say. 'Don't want to get stuck half-way, do ya?'

His feet were jammed against the brickwork of the chimney, his elbows finding purchase on a small ledge. He felt so tired, so very tired. He wondered if he would be able to hold on much longer.

Looking down, he saw the tiny, vague shape of the hearth way below. How could it be so far? He gulped with fear, gagging on the dry soot. A fall now would be the end. All he needed to do was let go and it would all be over.

Billy looked up and saw daylight above him, visible through the chimney-pot opening like a full moon in a black, black night. He dropped his brush, letting it clatter far below, and began to climb towards the light.

CHAPTER III.

Billy woke with a start, as he always did. He was catlike: almost as alert in sleep as he was awake. But he was drowsier than usual. He tried to concentrate. A dream ... A strange dream ...

Lemon-coloured light was raking the gloom with long beams, illuminating galaxies of dust motes swirling in infinity in front of his waking eyes. At the far edge of this universe sat the giant who had made such a mess of Fletcher and his gang.

Billy jerked back, scrabbling with his feet until his back hit a wall and he came to a sudden halt. The movement had been a mistake. His head reeled and he felt sick. Where was he?

'Rrrrest,' growled the giant.

'What?' said Billy groggily. 'You can talk?'

The giant nodded. Billy tried to get up, but the dizziness overcame him and he sank back down.

'Fever,' said the giant.

Billy's mind seemed to be filled with the same tumbling dust motes as the room.

'Fletcher,' he said, frowning. 'What happened?'

'That was three days ago.'

'Three days ...' But Billy did not finish. He shook his head and closed his eyes, half expecting the giant to be gone when he opened them, but he was still there. This was no fever dream.

'Wait,' said Billy, squinting. 'I know this place. We're in the attic above the baker's in Chalk Street.'

This was one of Billy's favourite hideaways, something he had managed to keep to himself. The heat from the baker's ovens made it unbearable in summer, but in winter it was a lifesaver.

'You brought us here,' said the giant.

'What?' said Billy. 'Yes. I remember. I was floating.'

Billy still felt like he was floating. His head seemed light. His own voice caused him pain, it sounded so loud. The giant's growl was deafening. Billy winced, narrowing his eyes.

'I carried you,' said the giant.

His voice was thick with an accent – the accent of the French weavers in Spitalfields.

'And you looked after me?' said Billy.

The giant nodded slowly.

'Why? Who are you?'

'Sleeeeeep,' said the giant, leaning towards him.

It seemed more of a command than a recommendation, and Billy had no desire to argue with whoever – whatever – this stranger was. Besides, sleep did seem appealing all of a sudden . . .

———————

Billy looked around for the giant. He was not always there when Billy woke up and if Billy had been stronger he would have climbed out of the window and run for it. But he had already tried to stand and found that his legs did not share his enthusiasm for escape.

In any case, the giant was back. Billy could see him sitting at the far end of the attic. There was a pale yellow glow seeping through the window. Morning? Evening? It was hard to tell.

Billy's vision was clearer now and the fog that had clouded his mind had also begun to dissolve. Even so, he found it difficult to find the courage to speak.

'Hey?' he said.

The giant slowly raised his head and Billy saw his watery eyes twinkle in the gloom.

'You are awake?' said the giant.

He was so large that he would have put his head through the roof had he stood up. He moved slowly towards Billy on his hands and knees, and the sight of it made Billy take a sharp, stuttering intake of breath.

'Why are you helping me?' said Billy.

'You needed help,' said the giant with a shrug.

Billy raised a quizzical eyebrow.

'You think because of . . . how I look,' the giant said with a curl of his lip, '. . . you think I must be without goodness?'

'I don't know,' said Billy.

'You think I am a demon, no?'

'I don't know what you are,' said Billy, but he knew that he did not like the word 'demon' being mentioned.

The giant grinned unpleasantly.

'Maybe I am the Devil himself?' he snarled.

'What?' said Billy nervously.

'Yes . . .' The giant seemed pleased at the notion. 'I am surely cursed as Satan was cursed, shunned as he was shunned. There can be no heaven for me, on Earth or elsewhere. For me there is only hell.'

It ain't no fairytale for me neither, Billy thought. But he said, 'You certainly gave old Fletcher a taste of hell, and no mistake.'

A wave of dizziness came over him and he closed his eyes. When he opened them everything seemed far away and blurred.

'Fletcherrrr?' said the giant, rolling the syllables round in his mouth as if tasting them. Billy had never seen such white teeth.

'Yeah,' he said, struggling to concentrate. 'You remember – the one who was planning to winkle my eyeball out. Is he dead?'

The giant shrugged disinterestedly.

'Look, what do you want with me?' said Billy, wincing at the sound of his own voice and dropping it to a whisper. It felt as though someone had taken the top of his head off while he slept. His brain felt raw and tender, his thoughts exposed.

The giant did not reply. He was staring at his own massive blue-grey hands, turning them over and staring first at the palms and then at the backs – staring as if he had never seen them before or as if they belonged to someone else.

'Mister!' shouted Billy, the sound of his own voice rattling round in his head like dice in a cup. The giant turned and looked at him. 'Can you hear me?'

The giant tilted his head to one side.

'Yes,' he replied in a low rumbling voice.

'Who are you?' said Billy, blinking, trying to focus his sleepy vision.

'Who?' said the giant.

'You,' said Billy, jabbing his finger towards the stranger's face.

'Me?' said the giant, prodding his own chest.

'You,' repeated Billy. 'What do they call you?'

The giant frowned and mumbled a reply.

'Creecher, is it?' said Billy, looking surreptitiously for an escape route. 'Well, I suppose I ought to thank you, Mister Creecher.'

'Monsieur Creecher?' repeated the giant slowly. After a pause, he began to laugh – or at least that was what Billy assumed the strange wheezing sound to be.

Billy raised an eyebrow. Who was this strange foreign monster of a man? Was he from a freak show? Had he escaped from Bedlam?

'My name's Billy.'

'Bill-ly . . .' said Creecher.

'Will you stop repeating everything I say, for goodness' sake!'

Creecher stared at him malevolently. Billy let out a nervous laugh.

'Sorry, sorry. Didn't mean to shout at you. Where are you from?' he asked hurriedly. 'You ain't from London, are you? Or England neither. Where are you from?'

'Frrrrrom?' said Creecher. He looked puzzled by the question.

'Yeah,' said Billy, then speaking more slowly and carefully, in the voice he used on tourists before he relieved them of their watches, *'where are you from? Where did you come from to get here?'*

Creecher frowned and seemed lost in thought. Did he have to think about where he was from, or was he trying to come up with a lie? Billy wondered if the giant had been knocked on the head after all. *Maybe his brains have been scrambled*, he thought. Then something appeared to spark in the stranger's mind.

'Switzerland,' said Creecher.

'Swissland?' said Billy. 'I thought you was French. The accent. Sounds French. You sure you're not French?'

Creecher made no reply. Swiss? Billy was none the wiser. His geography was a little limited. He knew London like the back of his hand – rather better actually. But outside of the city was foreign to him. Switzerland, France, Wales – it was all the same to Billy.

'I was born here. In London,' said Billy. 'Ain't never been anywhere else.'

The giant said nothing and the silence was somehow dreadful and Billy felt obliged to fill it.

'I'm an orphan,' he went on. 'Mother died when I was eight. Never knew my father. He left when I was just a baby, or so my mother said.'

Billy was surprised to see a look of sympathy pass over the giant's terrible face. Creecher shook his head and tears welled in his eyes. Whether the tears were for Billy or for himself, Billy could not tell.

'What brought you here, then?' said Billy, raising himself up and rubbing his eyes.

'A ship,' said Creecher.

'No, no,' said Billy, shaking his head. This was going to be hard work. 'What I mean is – why have you come? You don't look like a tourist to me.'

The giant did not reply.

'So how come you were stretched out in Finsbury Square?'

'I do not know,' said Creecher, frowning, clearly trying to remember. 'I must have slept.'

'Slept?' said Billy. 'In that weather?'

Billy remembered how sure he had been that Creecher was dead when he had found him that night. His fear of the giant came back suddenly. He shuddered and felt his heart flutter like a trapped moth. Creecher must have noticed.

'Ugly,' he said, waving his hand towards his face.

'I've seen worse,' said Billy pointlessly. They both knew it was not true.

Creecher seemed to slip into a daydream once more and Billy thought about getting to his feet and making a run for it. But he did not have the strength.

He was a fearful monster, but he could have snapped him in two an hour ago if that was what he wanted, Billy reasoned. Besides, had not he saved Billy's life? Not once but twice: from Fletcher and then from the fever.

'What do you want with me?' said Billy.

'Rest,' said Creecher. 'I will fetch food. When it is dark.'

CHAPTER IV.

Billy drifted in and out of consciousness for the next few hours, before eventually sitting up and stretching his aching muscles.

The room was almost entirely dark save for a bluish glow coming through the partly opened shutters of the attic window nearby. Though the shadows were big enough to hide the giant, Billy was sure that he was alone.

He had not only awoken from sleep. He had completely shed his fever too, he sensed. He felt light-headed with hunger, but that was all. Now was the time to get out and away from Creecher and whatever he had planned.

Billy got to his feet a little too quickly and had to steady himself, bright spots dancing before his eyes. He was about to push open the shutters and climb out on to the roof when he felt his body stiffen. He began to limber up – to get his lazy muscles going. He needed to move before the giant came back.

But where exactly was he intending to go? Creecher did not seem to know if Fletcher was dead, and if Fletcher was alive then sooner or later their paths would cross. Fletcher wasn't going to be satisfied with an eye this time.

Billy found himself imagining how sweet it would be if Creecher were with him when he met Fletcher. Creecher might finish the job this time. Until Fletcher was dealt with, London was not safe for Billy.

But how safe was Billy with Creecher, whoever – whatever – he was? Just as he was sizing these thoughts up in his mind, he sensed that something was outside and heading his way.

Instead of opening the shutters, Billy returned to the pile of sacks and hessian rags that had served as his bed for the last few days and lay back down, trying to look as though he had never stirred.

No sooner had he done so than the shutters opened and Creecher dropped through the window. Billy marvelled at how it was possible for so large a man to move so quietly. He had heard nothing of the giant's approach across the tiles and he had a thief's hearing.

Creecher had dropped to his haunches and now rose up like a shadow and moved towards

Billy. The boy let out an involuntary whimper at the giant's approach and flinched as Creecher's hands thrust towards him.

'Food,' said Creecher. 'Eat.'

Billy now saw the loaf and grabbed it greedily. He had taken several mouthfuls before he remembered to say a muffled, 'Thank you.'

Creecher had withdrawn to his side of the attic and was eating his own loaf of bread. There was a small sack between them.

'What's in the bag?' Billy asked.

'Chicken.'

Billy was out from under his rags in a flash. He dashed across the filthy floorboards and pounced on the bag. He shoved in his hand and pulled out a whole roast chicken. The smell made him giddy and he had to sit down. He held it out to Creecher.

'Here,' he said. 'You ought to have first go.'

Creecher shook his head.

'I do not eat . . . flesh,' he said.

There seemed something particularly unlikely about this great hulking beast denying himself the taste of meat.

'You don't want any?' said Billy. 'You're sure?'

Creecher smiled and shook his head again.

'Yes,' he replied, pointing at Billy. 'It is all yours.'

Billy did not need telling twice. He retreated to his side of the attic with his prize and set about it with all the delicacy of a ravenous wolf, slumping back a little drunkenly when he had finished. The food sat heavily in his stomach, but he liked the feeling. It seemed to warm him from the inside.

Billy's wits had now fully returned, and now he was well fed he felt better able to cope with the strange situation he found himself in. He still felt a vivid, visceral fear of the giant, but it no longer seemed to immobilise him.

He belched and looked at Creecher. He had studiously ignored him while eating. The giant's monstrous form was not good for the appetite. Billy saw that he was now huddled over a book.

It was an extraordinary sight. The book looked tiny in the giant's massive grip. What was this weird creature, this frightful demon who did not eat meat, this growling brute who read books?

'How can you read in this light?' asked Billy. He could barely see the giant in that gloom.

Creecher shrugged.

'What's the book?'

'*Persuasion*,' Creecher replied.

'Yeah?' said Billy. 'What's it about?'

'It is about a woman who loves a man, but he is thought unsuitable by her family.'

'Why's that, then?' said Billy.

'He is not rich enough.'

Billy snorted.

'Sounds about right. Who wrote that, then?'

'Jane Austen,' said Creecher.

Billy laughed out loud. Even he had heard of Jane Austen. Creecher scowled at him.

'What is so funny?'

'That's a woman's book!' Billy said. 'It's a novel, ain't it? Only women read novels!'

Creecher gave him a withering look and turned back to his reading.

'Sorry, sorry,' said Billy.

Creecher ignored him.

'Seriously, I didn't mean to hurt your feelings.' Billy tried to suppress a snigger. 'I've just never seen a man read a novel before.'

'Lots of men write novels and lots of men read novels,' said Creecher. 'Besides – it helps me with my English.'

Billy observed that the giant's accent already seemed less noticeable than it had before.

'Any good?' he asked. 'The book, I mean.'

'Not bad,' said the giant. 'Don't you read?'

'Yeah,' said Billy defensively. 'I can read if I have to. My mother taught me. She said I'd never amount to anything if I couldn't read. Ha! Can't see the point of stories, though. They're for children, aren't they? And women.'

He could not stop himself laughing again. When he looked up he saw that the giant was studying him.

'You say your mother taught you,' said Creecher. 'You did not go to school?'

'No,' said Billy. 'I was brought up in the workhouse.'

'But your mother could read?'

'Yeah,' said Billy. 'She'd fallen on hard times and . . . and, well, she had me.'

Creecher nodded.

'Your father?'

Billy shook his head.

'I never knew him,' he said. 'He left me and my mother to fend for ourselves. Didn't care about her. Didn't care about me. I hate him. He's probably dead anyway. I hope he is.'

The giant seemed to take a moment to absorb all this information, and again, Billy was surprised to see a gentle look pass over his terrible face.

'And how did you come to be a thief?' said the giant.

'I was a climbing boy for a chimney sweep, but I ran away.'

'Why?'

Billy shrugged and looked away. 'We didn't get on.'

'And so you steal,' said the giant.

Billy bristled at the disapproving tone.

'What about you?' he asked.

The giant did not reply.

'How you paying for all this food?' said Billy. 'You rich, then, are you? You don't look rich.'

The giant frowned.

'I am not a thief. I take only what I need,' he growled.

'Don't we all, Swiss,' said Billy.

He leaned back against the wall, cradling his swollen belly in his hands, and winced. He needed to get away and think.

'Look, thanks for the grub. But you still ain't said why you're looking after me. It's not that I ain't grateful, you understand. I don't have you down as the charitable type, so I'm guessing you want something from me. What?'

The giant took so long to respond that Billy almost asked again, but just as he opened his mouth to speak, Creecher leaned forward. The giant might not eat flesh, but he smelled like a butcher's gutter.

'Yes,' he said quietly. 'I do have work for you. But you will need to come with me. Are you well enough?'

Billy nodded. He would be glad to get out of that stuffy room and fill his lungs with some cold London air – glad, too, to put some space between himself and Creecher. But what work could he possibly do for this monster?

CHAPTER V.

Creecher waited while Billy stood and climbed through the window and on to the roof. Billy had been this way so many times he did not need the moonlight to show him down to the alleyway behind the baker's.

Creecher's descent was as alarmingly silent as his approach had been, and he dropped noiselessly to stand next to Billy, his feet barely registering a sound. A ghost would have made more of a din.

'So,' said Billy, 'what are we doing? Where are we going?'

'We must walk towards the river, near to Waterloo Bridge.'

Billy hugged himself.

'Don't you feel the cold?' he asked.

'Oui,' said the giant, nodding. 'I feel the cold. It is in my bones always.'

'What's the name of the place we're going to, then?' Billy asked. 'What street?'

'Whale Street,' said Creecher. 'Come.'

Billy grabbed Creecher's arm as the giant set off and he spun round with terrifying suddenness. Billy recoiled and raised his hands defensively.

'Whoa!' he said. 'I know Whale Street, all right. But this way's quicker.'

Creecher looked at Billy and nodded. Billy headed off without saying another word. He did not need to look round to check if the giant was with him. He could sense it somehow.

Besides, he did not want to see Creecher behind him. It was all he could do as it was to stop himself from running. He did not want to turn and see that inky shape, smudged by darkness. The sight of him in clear light was bad enough, but what a horror it would be to see him vague and spectral.

Billy led the way, moving quickly and smoothly through narrow alleyways, down winding flights of weathered steps and out across deserted squares, pausing only occasionally at corners to check the wide streets.

The air was even colder down here by the river. Billy could feel it enter his lungs and linger coldly there, chilling his chest. He could taste the stink of it in his mouth. He coughed and spat and looked behind him for the first time to find Creecher almost standing on his heels.

'Don't do that!' hissed Billy. 'How can you be so big and creep up on someone like that? It ain't natural.'

Creecher made no response but motioned for Billy to follow him into an alleyway, where they stopped and looked back out into the street. The giant was staring intently at the building opposite.

When they had been standing like that for several minutes, Billy took a deep breath and let out as big a sigh as he could muster. Creecher did not break off from his vigil.

'What?' said Billy finally. 'What are we waiting for?'

'Be quiet,' said Creecher.

It was spoken with such understated menace that Billy's heart skipped a beat.

'Look,' said Creecher, pointing to the door of the building as two men stepped out on to the pavement and walked away towards Covent Garden. After giving them a head start, Creecher set off in pursuit, with Billy at his heels.

The men crossed the Strand and headed up Southampton Street. Billy knew these streets well. Tourists and drunks were easy pickings and there were plenty of both here. He stayed close to Creecher. If Fletcher was alive, he was as likely to be here as anywhere.

Creecher kept away from the lamplight's glare. Billy marvelled at how darkness seemed to cling to him. Those who caught a glimpse of the giant saw only a fleeting phantasm of blackness and chose to question their senses rather than accept the unnerving truth of what they had seen.

The two men walked into the throng of people and disappeared now and then among them. They stopped by the columns of a church. Billy and Creecher were near enough to hear them talking to one another in what sounded like French to Billy's ears. Had Creecher followed these men from Swissland? A busker sang mournfully nearby.

'Do you see those men?' asked Creecher, as if he and Billy had not been following them for the past half hour.

'Course I see them,' said Billy. 'What of it?'

'I want you to follow them,' he replied.

'Why?'

'That is of no concern to you,' said Creecher. 'If you follow them, I will reward you.'

Billy looked at the men and wondered what connection Creecher could have with them.

Unlike him, they seemed perfectly normal. They also appeared to be wealthy.

'Why can't you follow them yourself?' he asked.

'By day I am . . . too visible,' said Creecher. 'And I am known to one of them.'

Billy was intrigued. But not intrigued enough to want the job. He screwed up his face.

'I don't think so,' he said.

'You don't think so?' said Creecher.

'Look,' Billy explained, 'like I said – I'm grateful to you for looking after me and if I had some way of paying you I would.'

'I don't want money,' said Creecher. 'I want your help.'

There was something in the giant's tone of voice that made Billy think twice about arguing. But still, he saw no reason to get mixed up in whatever it was that was going on here.

Billy spat at the gutter and sent a rat scurrying from its hiding place into the glare of the gas lamps. It paused briefly in its headlong sprint to look for the nearest shadows, its black button eyes squinting at the lamplight.

The two foreigners were being swallowed up in the crowd of theatregoers spilling out of the opera house. Beggars and thieves buzzed about like flies round a cowpat.

'Well?' said Creecher.

But Billy's attention was elsewhere. Two boys lurked in front of a chestnut-seller's brazier. They were hardly more than silhouettes but he recognised one of them straight away by the bite-sized chunk missing from his left ear.

Warner was one of Fletcher's boys and no sooner had Billy registered the fact than Warner saw him. He pretended that he hadn't, but he had, Billy could tell.

After a minute or two, Warner tapped the other boy on the arm and leaned towards him, whispering. The other boy wasn't as practised as Warner and could not resist a sideways glance at Billy and got a swift kick in the ankle as reward. The two boys slunk away into an alley like lizards into a crack in a wall.

Billy turned and walked away in the opposite direction. He walked with an unhurried air completely at odds with the drum roll of his heartbeat. But he had not gone more than a few strides before he heard a familiar rumbling voice.

'Where are you going?'

Billy did not turn round, but quickened his pace. The giant overtook him in the blink of an eye and blocked his way. Billy looked up at him and was shocked anew to see that pallid, wrinkled face and the watery gleam of those eyes. A woman came out from a doorway, took one look at Creecher and dropped to the floor in a faint.

'Where are you going?' Creecher repeated softly, stepping over the woman.

'Fletcher ain't dead,' said Billy. 'I can feel it. I've got to keep moving.'

'Those two boys?' Creecher asked.

'They're in Fletcher's gang,' said Billy. 'They'll go straight to him.'

He tried to walk on, but the giant placed one of his huge hands on Billy's shoulder and he had to stop himself from whimpering at its cold and heavy touch.

'Leave me alone,' said Billy, his voice quavering now like he was eight years old and a climbing boy again, pleading with the sweep not to beat him.

'I can protect you,' said Creecher.

'You can't be around all the time. Even you have to sleep, don't you?'

'Yes,' said Creecher with a slow nod. 'I have to sleep. But will you be any safer without me?'

Billy swore and put his face in his hands.

'If you hadn't –'

'If I hadn't stopped him, the one called Fletcher would have taken your eye.'

'Well, he ain't going to stop at an eye now, is he?' Billy snarled. 'He's gonna kill me for sure. And not quick, neither.'

'No,' said Creecher. 'He will not kill you. I will see to it.'

Billy squinted up at the giant, but his horrible face seemed devoid of any expression.

'I ain't asking you to kill him!' said Billy.

Creecher did not respond.

'Not that anyone would mourn him,' Billy added. 'But still – I never said I wanted him dead. You can't say I did, cos I didn't!'

Billy looked at the giant, who once again seemed to have edged into the darker side of the alley, as if he carried his own shadow with him.

'And all I have to do is follow these two men round London?'

Creecher nodded.

'How will I know you'll keep your side of the bargain?' said Billy. 'How will I know that Fletcher won't jump on me one –'

With horrible suddenness, Creecher moved towards Billy, grabbing him by the throat and pinning him to the wall.

'Because when I say I will do a thing, I do it,' he hissed, his rancid breath making Billy blink. Again the giant looked back towards Covent Garden and the two foreigners. 'Unlike some.'

His fingers tightened their grip on Billy's throat. He seemed to be lost in thought and Billy tugged at his arm to try to pull him away as he gasped for breath. It took several hard punches at the giant's forearm before Creecher looked back at Billy and released him.

Billy slumped down, choking. Creecher stood over him, watching without a trace of emotion.

'We are bound together, you and I,' growled the giant. 'Our destinies have become entwined for the present.'

Billy rubbed his throat and took special note of that 'for the present'. What would this devil do to him when his use was over? Crack his neck and hurl him in the Thames, most like. Billy felt as though he were running along a high rooftop, each tile slipping at his footfall and ever on the verge of plunging to his doom.

The woman who had fainted moaned and began to get up from the cold cobbles. She blinked and peered at Creecher, who turned to her and growled. The woman whimpered and swooned once again.

'I will meet you back at the attic,' said Creecher.

With that, the giant walked away. Within moments, Billy was alone in the alleyway and, for the first time since those early days on the streets as a runaway, he began to sob.

CHAPTER VI.

Billy stole a loaf on the way back to the room above the baker's. He almost hoped he would get caught. Maybe that was the only way to be free of Fletcher and the giant both: to get thrown in Newgate and transported.

But Billy was incapable of being a bad thief. It was like asking a falcon to slow its flight. It just wasn't in his nature. *You are what you are*, thought Billy. *That's all there is. That's all there ever is.*

He slept, though he thought he would not, and dreamed like a dog, twitching and muttering at the passage of the day's events.

Then, what seemed like seconds later, it was morning and he awoke with Creecher's pale blue-white face huge and filling his view.

'I wish you wouldn't do that!' said Billy, recoiling.

Creecher stood up and tossed a pie at Billy's feet before walking to the other side of the attic and dropping to his haunches.

'Eat,' he said.

'Give us a chance,' Billy replied, yawning.

He picked up the pie and took a bite out of the pastry crust, crumbs tumbling to the floor. He nodded his approval to the giant, who smiled back out of the gloom, his white teeth glowing horribly.

'Well, you seem to be in a good mood at any rate,' said Billy.

The giant's white smile was instantaneously eclipsed.

'You are feeling stronger today,' he said.

It was less a question than a statement of fact, and Billy nodded in agreement.

'Bon. Then tomorrow you are ready to work?'

'I suppose,' said Billy.

'You will follow the men I showed you and tell me everything – *everything*, you understand.'

Billy nodded.

'I want to know where they go, what they do, who they speak to,' said Creecher. 'I want to know –'

'Everything,' interrupted Billy. 'Yeah – you said.'

The giant looked as though he was going to say more but thought better of it and sat back, head bowed. Billy swallowed the last mouthful of pie and stared at him, trying to work out what was going on in that head of his.

'Won't you even tell me a little about them?' Billy asked. 'It don't have to be no great secret, but it might help for me to know something about them.'

Creecher made no response.

'All I'm saying,' continued Billy, 'is that the more I know, the more advantage I have over them and the easier it gets to guess their moves. If I knew why they was here I might –'

'If you knew that, you would piss in your pants, English boy,' hissed Creecher.

'What's that supposed to mean?' said Billy. 'They don't look very frightening to me.' He cast a sideways look at Creecher. 'Leastwise not compared to you.'

Creecher lurched forward until his terrible face was only inches from Billy's. His dry, parchment-like skin seemed unable to contain the workings of his body and appeared slightly too large, gathering here and there in wrinkles. Billy could see the blood coursing through his veins.

'You do not know what you are dealing with,' the giant growled. 'You must believe me.'

Must I? thought Billy. What had he done to deserve his very own demon? Was Creecher really going to protect him from Fletcher? It was beginning to feel like, rather than being relieved of one peril, he was now placed between two.

'Why not kill them, then?' he said quietly, almost to himself.

'What was that?' asked Creecher, though Billy was sure the giant had heard him.

'If they're so dangerous,' said Billy more forcefully, 'why not kill them? You'd be doing us all a favour, wouldn't you? Why not kill them and be done with it? You obviously hate them.'

'Hate ... ?' said Creecher, shaking his head. 'No. If he had shown me but one drop of kindness, one tiny crumb of understanding – oh, then I would have loved him. No son would have been more loving.'

Billy frowned at Creecher, who seemed lost for a moment in the rapture of these thoughts. Who was he talking about? Billy strained to make sense of what it all meant but he could not.

'But no,' said Creecher. 'I was shunned. He treated me as though I were some sort of abomination, as if I am the one to blame. He recoiled from me in horror, yet it was he who made me as I am.'

'What?' said Billy. 'What do you mean?'

Creecher suddenly seemed to come to his senses.

'Enough!' he snapped. 'I have told you enough.' He slammed his fist into the floor, making Billy jump.

Billy knew when to hold his tongue and stared sullenly at the new crack in the floorboard in front of him. A spider emerged from the hole, as if it had been waiting for a lull, and took the opportunity to scurry away.

'Please,' said the giant quietly. 'I am sorry about losing my temper. There are things I cannot speak of. If the world knew what kind of man Frankenstein was – what he had done – then he would be arrested, and I do not want that. He must remain free.'

'Frankenstein?' said Billy. 'That's one of the men?'

Creecher nodded.

'Victor Frankenstein,' said the giant. 'The taller one. The other is Henry Clerval. He is harmless. It is Frankenstein you must watch closely.'

'All right, then,' said Billy.

'So tomorrow you will follow them?'

Billy nodded.

'Bon,' said Creecher with a smile.

Yeah, thought Billy. *I'll follow them for you, you murderous freak, until I can figure out some way of getting rid of you.*

CHAPTER VII.

Billy's stomach flipped nervously as he stepped through the door. A place like the British Museum presented lots of opportunities for a thief and there were certainly plenty of wealthy and distracted people milling about.

But Billy had always made a point of never working inside. Montagu House was congested, and Billy needed a clear escape route should he be spotted. There were just too many unknowables here.

He had been on the trail of Frankenstein and Clerval for two days now. That morning he had followed them from their lodgings and now shadowed them as they wandered round the museum.

The two men seemed to find something called the Rosetta Stone inexhaustibly fascinating, but Billy could see nothing of interest in this great slab etched with rows of chisel marks. Educated people were impressed by the strangest things, he mused.

The foreigners moved on to studying a room full of broken sculptures. Billy listened to someone nearby and heard that the stone figures came from Greece and were very old.

He was embarrassed at first. Many of the figures were naked and, even when there was clothing, it clung to the bodies as though it were wet, revealing the form beneath.

Two fashionably dressed young women were standing in front of a scene showing a fight going on between a man and a creature half man and half horse. On closer inspection Billy saw that the women were not that much older than him. Their accents betrayed them as out-of-towners, up in London for the season.

'So I was, as it were, "How dare you talk to me in that insolent fashion!" And she was, as it were, "I'm very sorry, madam, it won't happen again." But they always say that, don't they? And then it does happen again and they are all, "I'm so sorry, madam," all over again. I told Mama. You can't be soft with servants. They only take advantage.'

'Oh my stars. You are so right, sister.'

'Incontestably.'

Billy shook his head. Rich girls. Some of them were pretty enough, until they opened their mouths. What was the point of all that education if at the end of it you came out speaking such drivel? He wanted to knock their silly bonnets off.

Frankenstein and Clerval had moved on and Billy followed them. He found them standing in front of a huge statue. Or rather it was a fragment of a huge statue brought back from Egypt.

The statue was of an ancient king of those parts. He was called Rameses II. He was stripped to the waist and wore an odd kind of headdress. His head had a sizeable piece broken from it, as if a great sword had sliced from crown to ear. His face was intact, smooth and handsome in a girlish way, with a strange scabbard-like beard stuck to his jaw. He seemed to be quietly pleased with something.

Billy could see that this was no bust. This was the remains of a whole figure, snapped at the waist, one arm taken off at the shoulder, another at the elbow. There was a hole near his right shoulder. A great crack arced up through his chest, as though a surgeon had opened him up.

Billy wondered who this strange king was and what he was like. He'd heard of Egypt – England had fought the French there – but this was from ancient times. How different he seemed to mad King George and his odious son, the Prince Regent. But perhaps he was just as bad as they were. Maybe he had not even looked like this. Maybe he had really been a fat old letch, like the Prince.

Whatever he was like, he had probably thought his statue was going to stand for ever, and now here it was, snapped and cracked and gawped at by tourists in London. Billy smiled at this idea. It was pleasing to see the mighty laid low, even if they were from another country and another time.

There was a man standing nearby. He was young, fashionable, but unkempt in the way that only the upper class could ever be. He had the soft-skinned look of a man who had never worked a day in his life.

He was pale and thin and his hair was long and a little wild. His eyes were like those of a bird, bright and intense. He was staring at the statue and muttering to himself under his breath, as though chanting some kind of spell. Then suddenly he seemed to snap out of his trance, and he turned to walk away, crashing straight into a stout woman. He apologised profusely before continuing on his way. Billy chuckled to himself.

'Run along now,' said an old man, looking down his nose at Billy. 'Go on. I simply can't understand why they would let a boy like you in here.'

Billy scowled at him.

'I got as much right to be here as you have,' said Billy.

'Such insolence!' said the man, grabbing Billy by the arm. A small crowd began to drift towards them. 'How dare you speak to me in that manner? I've a good mind to have my man flog you.'

'The boy is doing no harm, I think.'

Billy and the old man both turned at the sound of the voice and Billy was taken aback to see Clerval standing beside him.

'I would thank you, sir, to look to your own affairs,' said the old man briskly.

'I meant to cause no offence, sir,' said Clerval with a small bow. 'But surely it is to be welcomed that a boy such as this would come and spend his time looking at things of beauty?'

'Pah!' said the old man. 'Beauty? Beauty? He's here to thieve, like all his kind. Perhaps where you come from, sir, you take a more lenient view of scum like this, but this is England and we know how to deal with his type.'

There were murmurs of agreement among the

onlookers at this outburst. Billy saw Clerval's usual smile leave his face.

'With respect, sir,' said Clerval. 'I saw this boy myself not ten minutes ago, staring in wonder at the Parthenon sculptures. I noticed because it seemed so moving that a boy of his kind would come to a place like this.'

'Ha!' said the old man. 'You wouldn't last five minutes in this city with that attitude, sir. God bless you for your good nature, but kindness will cost you dearly in London.'

The small knot of listeners muttered and nodded. An attendant arrived but Billy was already walking towards the door.

'And I don't want to see you in here again!' the attendant called after him.

Billy strode away and did not look back. He was annoyed with himself. He had allowed himself to become distracted and now Clerval – and maybe even Frankenstein – had noticed him. Following them would become harder.

He stepped out into the courtyard, blinking in the sharp sunshine, and walked towards Great Russell Street. He would simply have to wait outside for Clerval and Frankenstein to emerge.

Despite the sunshine, it was cold and Billy hugged himself, shivering, opting to walk up and down the street rather than freeze in one place. The sun was still low and the shadows long and dark. The street muttered with the usual morning chorus of horses' hooves and creaking handcarts. A delivery boy whistled at a maid and she blushed and quickened her pace.

The minutes ticked away and, though Billy had no watch, he felt he could hear their dull and tedious passing inside his head. And even if he could have shut that out, the church bells were there to remind him of just how long his wait had been.

Billy's boredom soon gave way, as youthful boredom will, in time, to frustration and annoyance. When Creecher was with him, Billy could see no alternative other than to do as he said. But here in the dazzling sunshine on a busy street, Creecher seemed more like a bad dream: something that belonged to the fog of sleep and nothing more.

What purpose was there to be served by Billy watching two tourists on their sightseeing expeditions? Sooner or later – whatever Creecher said – Fletcher or one of his cronies was going to find him.

Besides, it was just plain unnatural for a thief of Billy's skill to watch so many opportunities go by. It was a kind of torture.

Then, just as Billy walked past the entrance

to Montagu House, who should appear from the museum but the same eccentrically dressed toff he had seen earlier by the statue of the Egyptian king. It was just too tempting.

Billy strolled nonchalantly by and reached out towards the man's purse. In his mind he had already pocketed the purse and so it was a great shock when he felt a hand grab his wrist.

Billy was about to kick the man in the shin and run for it, when to his surprise the man smiled and let go of his arm.

'Don't worry,' he said. 'I have no intention of arresting you.'

Billy backed off to a safe distance in case the man changed his mind. He was intrigued.

'Why not?'

'I would not be the cause of your suffering,' said the man with a kind smile. 'It would bother my conscience.'

Billy raised his eyebrows.

'You religious, then?'

'Oh, dear me, no. Did you hear that, Mary?'

A woman walked forward.

'Yes, I did, my dear,' she said with a chuckle.

She was so different from the bonneted girls in the museum, though she could not have been any older. Thin and pale, like the man at her side, with a high forehead and long nose, she was pretty, but in a cool way, like a marble bust.

'So our French friend was right?' said the man. 'You are a thief.'

'He's not French,' Billy replied. 'He's from Swissland.'

'I told you he sounded Swiss,' said the woman called Mary.

'I'm intrigued that a boy like you has such an acute ear for accents,' said the man. 'Do you know him?'

Billy muttered something under his breath and began to walk away.

'Wait!'

Billy turned and the man opened his purse. He took out a coin and tossed it to him.

'That should stop you picking pockets for the rest of the day, at least!'

'Shelley,' said Mary, 'you are as soft-hearted as an old woman.'

'Come,' he replied. 'What harm can kindness do? Would you have me be hard-hearted, then?'

'Of course not, my love.'

Billy stood there looking at them, not knowing what to say. From the corner of his eye he saw Clerval and Frankenstein emerging from the museum gates. He began to move away.

'Do you see?' he heard the woman say. 'He doesn't even thank you for it.'

'He thanks me in his heart,' said Shelley, with a chuckle.

'In his heart he thinks you are a fool.'

'Ha!' said the man. 'You are probably right, dear wife. You usually are.'

'Only usually?'

'Always,' he replied.

From across the street, Billy watched him lean over to kiss her. An elderly couple tutted in disgust and Shelley and Mary burst into laughter. *What must it be like?* Billy thought. *What must it be like to be happy?*

CHAPTER VIII.

Billy got back to the museum gates in time to see his two targets leave, and he followed them for the rest of the day as they wandered the shopping streets of Piccadilly.

As the sun went down that afternoon, and the chill of night was once more ushered in, Creecher's invisible grip on Billy returned and he was in no mood to test its potency.

He made his way back to the bakery attic and found the giant standing waiting for him. Billy sat down and began to tell Creecher about his day. He told him that he had been thrown out of the British Museum, but not that Clerval had become involved. Nor did he mention his odd encounter with the man outside. He did not think the giant would look favourably on his risking arrest by a return to pickpocketry.

Besides, Creecher did not seem best pleased as it was. He had gazed at Billy expectantly when he had begun his report, but his expression grew grimmer and grimmer, as though a great shadow was passing across his face.

When Billy had completed his observations about the two men's shopping expedition, Creecher sat in silence for a long while. Billy could sense anger, but there was also disappointment – as though he had hoped to hear something but had not.

'You need new clothes,' said Creecher finally.

'No, I don't,' said Billy defensively. He looked down at the threadbare rags he was wearing and sighed. 'Well, maybe a coat wouldn't go amiss. Some better shoes maybe.'

'You need *new* clothes,' repeated the giant. 'You are following two gentlemen tourists. You need to be able to go where they go without being thrown out.'

'Yeah?' said Billy. 'Well, if you don't mind me saying, you're no Beau Brummell yourself.'

It was Creecher's turn to look at the poor and ill-fitting clothes he was wearing. He nodded, pouting a little.

'Agreed. We *both* need new clothes.'

'And you've got money, have you?'

Creecher shrugged.

'I have no need for money,' he replied.

'Well, ain't you the lucky one,' said Billy. 'You might be able to snatch a pie or what-have-you, but you can hardly stroll into a tailor's and make off with new suits for us both now, can you? Besides, you ain't exactly your standard measurements.'

Creecher took a deep breath and stared hard at Billy from under his hat. Billy caught his breath, wondering if he had spoken too boldly.

'Do you know a place where we can get clothes?'

Billy nodded.

'Somewhere discreet?'

Billy nodded again.

'I know just the man down Clerkenwell way: Gratz is his name. He's all right. He'll sort us out, I reckon. But he'll want money or the like in things he can sell. He gets a good price.'

'Let's go, then,' said Creecher.

'What, now?'

But Creecher was already through the window and Billy felt compelled to follow.

'How shall we get the money we need,' said Creecher, when they were in the alley, 'to pay for the clothes?'

'Well,' said Billy. 'As it happens, I think that might be the easy part.'

He grinned. For once it was going to be him taking the lead. Billy had spent days doing whatever Creecher told him to do – now he was going to get some fun out of this terrifying giant, on his terms.

He walked to the end of the alleyway and peered round the corner. It opened on to a street where he knew there was a gambling house frequented by the Mayfair set when they wanted to slum it a little. Two dandies were strolling towards him at that very moment, cravats wound round their necks, corsets pinching their waists. Billy looked back at Creecher, put his finger to his lips and then stepped out in front of them.

'Give us your money,' he said matter-of-factly.

The two men had been startled by Billy's sudden appearance, but seeing that he was alone and unarmed they turned to one another and laughed uproariously. Billy smiled.

'I asked nicely, gentlemen,' he said. 'Now give us your cash. I ain't got all night.'

'I really would rather not,' said the taller of the two, 'if it's all the same to you.'

'Yes,' said the other. 'If it's all the same to you.'

'And now I think I'm going to thrash you, boy.'

The dandy stepped forward, bringing his cane up over his shoulder. He was about to swing it down in an arc that would have ended in the splitting of Billy's skull, when an arm reached out and grabbed it, snatching it and pulling the man with it into the alley. His friend opened his mouth to shout, but he, too, was grabbed and pulled off the street.

Billy smiled to himself and followed them into the shadows. The two men were staring, open-mouthed and wide-eyed, at the giant who stood before them. Billy could smell that at least one of them had urinated.

'This is my associate, gentlemen,' said Billy. 'Now I'll ask again – your cash, if you please.'

The men could not move quickly enough, thrusting their purses towards Billy as if they were on fire, all the while staring incredulously at Creecher.

'I'll have your watches, too,' said Billy. 'And your neckties and handkerchiefs.'

They were as happy to part with these as with their purses if it meant getting away from Creecher.

'And your boots,' said Billy.

The two men paused and looked at each other.

'Your boots!' repeated Billy fiercely.

They jumped into action, whimpering as they did so, looking at Creecher while they clumsily removed their boots and held them out with shaking hands for Billy to take. They stood there quivering with fear, the cold seeping into their stockinged feet. Billy bowed elaborately.

'My associate and I will bid you farewell, then, gentlemen,' said Billy.

The two men took their chance and ran away as fast as their legs would take them. Billy hopped about, yelping with excitement.

'Ha!' he cried. 'Did you see their faces? I thought the one with the red nose was going to keel over!'

Billy chuckled to himself as he and Creecher walked away with their haul. Once they had gone a sufficient distance and Billy was confident they had turned enough corners, they stopped and Billy looked through the goods, making the odd appreciative noise as he did so.

'You are cruel,' said Creecher.

'What? That's rich coming from you.'

'I do what I have to do,' the giant replied. 'I take no pleasure in doing harm. I did not choose to be this . . . this . . .' He waved his hands, indicating his massive form, but words seemed to fail him.

Billy spat and muttered a curse.

'You think I *chose* to be a thief?'

'That is not what I meant,' said Creecher. 'It is –'

'You don't know what it's like here,' interrupted Billy, 'for the likes of us. For the likes of me. I've had my share of beatings and cruelty. You'll get no guilt from me.'

Billy felt Creecher's limpid gaze on him but did not return it.

'If you only knew how much I would give to swap places with you,' said the giant gently.

'You'd rather be me?' said Billy incredulously. 'I don't think so.'

'I'd rather be *any* man than the thing I am,' he answered forlornly. 'I am jealous of the leper.'

Billy looked across at Creecher and for once saw something other than the fearful freak. For the first time he saw some vulnerability in this monstrous hulk.

'Let's go,' he said, changing the subject. 'Those dandies wouldn't come back here for a knighthood, but they may have friends or they may find a Charley –'

'A Charley?' said Creecher.

'A watchman,' said Billy. 'Or a constable. Either way, we ought to move. Never linger. That's the first rule.'

Creecher nodded.

'For me too.'

CHAPTER IX.

Billy took Creecher on a convoluted route to Clerkenwell. The lamps were already lit in the busy shopping streets of the city, but lights were few and far between in these parts.

The wide, bright thoroughfares of the centre branched and forked into narrower and narrower, darker and dingier streets and courtyards. Rickety bridges arched across stinking black ditches to filthy alleyways.

A drunkard reeking of gin took one look at Creecher as he strode past and fell to the floor, gibbering, his hands clasped together in prayer.

Eventually Billy led Creecher to the end of an alley that opened out on to a wide street of warehouses. The bone-melters, glue-makers, leather-tanners and cloth-dyers were all closed up for the day. The owners lived elsewhere. No one with any money or sense would choose to live amid that putrid stink.

But some people did not have the choice and one such was old Gratz. He was a tailor by trade – or so he had been in the old days, back in Prague where he had lived as a young man. There were more lucrative ways to earn a living in this stinking town.

Billy had known Gratz since he was a boy – since his first days on the street. It was Fletcher who had brought him to the old man.

Gratz had fed him and given him a roof – albeit a leaking one – over his head. All he had had to do to continue taking advantage of Gratz's hospitality was to bring the old man a steady stream of trinkets. Billy's life as a thief had begun.

Billy took a long look up and down the street and then nodded to Creecher to follow him across to a small courtyard on the other side. The buildings at the back were walled with rough planks, as rotten as the hull of a prison ship. It reeked of the sewer, of death, of decay. Even Billy's dulled nostrils were always caught off guard by the potency of it.

'This way,' he said, leading Creecher under a couple of great wooden buttresses and into a building that looked as though it was on the verge of collapse. It appeared deserted. It always did.

'Mr Gratz,' whispered Billy. 'It's me – Billy. I got some business for you.'

At first, nothing seemed to happen, and then a shape began to move towards them in the dark. Its movements were slow and soundless. Billy could sense Creecher tensing. A thin young man appeared, a curved yellow smile on his shadowed face, like a crescent moon at dusk.

It was Gratz's nephew. Billy had met him a few times before. He was a good few years older than Billy, but so much younger than Gratz that this age difference barely registered. They were wary of each other, but always grudgingly appreciative of how useful the other might be. Billy nodded a greeting.

'He's through here, Billy,' said the nephew and he moved away towards a door nearby and disappeared through it. Billy followed warily, with Creecher behind him. The giant had to stoop almost double to get through.

In the centre of the room sat an old man as lined and time-worn as an old leather shoe, illuminated by an oil lamp – a dim light, but so surprising that Billy found himself squinting as though it were a burst of sunlight.

'Billy,' said the old man huskily. 'Come closer, my dear. Come closer.'

'Evening, Mr Gratz,' said Billy. 'Are you well?'

'Can't complain,' croaked Gratz. 'Well, I could, but it wouldn't make no difference now, would it?'

Gratz cackled throatily at this, as he always did – the exchange was an oft-repeated one.

Billy indicated to Creecher that he should stay back in the shadows, then stepped forward into the little bubble of light from the oil lamp.

'Well,' said the old man. 'Have you got something for us, Billy?'

Billy smiled and put the sack down between them. Gratz gave a nod to his nephew, who scurried over and lifted the sack, tipping the contents on to the floor. Billy saw the old man's tiny eyes widen in their shadowed sockets.

'That had a nice, healthy sound to it,' he said. 'What's in there, my dear?'

'Couple of canes, Uncle – good ones. Silver tipped, maybe. Silk handkerchiefs. Neck scarves. Two nice watches, one of 'em gold, or gold-coloured, anyways.'

'That's silver and gold and you know it,' said Billy. 'But if you ain't interested . . .'

He made to pick the items up. The old man clapped his leathery hands and said, 'Billy, Billy. No need for that . . . How long have we known each other now? Three years? Four?'

'More like five,' said Billy, without looking at the old man.

'He was such a skinny young thing when he came here,' said Gratz to his nephew. 'He ain't much to look at now – but you should have seen him then. Always sharp in the head though. Always had a thief's brain in his skull. You can't teach that.'

'Ha!' said Billy, still gathering the things together. 'Any thieving brain I have, you put there, old man. I weren't no thief before I met you. And you're even worse. You thieve from thieves.'

'Billy!' called Gratz. 'Enough now. You know you'll get a fair price here. Ain't I always been fair?'

'Fair?' said Billy. 'Let me see. It's me that takes the risks and you that has a roof over his head. If that's fair, then I suppose you are.'

'Billy, Billy, Billy,' said the old man, wheezing a little. 'It's like a rusty knife in my heart to hear you talk this way. You was always my favourite. Always.'

Billy smiled and stood up straight once more.

'A fair price mind,' said Billy. 'None of your nonsense.'

'Of course, of course,' said Gratz. 'Anything else in there?'

'Couple of pair of boots, Uncle,' said the nephew. 'Gentlemen's.'

After a moment the old man burst out laughing – a wheezing, spluttering laugh that quickly descended into a hacking cough. It took a while for him to compose himself with deep rasping breaths.

'You took their boots, Billy?' said the old man, waving an admonishing finger at him.

'Took whose boots?' Billy replied. 'I found these things. They must have been dumped.'

The old man nodded and chuckled.

'Of course, of course,' he said holding up his hands. He cleared his throat noisily and squinted into the shadows behind Billy. He held out the lamp at arm's length and peered past it.

'You've brought someone with you, Billy?' said the old man. 'You know I ain't one for strangers.'

'He's all right,' said Billy.

'I'm sure he is, my dear,' Gratz replied, in a voice that did not share the meaning of the words. 'Ain't you going to introduce us, then?'

'He's foreign,' said Billy. 'From Swissland. He don't speak English that well and –'

'Even so, my young friend,' said the old man. He beckoned to Creecher. 'Even so . . .'

Billy nodded and Creecher stepped forward into the dim light, his huge frame even more exaggerated in this confined space. Gratz recoiled in horror.

'A Golem!' he shrieked. 'Why have you brought a Golem to my house?'

'A what?' said Billy.

But the old man was screaming now.

'Get out! *Get out!*'

Billy froze, startled for a moment, and then quickly began gathering up the hoard and replacing it in the sack, while the old man was comforted by his nephew. He took a sideways look at Creecher, who was now nothing more than a massive inky shadow.

'Come on,' Billy said. 'I'll think of something.'

They retreated back through the door and were about to leave the building when they heard a voice behind them.

'You're not leaving, I hope.'

It was the nephew, holding a candle. He gently closed the door on his uncle's room.

'I thought, with old Gratz that way –' Billy began.

'That?' said the nephew, waving it away as though it happened every day. He dropped his voice to a whisper and took hold of Billy's sleeve.

'Between you and me,' he said, 'my uncle is not a well man. Not a well man at all. He is easily upset.'

'But not you?' said Billy, with a quick glance towards Creecher.

The nephew looked at the giant and then smiled, putting the candlestick down on the top of a wooden chest.

'I takes as I find,' he said. 'And it takes all sorts.'

He clasped his hands together, his long fingers coiling around each other like snakes.

'What was that Gratz said about a Golem?'

'Pay no heed,' said the nephew. 'The old man is – how can I put it? – a little *confused* from time to time. It's a superstition with our people. A fairy tale. It wouldn't interest you.'

'It would interest *me*,' said Creecher, stepping forward. The giant seemed to bring a blast of cold air with him as he did so, and the nephew flinched as Creecher moved into the light. Even so, Billy was impressed with his calmness. Creecher was a troubling spectacle at the best of times, but in that gloom he seemed all the more terrifying: like the embodiment of everything a person fears when they are trapped in a dark place.

'Well,' began the nephew, his voice now a

little more strained and his smile a little more forced. 'The Golem is a man made from clay. He is brought to life by means of magic and serves as a slave to his master.

'There is a story of Rabbi Loeb in Prague many, many years ago, who created such a Golem and brought it to life, and it served my people there, guarding them and doing work for them. He was a giant, you see – much like your good self – and very strong.'

'And what happened to him?' said Creecher, seemingly fascinated by the tale.

'The Golem?' said the nephew, rubbing his clammy hands together. 'Well, he ran amok, I'm afraid, and the rabbi was forced to destroy him and return him to the dust from which he had come. It is a fairy tale. Nothing more. But my uncle is from that part of the world, you see, and these things have a special grip on his mind.'

Creecher made no response, but Billy could sense that, for whatever reason, he had attached some significance to this yarn.

'Between me and you, my friends, Uncle is not much longer for this world.'

He opened his hands and shrugged.

'But I am here to do what I can to help keep

the business afloat,' he continued. 'So what can I do for you, gentlemen – in return for those goods you offered us?'

'I need new clothes and shoes,' said Billy. 'Nothing too smart, but smart enough. I need to be able to pass as a servant or a delivery boy. Respectable, but not too much. I want to blend in.'

The nephew nodded his way through Billy's specifications.

'You want to be invisible. I understand. You're pretty much my height and build,' said the nephew, looking Billy up and down. 'We can find you something, I'm sure.'

'Hey!' said Billy. 'I don't want your cast-offs, mind. They don't have to be new, but they need to be decent.'

The nephew recoiled theatrically, clutching his heart.

'I'm offended that you would even think I'd pull a trick like that.'

'Him, too,' said Billy, ignoring the protests. 'He needs new clothes and all.'

The nephew raised his eyebrows and tapped his fingers together. 'That will be more of a challenge,' he said with a grin.

'Yeah – but you can do it?' asked Billy.

The nephew nodded.

'Everything is possible, my friend. We do a little business with Mr Bartholomew down the road.'

'The undertaker,' Billy told Creecher.

'He had a fearful tall man through his hands last week. I was wondering where we'd find a buyer for those clothes. You ain't got no objection to wearing a dead man's clothes?'

'None,' said Creecher, with a wry smile.

'Very well, then,' said the nephew. 'He wasn't quite your height, of course,' he continued with a nervous chuckle. 'But with a few alterations here and there. If I can just take a few measurements?'

Billy looked at Creecher, who after a moment nodded his assent. The nephew took a pencil and small pad from one waistcoat pocket and a tape measure from the other.

'Now then, now then,' he said, dragging a chair noisily over to Creecher. He passed the candle to Billy and climbed up to stand on the chair. He was still not as tall as the giant, his eyes level with Creecher's teeth. Billy saw him recoil from the foul breath and grinned.

'I . . . I . . . I feel a little dizzy,' said the nephew shakily. 'What a curious view of the world you must have, my friend.'

'His name's –'

'I don't need to know names,' said the nephew, putting a finger to his lips. 'No need to know more than you need to know, eh? Knowledge is a fine thing, of course, but it can stretch your neck, too. Or those of your acquaintance.'

Billy nodded.

'Now then, my mighty friend,' said the nephew, 'if I could just ask you to raise your arms.'

He passed the tape round Creecher's chest, not without a little difficulty, and wobbled on his chair. Once the measurement was taken he jotted it down in his notebook with a whistle.

'If you could hold that there,' he said to Creecher, asking the giant to hold the tip of the tape to the back of his collar while he hopped from the chair and straightened the tape out to measure the length from the collar to the floor. Again he noted the measurement and again he whistled, half in admiration and half in amazement.

He measured the giant's boots from heel to toe and across the width.

'Bigger than these,' said Creecher. 'They crush my feet.'

'They will have to be specially made, of course, but I know a cobbler who will do a good job.

He'll be happy to take the two pairs of boots in payment, if that's all right with you?'

Billy nodded.

'While I'm down here,' said the nephew, putting the tip of the tape to Creecher's groin. The giant roared and shoved him away.

'Easy, easy!' said the nephew. 'I meant no harm. It's what we do to measure the trouser length. It does make you wonder, though, don't it? The size of him and what not.'

Creecher clenched his fist and moved forward. Billy chuckled, then Gratz called from the next room.

'It's all right, Uncle,' shouted the nephew. 'The gentlemen have almost finished.'

Creecher calmed himself and stepped back, scowling.

'I think maybe you ought to guess,' said Billy, grinning.

'I think we'll guess at the waist, too,' said the nephew breathlessly. 'That's enough measuring for one day.'

'When will they be done?' Billy asked.

'Beginning of next week good enough?'

'The end of this week,' said Creecher.

'Of course. Right you are, gentlemen,' said the nephew. 'You know the way out, don't you?'

Creecher walked to the door and Billy followed him.

'Terrible thing about Fletcher,' said the nephew as Billy was about to leave.

'Yeah?' said Billy, with all the disinterest he could muster.

'Found him in Fleet Ditch, they did. Skull crushed in like a walnut.'

'He had a lot of enemies,' said Billy more coolly than he felt.

His mind reeled. So Creecher had dealt with Fletcher, after all. Billy could not deny it was a relief to be rid of him, but this reminder of the dreadful power of the giant unnerved him.

The nephew smiled and nodded, studying Billy's face intently.

'So he did, my friend. So he did.'

CHAPTER X.

A rancid mist drifted in from the river. It tasted of rotten fish. Billy coughed and spat on to the pavement, yawned and stretched.

It was a cold morning: crypt cold. Horses made their way warily over the treacherous cobbles, steam rising from their sweating flanks. Cartwheels skittered and squeaked. Hunched drivers clenched their teeth.

Billy stood under an archway waiting for Frankenstein and Clerval to emerge from their rooms on the opposite side of the street. He stomped his feet and blew into his clasped hands, trying to warm them.

The air was so chilled he could feel it stinging his flesh, biting into his fingertips, his nose, his ears. It seemed to have sucked the life out of everything and everyone around him, slowing the world down to a snail's pace and painting it a dozen shades of dull grey.

Billy cursed the two foreigners, who he was sure were sitting next to a raging fire, eating a warm and hearty breakfast while he stood freezing his balls off outside.

All this waiting for Frankenstein and Clerval had given him time to think – perhaps too much time. Rumination was a novelty for Billy. He had rarely had great cause to think much beyond where his next meal was going to come from, or where he was going to sleep.

But since meeting Creecher, when his life had taken this new course, he found more and more that his head was full of thoughts, all crowding in on each other.

Sometimes he thought about his mother, although he tried not to. Thinking about his time with her was like holding his hand over a flame: he could only do it for so long before the pain became unbearable.

Other times he thought about the sweep and the beatings he took at his hands, and the memory filled him with shame and anger.

But today he thought mostly about Fletcher. The vision of his crushed head flashed with unwelcome vividness into Billy's imagination. He replayed the events of the night he first met Creecher over and over again, so dreamlike did they seem now.

Who, or what, was Creecher? Why did he look the way he did? Some wrong had been committed, of that he was certain. But what and to whom? And if he was right and some wrong had been done, was he helping the victim or the perpetrator?

He thought of Gratz screeching about the Golem and then he thought of Fletcher again. What the hell had he got himself into? He should just walk down to the docks and sign himself up on a ship bound for the Americas and be done with it all.

But Billy could not let go. He rattled the coins in his pocket. The giant might not be the most enthusiastic of robbers but his presence was better than a pistol – hell, it was better than a canon! One sight of Creecher and the hapless victims were only too eager to hand over their valuables. Billy was already richer than he had ever been.

And he had a protector. Sticking around the giant had paid off so far. Fletcher might be gone, but his sidekick, Skinner, was still out there somewhere and he wasn't the kind to let bygones be bygones.

But then Billy thought of old Wicks, who used to live down by the Fleet Ditch and who had a fearsome bulldog that terrified the living daylights out of everyone who saw it. And then one day the dog had leapt at Wicks and bitten half his face off.

Frankenstein and Clerval finally emerged and, after a moment, Billy followed in their wake. He had followed many people in his time. It was all part and parcel of being a thief. Just as the wolf or the lion picks a target from the herd, so too does the thief learn to spot a potential victim in the crowd.

Life as a pickpocket had made Billy a keen observer of people – and he could tell that Frankenstein walked with the hunched gait of a guilty man. But what was the source of that guilt? Was it for something he had done or for something he was about to do? And how did Creecher fit in?

Whatever it was, it was clear that Clerval knew nothing about it and that Frankenstein had another secret life, hidden from his friend.

Billy had come to like Clerval over the few days of following him. As guilty and world-weary as Frankenstein seemed, by contrast Clerval seemed carefree and full of life and hope. Billy had been amazed to find that he had noticed things in London that he must have walked past a thousand times and not seen, simply because he was now allowed to share in Clerval's excitement and enthusiasm for the city.

But seeing the city through Frankenstein's eyes was a different matter altogether. As soon as he was apart from Clerval, he had the air of an escaped convict.

Not far from Charterhouse Square, the two men separated. Billy dropped Clerval and stayed with Frankenstein, keeping far enough back from his quarry to avoid any suspicion, given that Frankenstein turned around frequently as he walked.

The crowds slowly began to thin and following him became more difficult. But Billy knew these streets by heart and took shortcuts and detours, confident that he would not lose this foreigner on his home turf.

The more they walked, the more Billy began to wonder where on earth the Swiss was taking them. Indeed, he began to wonder if the man was lost. The area they were entering was a long way from the tourist trail.

But Frankenstein appeared to know exactly what he was doing, and occasionally took out a piece of paper – a map, Billy supposed – and consulted it, making sure of his bearings before proceeding.

Frankenstein paused at the intersection of a crossroads and walked diagonally across, so intent on where he was going that he was almost hit by a wagon and certainly felt the full force of the driver's annoyance. A little ruffled, he continued on his way and, once safely across the filthy street, he made straight for a covered alleyway.

Billy waited a few moments for him to disappear from sight and then crossed the street himself, stepping straight into a pile of horse dung, courtesy of the passing wagon. A few whispered curses and boot shakes later and he was peering into the alleyway.

Frankenstein was in the courtyard beyond, seemingly eyeing up the place. One building in particular occupied his attention and he walked its length, looking at the walls and up at the roof, before reaching into his pocket and pulling out a bunch of keys.

Frankenstein looked round, causing Billy to duck out of sight. When he felt he was able to look again, the Swiss had gone.

Billy crept forward. The door was still swinging back and forth on whining hinges. He came as near as he dared and peered inside.

There was no sign of Frankenstein, but he could see that there was a set of steps leading downwards just beyond the door. The building looked like a warehouse that would be filled with barrels and clutter, but from what little Billy could see of it – there were no windows save for greasy skylights high above – it was in fact surprisingly tidy and clear except for two or three large tables and several crates. What was Frankenstein doing in a place like this?

While this question was still forming in Billy's mind, Frankenstein suddenly began to ascend the staircase. Billy's heart leapt into his mouth. He ran out of the alley as fast as he could and stood panting in a doorway nearby, his back pressed against the door, praying that the shadows would conceal him.

A minute later, the Swiss emerged from the alley. Billy heard his familiar footsteps clip across the cobbles. After a nervous few moments, he peered round and saw Frankenstein's silhouetted figure walking away and then disappear round a street corner. Billy waited a second and set off in pursuit.

CHAPTER XI.

That evening, when the sun was setting and the clouds were blood-soaked swabs and the chill of night had begun to descend on the city streets, Billy and Creecher made their way back to Clerkenwell to collect their clothes from Gratz's nephew.

For the first time, Creecher had been pleased by one of Billy's reports. When he had told the giant of Frankenstein's mysterious visit to the warehouse, Creecher clapped his hands together.

'Finally,' he said. 'This is good news, mon ami. This is excellent news!'

But he had given Billy no clue as to why this was such excellent news. For his part, Billy was happy to enjoy the giant's lighter mood and saw no reason to ruin it.

Gratz's nephew was standing outside as they arrived, his sharp shadowy form like a stick man drawing. There was a group of children with him.

'All right, then, boys and girls,' he said, seeing Billy and Creecher approach. 'Off you go.'

Billy looked at the ragged urchins who clustered around the doorway, with their tattered clothes and filthy, half-starved faces. A small boy turned to face him and Billy felt as though he were looking at his younger self. He smiled, but the boy simply stared back at him, dead-eyed. When the children noticed Creecher, a couple of them stared up in wonder, until they joined the others in running away as fast as their legs would carry them.

'And make sure you work hard,' Gratz's nephew called after them, 'or I might have to set the giant on you!'

He cackled as the children disappeared. Billy stared after them. Was he ever that young? He felt a chill go through him, as if the blood was freezing in his veins.

'Gentlemen,' said the nephew, peering at Billy. 'I've been expecting you.'

He opened the door and they followed him through to the main room. Billy looked around for Gratz, but there was no sign of the old man. The air smelled of dust, damp clothes and decay.

'Uncle sends his apologies,' said the nephew, with a hunch of his shoulders. 'He is feeling a little bit under the weather and has taken to his bed early this evening.'

Billy looked at the door that led to the private chambers upstairs and imagined the bolts and locks that lay on the other side and Gratz trembling above them.

'Have you got the clothes?' he asked.

'Would I let you down?' said the nephew, hand to his heart.

He opened a wooden chest nearby and brought out two piles of clothes and shoes, placing each on top of the chest once it was shut.

'I think the cobbler rather enjoyed making your boots, my friend.'

He handed a pair to Creecher, who took them and turned them over, nodding appreciatively.

'Good,' he said. 'They are well made.'

'Oh – he knows his stuff all right,' said the nephew, turning to pick up a coat. 'Now this was a little harder. It took a bit of careful opening out here and there, and a lengthening of the sleeves with these cuffs and so on. It ain't a bad sort of a coat. And warm, too. That's good quality that is.'

Creecher took his coat off and dropped it over the wooden counter beside him. He put the new coat on and, again, nodded approvingly. Billy was less sure. The coat was dark and made the ghastly pallor of the giant's skin even more noticeable. But at least the high collar helped hide his face.

'And I thought a hat might help ... well, it might assist ...'

Creecher took the hat. It was broad-brimmed and, together with the collar, did indeed help. It helped mask the worst of Creecher's terrible face. It was Billy's turn to nod with approval.

'Very good,' said Creecher. 'You have done well.'

'There, you see,' said Gratz's nephew, with evident relief.

Creecher picked up a book that was lying on the counter.

'You are a scholar, sir?' said the nephew. 'I thought you might be. I said to myself, there's a man with a brain if ever I saw one.'

'How much?' said Creecher.

'My gift, my dear.'

'Good,' said Billy. 'We'll be off.'

'I hope you gentlemen will think of us should you have anything else you might want to exchange.'

'Maybe,' said Billy, without turning round.

'It's been a pleasure to do business with you, my friend,' the nephew called from the doorway as Creecher walked away after Billy.

Creecher looked at him but said nothing. Glancing up, he saw the face of Gratz staring down from a window for a few seconds before the old man jumped back into the darkness, letting the filthy curtain fall back into place. Creecher nodded at the nephew and he and Billy left.

They walked back to the city and returned to the attic to change. They each went to the furthest reaches of the room to strip but Billy could not resist a quick glimpse of the giant's naked form.

Creecher had his back to Billy and was stripped to the waist. Billy had never seen muscles like it – not even on builders or the bare-knuckle boxers at the fair. Samson himself could not have been more powerful.

But no living man ever looked like Creecher: the rippling muscles that looked as though they had been flayed, the dry, parchment skin more like the casing of a chrysalis than the hide of a human being.

Creecher turned as he picked up his shirt and Billy looked away, embarrassed. It was just a glimpse, but there was something odd about that muscled torso – something not quite as it should be. Billy just could not settle on what, though.

Half an hour later, they stood in their new clothes at the end of the alleyway at the back of the baker's, illuminated by the mellow light from a window above them. Billy had persuaded Creecher that another robbery was needed to refill his empty purse.

'How do I look?' asked Creecher, noticing Billy's expression.

'Better,' said Billy. 'It's just . . .'

'What?'

'You'll get annoyed with me. And then you'll throttle me.'

'I will not get annoyed,' said Creecher. 'I promise.'

Billy took a deep breath.

'Look, there's nothing wrong with the clothes,' he said. 'It's more the way you wear them.'

Creecher frowned.

'I do not understand.'

Billy scratched his chin and tried to think of the best way to word what he was about to say.

'You need to have a bit more style about you,' he said. 'Look at you. You standing there. You're so . . . stiff.'

'Stiff?' said Creecher.

'Yeah, like you was about to read a sermon or something.'

Creecher looked baffled.

'If I was your size, I'd really . . . I'd . . . Well, I wouldn't stand like a trooper on parade anyway. Bend your neck a bit. Get your head lower. Look out from under your eyebrows. Stick out your jaw like you're daring someone to thump it. Let your arms swing,' said Billy, all the while miming these words with growing enthusiasm.

'And when you walk, you should roll,' he added. 'Like you're walking along a ship in a stormy sea. Let that coat flap around like a sail. You need a big walk to go with your size: big, slow steps, like you was wading through mud. You ain't in no hurry cos you ain't afraid of nobody. You get what I'm saying?'

Creecher nodded and, taking a deep breath, lowered his head, stuck out his jaw and set off down the alleyway with a big loping stride, arms swinging, coat flapping.

Billy collapsed to the floor, howling with laughter. Creecher slowly came to a halt and turned to face him, glowering from under his eyebrows. It was a little while before Billy could get to his feet and speak.

'That is the funniest thing I've seen in a long time,' he said between pants, holding his stomach as if winded.

'But you told me –'

'I know,' said Billy, patting him on the back. 'I know I did. You just need a bit more practice, that's all. I'm sorry I laughed. Really.'

Creecher nodded.

'Then I would very much appreciate it if you would consider recapitulating for me.'

'What?'

'Show me again,' said Creecher.

'Oh, right,' said Billy. 'We really ought to do something about the way you talk as well.'

Creecher frowned.

'All right, all right,' said Billy. 'One thing at a time.'

Billy's swaggering lessons continued for the next twenty minutes, the first five of which were mainly taken up with Billy's efforts to resist laughing.

Slowly, though, the giant seemed to grasp the coordination necessary and Billy sent him away to one end of the alley and told him to strut his way back.

Creecher disappeared into the darkness and there was a long pause. Then all at once the giant emerged into the light, head down, eyes glinting from under his furrowed brow, his coat sweeping back and forth as he took long rolling strides towards Billy.

'Good,' said Billy, his mouth a little dry. 'That was good.'

'Shall I try once more?' asked Creecher.

'No,' said Billy, putting his hat on and walking towards the light at the alley's end. 'I think you've got the idea.'

CHAPTER XII.

The cloud that for months had covered the city like a filthy blanket momentarily developed a ragged tear and a beam of light poured through, hitting the soot-blackened dome of St Paul's and polishing the golden cross at its summit. It gleamed like a crucifix on a priest's black cassock.

The effect was startling, if short-lived, and even Billy, who was normally immune to the architectural delights of London, joined the tourists in looking up in wonder.

For a few seconds it was as if the whole of the City stopped to watch, but as soon as the clouds rolled back and the light faded, each one of the crowd – lawyer, con man, banker, thief – went back to their allotted tasks.

Billy, too, returned to his employment. Frankenstein and Clerval were sightseeing in the City and Billy was in slow but dogged pursuit.

Billy had already accompanied the men on a visit to the docks, where Clerval had arranged meetings with several importers and exporters.

From there Billy had tailed the two men up the winding narrow streets to the hill on which London's great cathedral stood, dominating the skyline for miles around.

Frankenstein and Clerval walked up the steps and into the cathedral entrance. Billy followed moments later and saw the two men strolling down the nave, stopping below the dome, looking up and pointing.

Clerval, as usual, was the most animated, constantly tapping Frankenstein's arm to show him some new feature he had spotted. For his part, Frankenstein seemed relaxed for a change and bore his friend's enthusiasm with an amused indulgence. After looking at the choir stalls and the altar, the men headed towards the crypt.

Billy followed them down the stairs. He had never been to the crypt before. He had been to the cathedral many times: the exiting congregation, chatting, distracted, provided easy pickings. But the crypt had always felt too enclosed, too much of a potential trap. Billy felt nervous.

He watched from a safe distance as the two men studied a large tomb in the centre of the vaulted room: a huge monument, topped with a black sarcophagus. Only when they moved away did Billy see that it was Lord Nelson's tomb.

He was taken aback by the sudden surge of emotions that threatened to overwhelm him. One of Billy's earliest memories was standing on the bank of the Thames, watching the funeral barge sail down the river. They had been allowed a day away from the workhouse for the occasion.

It was a painful memory, not because he had any special feelings for Nelson, but because it came as such a vivid reminder of his mother. He could almost feel her hand in his – as though they were standing together once more amid that great crowd of mourners thronging the waterfront.

But like a dream it slipped away and Billy was left with all that desperate loss renewed. Tears blurred his vision and, as always, his sadness changed in moments to anger, to a bitter and violent resentment of the whole world about him.

He stomped out of the crypt. Frankenstein and Clerval continued their tour and headed for the stairs that would take them to the top of the dome and the great view of London that attracted so many visitors.

Billy did not follow them. He would be too easy to spot in such a confined space. He knew where they were and he simply had to wait for them to come down again. He sat on the steps by the entrance, the image of his mother at the waterfront still clinging to his mind.

All those thousands of people and yet it was *his* mother who had to die. Billy wondered how many of the people milling around the cathedral were there that day. Why did they live and not her? He would have killed any one of them with his bare hands if it could have brought her back to life.

The image of Creecher's mighty hands around Fletcher's head came fleetingly into his mind's eye again, but he was able to waft it away. He would not feel remorse for that animal. Creecher had done the world a favour.

Billy spotted Frankenstein and Clerval leaving the cathedral and as he got to his feet to follow them, he noticed a familiar figure walking east. Even from the back he could tell it was Skinner, together with a couple of his cronies. Sooner or later, Billy knew he was going to bump into Skinner. He could only hope that Creecher would be on hand when he did.

He cursed and looked around for Frankenstein and Clerval, and saw them strolling down the hill. The clouds above were dense and it was oppressively dark. The sky, the soot-blackened buildings and the granite cobbled streets filled Billy's entire view with a grimy gloom.

At the point where Ludgate Street became Ludgate Hill, a great crowd was gathering. Billy could see that they were clustered at the end of Old Bailey and he sped up so that he would not lose sight of Frankenstein or Clerval as they became part of the throng.

The crowd was ragged at the edges and surged gently back and forth, like waves against a shore. Frankenstein and Clerval, clearly curious as to what the attraction might be, decided to take a closer look. Billy, who knew all too well what was going on, followed them in turn.

Sure enough, a scaffold had been erected outside Newgate Prison. A hanging always drew a large and enthusiastic crowd. Billy often worked these congregations too, thieving in the shadow of the gallows.

Three of the four on the scaffold had already had their heads covered by the time they joined the crowd. The last was a young woman who Billy guessed must have been nineteen or thereabouts. Her pretty face was marble pale, her eyes wide and shadowed. Her lips were fluttering but Billy couldn't hear what she was saying above the noise of the crowd.

The hangman covered her face with a night-cap, stepped back and dropped the trapdoors. Suddenly all was silent. Billy looked away. He'd seen that dance before and had no wish to see it again. He wished his ears had not caught the creak of the hemp ropes as they took their weight. Then the crowd roared to life.

He turned towards Frankenstein, who was staring at the hanging figures with an expression so moved that it could not have been stronger had a member of his own flesh and blood been dangling on the scaffold.

Clerval looked sour and shook his head wearily and then leapt to the aid of Frankenstein, who collapsed backwards and would surely have fallen had his friend not held him.

A couple of people chuckled at the sensitive foreigner. Clerval helped his friend to a quieter courtyard nearby and sat him down while Billy watched from the shadows.

Frankenstein fumbled in his pockets and took out a small bottle. Clerval grabbed his arm and said something in French that Billy could not understand, though he could guess what the bottle contained without catching the word opium.

Frankenstein pushed his friend away and, pulling the stopper from the bottle, took a swig while Clerval turned away angrily. Frankenstein looked back in the direction of Newgate and the scaffold and took another swig.

Was this man – a man who fainted away at the sight of a stranger's death – the dangerous man that Creecher spoke of? It seemed hard to believe.

———•••———

When Billy recounted the day's events to Creecher that evening in the attic, the giant listened in silence until Billy reached the part about the hanging.

As soon as he mentioned the woman on the scaffold, Creecher let out a strange moan, like a wounded dog. His hands flexed, his fingers falling in and out of fists. Billy grew nervous. This was the way the sweep would get just before he gave Billy a beating.

'You all right?' he asked.

'Oui,' said Creecher almost inaudibly. 'Go on.'

Billy took a deep breath and told Creecher about Frankenstein's reaction and how Clerval had settled him. He told him, too, about the opium. Creecher nodded and snorted derisively.

'Opium,' he said. 'Pah! The coward cannot even

look the world in the eye without this drug to dull his nerves.'

Creecher put his hands to his face and shook his head. He ran his fingers through his long, lank hair and then suddenly stood up and banged one of the beams with the flat of his hand, sending a mist of dust across the attic. He strode through this fog towards Billy almost doubled over, seeming to fill the whole space. Billy scrambled backwards.

'When will he keep his promise to me?' he growled, coming right up to Billy's face. 'How long must I wait?'

'Wait for what?' said Billy, flinching and turning away.

Creecher came to a halt and looked down, muttering to himself.

'Spends his days dosing himself with poppy juice, while I –'

'Wait for what?' repeated Billy. 'I don't understand.'

Creecher fell silent, his head hanging. Billy could see his great shoulders rise and fall, slowing now as his breathing calmed.

'I have already told you,' said Creecher, the threat gone from his voice. 'It does not concern you.'

Billy knew that he should leave it there, that picking at this scab could be dangerous, possibly deadly. But his curiosity was too hungry now. It needed feeding.

'Can't you at least tell me why you and this Frankenstein fellow seem so troubled by the hanging? You don't neither of you strike me as the sentimental type, if you get my drift.'

Creecher turned with a half-smile that Billy found particularly unpleasant on that long, grim face. The giant sat down on the dusty floorboards. Billy could see that a story was coming.

'There was a girl in Switzerland,' said Creecher. 'Her name was Justine. She was young and pretty.'

He stared off into the distance, lost in thought. Billy raised an eyebrow. Was Creecher love-struck? It seemed hard to imagine.

'And you knew her?' asked Billy, prompting the giant to continue his story. It seemed so unlikely that he would know any girl, young or old, pretty or not.

Creecher shook his head.

'No,' he said softly. 'I did not know her. How could I? A brute like me. No, no. But I saw her. Once.'

Creecher stared away again and Billy watched him in wonder. Creecher's face was not made for delicate emotions, but there was a yearning there, Billy was sure of it.

'Who was she,' said Billy. 'This Justine?'

'She was a servant in the Frankenstein household,' continued Creecher. 'More than a servant, I should say. They treated her like one of the family.'

'So?' said Billy, concerned that the story was going to end there. 'What has she to do with a hanging?'

Creecher licked his thin black lips.

'Frankenstein had a young brother – much younger – only a small boy. There were many years between them. His name was William.'

'Had?' said Billy. 'Is he dead, then?'

Creecher nodded grimly.

'And what's he got to do with this Justine?' Every word that Creecher spoke seemed to confuse the matter.

The giant's face took on a new level of paleness.

'The boy,' he said, 'was murdered. Justine was convicted of William's murder and hanged.'

Billy raised his eyebrows and puffed out a breath.

'No wonder Frankenstein was a bit shaky,' he said. 'Must have brought back some bad memories for him. His brother and –'

'It was *guilt* you saw,' said Creecher between

gritted teeth. 'Do not credit Frankenstein with pity. You do not know him.'

Billy was about to ask why Frankenstein would have felt guilty about the murder of his baby brother but there was something about Creecher's tone of voice that made him think twice.

But it certainly explained why the hanging of the girl at Newgate had such a profound effect on Frankenstein. Billy shook his head.

'What sort of person would kill a little child?' he said with a curl of his lip. 'Hanging's too good for 'em, that's what I think.'

'Nobody cares what you think!' hissed Creecher.

Billy lowered his head and scowled at the floor, unwilling to look at the giant's snarling face. He was annoyed with himself at how upset he was by Creecher's reaction. He could feel tears stinging his eyes.

'I'm sorry, mon ami,' said Creecher quietly, after a few moments.

'Yeah, yeah,' said Billy.

'It is Frankenstein I am angry with,' said the giant. 'Not you.'

'Didn't feel like that,' said Billy.

'No,' said Creecher. 'I apologise.'

Billy continued to avoid eye contact and

glowered sulkily at the dusty attic floorboards.

'What if we robbed someone?' said Creecher. 'Would that cheer you up?'

Billy looked up with a half-smile. Creecher was grinning back at him.

'It might,' said Billy. 'It just might.'

CHAPTER XIII.

February came and went. Billy's life had now settled into a new and more profitable pattern: every day he would follow Frankenstein and Clerval on their excursions around the capital, and every evening he would tell Creecher what had occurred.

Creecher had taken to reading to Billy and Billy was surprised by how much he enjoyed it and looked forward to it. And every now and then, he and the giant would relieve some gentlemen of their purses.

Thievery had, until then, been a means of survival for Billy and no more. It was not that he had been a bad thief – bad thieves did not survive long; it was just that pickpocketry was never going to make a boy like Billy rich.

And rich was what Billy was now – at least in comparison to anything he had previously known. Only months before he had looked on what he stole simply in terms of what food it might buy once he had exchanged it for a few coppers from Gratz. But now Billy found he had money to spare – a lot of money.

He did not have to risk stealing food any more. He could eat whenever he was hungry and eat well. He had gradually replaced the clothes that Gratz's nephew had given him all those weeks ago, and for the first time in his life he had brand new clothes. However terrified Billy had been of Creecher when they first met, his life was immeasurably better than it had been before.

The change that had come over him was remarkable to see, and none but the sharpest-eyed of his old acquaintances would ever have associated this respectable-looking lad with the rat-eyed thief he had been.

He was a long way from being a dandy, but he had begun to take an interest in his appearance. His clothes were clean and pressed and his shirt was now white. His neckerchief was knotted with a fashionably complex triple knot. He carried a cane.

This change was taken a step further when, one day, he asked Creecher if there was any reason that he could not rent a room, rather than live in the attic.

'Why?' growled Creecher.

'Why not?' said Billy. 'You'll still know where I am.'

'This is all we need,' said Creecher.

'It's all you need!' said Billy.

'It was good enough for you when we first met.'

'Yeah – well, things are different now. I never chose to live like this. I've got money now. I don't need to live like an animal.'

Creecher glowered at him.

'You think I am an animal, then?'

'What?' said Billy nervously. 'No, no. I didn't mean that. I just meant –'

'Look at you,' said Creecher angrily. 'Who are you to sneer at me? You think you are better than me, is that it?'

Billy bit his tongue. He took a deep breath and let it out slowly before speaking again, quietly and calmly.

'I never said nothing of the sort. I ain't better than anyone. I just want a proper bed to sleep in. Is that so hard to understand? What's the point in having money if you ain't any better off?'

Creecher sighed and looked away sulkily.

'Very well,' he said finally. 'Rent your rooms if you must.'

Billy grinned.

'Really?' he said. 'You don't mind?'

'I have said you can do it, haven't I?' said Creecher grumpily, with a shrug of his great shoulders.

Billy thought it wise to leave the conversation to die there and then. He did not care whether Creecher liked the idea or not; Billy was determined to enjoy his new-found wealth.

He looked at several rooms before he chose one. To begin with he was nervous, assuming the owners would see through the mask of respectability to the grimy thief beneath. But this was London. You could be Satan himself, but if you had clean clothes on your back and money in your purse, any door would open.

The first few places he looked at were dingy and flea-ridden, though he would have regarded them as impossibly grand only weeks before. In the end he spent more money than he had intended to rent a couple of small but clean rooms in Soho.

The owner spent a ridiculously long time showing him round the few square yards that would now be his to live in, and when Billy was finally left alone he felt a little faint with the excitement of it all.

He looked out of his window across Soho Square, grinning so hard his face was beginning to ache. Turning towards the door, he saw a key in the lock.

Billy strolled over and turned the key, hearing the mechanism clink into place. He pulled the key out and weighed it in his hand, tears coming unbidden to his eyes. He had never had a space he could call his own and now here he was, a lock on the door and his own clothes in a trunk on the carpet.

He went to the washstand and poured water into the bowl and washed his face. He felt as though he were washing the old Billy away with every splash. He dried his face and looked in the pockmarked mirror.

This is a new beginning, he thought and he made a pledge to himself that he would never ever sink back into his old life, living on the streets. It had seemed that Fate had laid out a set of cards for him, but he was going to sweep them aside.

CHAPTER XIV.

The following morning, Frankenstein and Clerval went their separate ways, and again, rather reluctantly, Billy followed the morose Frankenstein and let the good-natured Clerval go about his day.

Frankenstein once again adopted his familiar wary gait, constantly stopping to turn round as if expecting to be followed – as indeed he was, though Billy took pains never to be seen, pulling down the brim of his hat and studying a newspaper, or reaching for an apple on a market stall.

He followed Frankenstein to a very rough public house in Shoreditch, the kind of place that even a thief like Billy would think twice about entering. The windows were stained to the point of opacity by tobacco smoke and a century of filth. The weatherboards were rotten and riddled with worm.

What was Frankenstein doing there? Slumming it, maybe? Tourists did do that, Billy knew – they liked to get some of the authentic London experience. Some got more than they bargained for.

But Frankenstein would have taken Clerval if he'd been on an exploration of that kind. No – he was up to something, and Billy had a bad feeling about it.

He waited outside. He couldn't risk going in for fear that Frankenstein would notice him. He could hear the sound of rough voices coming from inside, the sound of a glass being broken and a great merry cheer going up at the sound.

The door opened and two men stepped out, collars turned up, hat brims pulled down. One of them looked threateningly at Billy until the other tapped his arm and urged him away.

Frankenstein left about ten minutes later and Billy set off in pursuit. After a few streets Billy guessed where Frankenstein was going and following him became much simpler. He was headed for the small warehouse he had rented.

A grey morning had darkened into a dismal afternoon, the sky like filthy pewter above, the streets dusk dark. Billy stood across the narrow street as Frankenstein disappeared into the gloom of the courtyard. He could hear the keys grate in the lock and the rusty hinges groan their complaint.

Billy couldn't help but be intrigued by the nature of what it was Frankenstein was engaged in. It was clear that whatever he was doing, he did not want any witnesses. Billy waited nearly an hour before curiosity got the better of him.

He crossed the road with his easy, assured tread and slipped silently into the shadows of the covered alleyway.

He edged towards the door and, taking care not to apply any pressure to it and risk a creak, put his face to the keyhole and peered nervously in to see . . . to see . . . nothing!

Frankenstein had not only locked the door, but had been guarded enough to leave the key in the lock and keep the view obscured.

Billy had to stop himself from cursing. He looked again at the wall and tried to think of any possible way that he might be able to glimpse inside, but it was futile.

Then he heard a noise behind him and realised straight away that something was approaching from the direction of the street. Billy quickly moved to the other side of the courtyard.

He moved just in time. Three men, one pulling a handcart, suddenly entered the courtyard. They

were as wary as polecats, twitching and sniffing
the air. Billy knew criminals when he saw them
and he knew when they were dangerous ones,
too. He had a strong suspicion that at least one
of them had stepped out of the inn Frankenstein
had visited.

He held his breath. He could see the men but
they couldn't see him. A bat would have struggled to notice his dark form in the black of that
courtyard.

One of the men rapped at the door. It was a
soft, musical little rap and clearly a signal that
Frankenstein knew, because Billy heard the
jangle of the keys almost immediately and the
door swung open.

Billy could just make Frankenstein out
through the group of men and was surprised to
see that he had no coat on and appeared to be
wearing an apron of the sort a fishmonger or a
butcher might use.

He talked to the men, but Billy could not hear
what was said. He did see Frankenstein hand
over a small bag that he was sure must contain
coins.

After more conversation, two of the men moved
to the handcart and busied themselves with
something on the back. Whatever it was, it was

heavy, because Billy could hear the effort in the men's breathing as they heaved it off and carried it towards the door of the warehouse.

Billy could now see that the bundle was large, too, and covered in some kind of sacking, it seemed. Before he could see more, the men and the bundle they carried disappeared inside and out of view. The third man remained by the hand-cart, waiting for his colleagues.

Billy heard a noise at his feet and, peering into the gloom, saw a rat inspecting the toe of his boot. He clenched his teeth. He hated rats.

He dearly wanted to kick the beast into the neighbouring courtyard but knew that any move-ment from him would alert the man by the hand-cart, and so he had to keep still and allow the rat to go unhindered about its business.

The rat, for its part, seemed to sense Billy's predicament and took full advantage, climbing over his feet, sniffing at his boots and nibbling at the laces.

All of this Billy endured with grim resolve until the rat decided that the leather of Billy's boots might be a tasty snack and set about gnaw-ing one with a real sense of purpose.

That was too much. Billy lashed out and sent the rat skittering, head over tail, across the courtyard. The movement was swift and over in an instant, but the man by the handcart was as vigilant as a spider in its web. He lurched forward, opening a clasp knife as he did so, its huge blade a magnet for any light there was.

Billy saw its steely glint and silently cursed his own stupidity. He was trapped now and there was something about the stance of the man that made Billy sure this was not the first time he'd used that knife.

What was best? To brazen it out and hope the darkness would still conceal him, or to bolt now while there was still some chance of making it to the entrance ahead of the man and his knife?

The closer the man got, the bigger the knife became and the more Billy knew that it would only be a matter of time before he was spotted. His only chance was to run.

He had just tensed his muscles for the race when the man's colleagues reappeared from Frankenstein's warehouse. The man turned at the sound and it was just as well, for the feeble light from the open doorway raked across the courtyard like a searchlight and he would have seen Billy for sure.

'Matt!' called one of the men. 'What you doing?'

'Looking for something,' he said. 'I heard a noise.'

'There's nothing here,' said the other man.

'And I thought we said no names,' said the one called Matt.

'Yeah – sorry,' said the other.

'Don't do it again. Or I'll cut you so as you can't.'

'No need for that,' said the third man. 'Come on. No sense in hanging around. The Frenchman's got his goods and we've got the cash. I'll buy you a drink.'

The man called Matt took one last look into the shadows and, putting his clasp knife away, joined the others in rolling the handcart out of the courtyard and into the street. The sound of its wheels retreated into the night.

For the first time in what seemed like minutes, Billy let out a long sighing breath. But it was even longer before he could move his feet, and then only tentatively, edging his way out of the courtyard as silently as he could, fearful that the men might still be waiting. But happily they had gone and, in seconds, so had Billy.

CHAPTER XV.

Winter's grip was loosening, but spring had yet to make itself felt. The freezing fogs that had choked the city streets were less frequent now, but there had been no respite from the dark overcast days.

Billy couldn't remember the last time he'd seen blue sky and, in his mind, had begun to blame Creecher for the weather. It was as if the giant carried the gloom with him.

On one such dull afternoon, Billy found himself once more outside the gates of Montagu House. Frankenstein and Clerval were paying another visit to the British Museum and he, as usual, was in pursuit.

He paused at the doorway, remembering the scene he had caused the last time he was here. He smiled at the very same attendant who had shooed him out of the building and received a good-natured smile in return. A new suit of clothes and a wash were all that was required to fool these idiots, thought Billy to himself.

He let Clerval and Frankenstein get well ahead. He did not want to risk Clerval being sharper-eyed than the attendant.

They took a different route through the building, pausing to look at some stuffed giraffes. Billy had seen a drawing of a giraffe in a book but had never expected them to be so huge. He wished he could see one alive.

He noticed that Frankenstein seemed absolutely fascinated by a particular exhibit and he waited until he and Clerval had moved on before going to find out what it was.

Billy was amazed to see a large box, like a coffin, containing the shrivelled remains of a human being. He was even more amazed to read that it was hundreds and hundreds of years old. It was an Egyptian mummy – a preserved body from ancient times.

How could a body last so long without rotting and getting eaten by worms? It didn't seem possible. It gave Billy the shivers. And to make it worse, there was something about its wrinkled, desiccated skin and sunken features that was horribly reminiscent of Creecher.

He continued to follow Frankenstein and

Clerval around the exhibits for a while, but his interest became exhausted long before theirs. As he was strolling along Great Russell Street, waiting for them to reappear, he saw the pale gentleman whose purse he had tried to snatch when he was last there.

Billy smiled at the reminiscence as though he were an old man looking back at the fondly remembered wild days of his youth. It seemed like another Billy entirely. A clap of thunder boomed in the distance. The sky was black now, the air strangely clear and still.

He was sure he could have walked straight up to the gentleman and his wife and never been recognised as the filthy street urchin he had been when last they met. The man was standing on the pavement reading *The Times*, seemingly oblivious to the drops of rain that now began to fall.

'Listen to this, Mary,' he said. 'It says here that a Captain John Ross is to sail to the Arctic seas next month to map the north of Canada. Just imagine, all that ice. A frozen desert from horizon to far horizon. Let's hope he doesn't suffer the same fate as Walton, eh?'

'The frozen north is all well and good, my love,' his wife replied with a smile. 'But if you have any hope of getting your family to the warm south, then I am going to require that you please pack your books away.'

'I am at your service as always, my dearest,' he answered, tucking his newspaper under his arm and following her into a house further along the street. The pavement gathered dark spots silently in his wake.

Billy walked up to the building and looked in at the window. A fire was burning in the hearth and candles were lit, and the whole interior glowed with warmth that held Billy in a moth-like thrall. And, like a moth, his heart seemed to flutter in his chest.

Inside he saw the woman walking here and there, doing her best to organise. Another woman about her age sat with a baby on her lap, while a small boy stood alongside, laughing at the baby.

The pale gentleman walked by with a stack of books, and a maid held another baby in her arms, rocking it from side to side, while another young servant girl was polishing candlesticks before putting them in a trunk.

The scene was one of such sweet domestic happiness to Billy's eyes that he wanted the walls and windows to melt away and let him tumble in among those pretty women and laughing babies.

That man, thought Billy, must be the happiest man alive.

He was in the midst of these thoughts when suddenly there was a scream from inside the house and he saw that the man was shouting and pointing at him. He turned and there was Creecher standing beside him. They made their escape round the corner, ducking into a back street. Lightning flashed overhead, followed by a loud explosion of thunder. The rain poured down.

'What are you doing here?' said Billy.

'I could say the same of you,' Creecher replied.

'You frightened the life out of that man.'

'You are not here to watch him,' said Creecher. 'You are here to follow Frankenstein.'

'I just . . .' Billy began, but the truth was he did not know what to say.

There was another flash of lightning and Billy turned to see the man from the house standing in the street, staring at them, his frozen figure reflected in the wet cobbles.

'Who are you?' he called, his voice faltering a little as he looked at Creecher.

A blast of thunder rocked the sky above them and the rain seemed to fall with an even greater violence. It sounded like gravel hitting the street.

'Who are you?' he shouted. 'What do you want here?'

'We meant no harm, sir,' Billy called back. 'Honestly.'

The man took a few tentative steps forward, his eyes fixed on Creecher. Lightning flashed again and illuminated the giant with alarming suddenness. The man staggered back, putting a hand to his face.

'What manner of creature are you?' he said. 'Speak!'

'You would not believe me if I told you,' said Creecher gloomily.

'You are French?'

'Swiss,' Billy interjected.

'No,' said the man, staring wide-eyed. 'No. It can't be. You are –'

'Shelley!' called a voice behind him. 'Come inside, my darling.'

The man turned to see his wife coming round the corner in a hooded cape, allowing Billy and Creecher to make their escape. When he turned back, they were gone.

Billy managed to peer unseen round the corner of the street and watched as the man staggered sideways and clutched at a railing for support. His wife rushed to his side.

'You have not been well, my love,' she said. 'Come in out of the rain. You're soaking wet.'

'Mary,' he said, staring back towards where Billy and Creecher had been standing. 'I thought I saw him . . .'

'Who, my dear?' she asked, following his gaze.

He shook his head.

'Nothing,' he muttered. 'It was nothing.'

'Come along. The lightning has befuddled you. It always does.'

He smiled weakly.

'Yes,' he replied, shaking his head and staring once more at the place where Billy and Creecher had been standing. 'The lightning. It must have been the lightning.'

CHAPTER XVI.

Billy stood across the street from the alley-way entrance to Frankenstein's warehouse. He was nervous. It was late and the businesses were closed up. Thieves like a crowd. Billy hated to be so exposed.

An owl was sitting on one of the chimney tops and Billy cursed. Everyone knew an owl was a bad omen. He was relieved when the bird finally hooted and flew off, with big, lazy flaps of its wings.

Billy walked across the street and entered the alley, its chill gloom gathering about him like a damp cloak. The door was, as always, closed and, were it not for the fact that he knew Frankenstein to be inside, Billy would have assumed it empty. Creecher had told him to leave Frankenstein alone when he was in the warehouse, and not to attempt to follow him in, but Billy's curiosity had become too great. He was tired of being kept in the dark. He had to know what Frankenstein was doing in there. He had to.

He found himself looking again at the walls, searching for a window he knew was not there. He walked the length of the building until it met the back wall of the courtyard, which he climbed.

Standing on that vantage point he could see that the gable end of the warehouse was also windowless and opened out on to a filthy ditch bordering a rubbish pit. The smell was foul, like rotting meat.

Turning away from the stench, Billy noticed a drainpipe that ran down the building near the corner where he stood. It was a stout contraption, old but strong enough to bear his weight, he was certain.

Billy was no burglar, but it looked an easy climb up to the roof and, once there, he would be hidden by a projection of the wall. His days with the sweep had numbed his fear of heights.

Billy needed no further thought and was already climbing before he could raise any objections. Within moments he was hauling himself over the wall on to a small, flat leaded area that ran around the whole roof.

Billy could see one of the large roof lights ahead of him, a honeyed glow coming from the window panes. He edged his way tentatively along, aware that his footsteps might be audible to Frankenstein below.

Once beside the dirty, grime-stained glass, Billy paused, knowing that he could not be sure that Frankenstein might not choose that very moment to look up from his work and see his face peering in. But knowing that meant he either had to take the risk or simply climb back down, none the wiser.

Billy had to know, so he had to look. Taking a deep breath, he rested against the roof slates and leaned round the window frame.

It was a disappointment: the glass was so filthy he could see nothing but a vague glow below. So slowly and silently, Billy began to rub his coat cuff against the grime. At first this simply made the situation even worse, but he persevered and, with the addition of a large drop of spit, he had soon worked a small spy hole in the filth.

Billy placed his face against the greasy glass and his eye over the hole of relative cleanness. It took a little while for him to make sense of what he saw.

Frankenstein was working at a table way below – further below than Billy had imagined and the effect of that was dizzying enough to distract him from what Frankenstein was doing.

Billy's eye widened as he realised that there was a naked body on the table. The body was dead, Billy could tell, even from that distance, and he was also able to see that it was female. Frankenstein was leaning over it, doing something that Billy couldn't see, obscuring the head and torso.

Just as Billy made the connection between the body and that mysterious delivery by the men with the handcart, Frankenstein walked away, returning after a moment with a bow saw. Before Billy had time to grasp what was happening, Frankenstein placed the jagged blade against the cadaver's forehead and, steadying himself for the effort, began to saw.

Billy looked away, but only to see that there were further horrors in that room – body parts on the other tables and in tinted glass jars. It was a butcher's shop of human meat.

The tabletops were smeared with blood and the apron Frankenstein wore was likewise stained and flecked with gore. Lamplight flickered across an arsenal of knives and saws and blades of all kinds.

The scene was nightmarish and made more so by the weird angle of view. Frankenstein walked into Billy's sight once more and he seemed to shimmer and stretch, distorted by the glass and the light.

He paused as if deep in thought and ran the back of his hand across his brow. Billy could see the trail of blood it left. Frankenstein slammed his hand down on the table and then threw a glass jar to the floor with a crash that sounded like it came from a mile away.

Billy didn't need to see any more. He edged away from the window as quietly as he had come, trying to rid his mind of the image of the white knuckles of Frankenstein's fist as he clenched that thin ragged blade.

———◆———

So Frankenstein was an anatomist, a corpse-butcher. Billy had the thief's hatred for that line of work. Surgeons were allowed to use the bodies of those who were hanged, as if the hanging was not punishment enough. Billy had seen men he knew taken to be chopped up by those ghouls.

But there were not enough hanged convicts to go round, even in these lawless times, and so surgeons were forced to employ resurrectionists to pull the recently buried from their rest.

But why was Frankenstein doing such work in England? Grave-robbing was a crime. And it made Frankenstein's reaction to the hanging seem even stranger. Why would a man who thought nothing of butchering the bodies of the hanged faint at the sight of an execution?

But maybe men like Frankenstein put the realities of such things out of their mind. Maybe when confronted by a hanging he was overwhelmed by guilt at the horror of what he was doing.

Billy doubted this somehow. There was something about Frankenstein's manner with the resurrectionists that did not suggest guilt so much as expediency. Maybe it was more the memory of his brother's murder and of Justine's execution.

But surely Frankenstein's work must contain some explanation for his relationship with Creecher. Had he done something to the giant? Was Creecher the victim of some kind of surgery that had gone badly wrong?

This seemed to be confirmed by the grisly pleasure that Creecher took in hearing Billy's report of the work going on in that warehouse. He quickly forgot his annoyance at Billy for taking such a risk.

He showed a particularly ghoulish interest in the sex of the corpse. The sight had made Billy queasy enough, but the grin on the giant's face made him feel even worse.

'So Frankenstein's a surgeon, then?' said Billy.

'Not a surgeon,' said Creecher. 'He is a scientist.'

'A scientist? What's that?'

'It is a person who studies natural philosophy.'

Billy looked baffled.

'They study the world and how it works,' said Creecher, by way of explanation. 'They study the Earth and the heavens and the forces that act upon them. They study the oceans and the forests and the animals that live there. They study the minute and the cosmic. They study life itself.'

'And is that what Frankenstein studies?' said Billy. 'Life itself?'

Creecher looked at him for a long time before replying.

'Yes,' he said.

And there the conversation seemed to end. Billy could think of nothing more to say and Creecher gave the distinct impression that he felt enough had been said already.

'You must leave Frankenstein to his work,' said Creecher after a while. 'We cannot risk disturbing him.'

'You don't want me to follow him any more?'

'Follow him to the warehouse, but there must be no more climbing to look in. I do not want Frankenstein to be scared off. Do you understand?'

Billy nodded. Frankenstein scared off? It would be no hardship to avoid looking in on those horrors.

'Follow him to the warehouse,' repeated Creecher. 'And anywhere else he goes. But no more.'

'What about Clerval?' asked Billy.

'I told you, Clerval is not important to me,' growled Creecher.

'Does he even know what Frankenstein's up to?' asked Billy.

'No,' Creecher replied. 'Frankenstein's work is a secret to all but him and to me, and must remain so.'

Billy nodded again.

'His work is of vital importance to me, do you understand? Vital.'

CHAPTER XVII.

The family in Great Russell Street were not the only ones leaving London. The season was ending and the lords and ladies and well-to-do would be thinking about packing up their London houses and travelling back to their country estates.

And Billy had his suspicions that Frankenstein and Clerval were about to move on, too. They no longer made calls on anyone and, though they still toured the sights of London, he had the impression that they had seen all they wished to see. He also noticed that the two men were buying new clothes – warmer clothes and stout boots. They were clearly envisaging walking in wilder terrain than the streets of London.

Then, one morning towards the end of March, the two men stood at the door to their lodgings and shook hands with the landlord. A cart was brought to carry their bags and boxes of scientific equipment.

Billy considered rushing back to the attic to warn Creecher, but thought it best to find out where they were going first. As soon as they were out of sight he knocked at the door of their lodgings.

The owner opened the door and smiled at him. 'Yes?'

'My master has sent me to deliver a message to Mr Frankenstein, sir.'

'Oh dear, I'm afraid you've just missed them.'

Billy put his hands to his face and pretended to sob.

'Now then,' said the gentleman at the door. 'What's this? Why the tears, lad?'

'My master, sir,' replied Billy. 'He'll beat me, sir. I dawdled when I should have run, sir. If I tell him I've missed them, he's going to be fearful angry. You don't know where they're headed, do you, sir? Maybe I could catch them.'

'If you're quick, you might,' he replied. 'They're going to catch the coach from the Strand.'

'Which coach, sir?'

'The one bound for Windsor, and from there on to Oxford,' replied the man. 'Delightful gentlemen. Foreign, you know – but wonderful manners. I have some forwarding addresses somewhere. They asked me to send on any mail they received. Let me write them down for you, just in case . . .'

Oxford? Billy had no clear image of Oxford, but found it hard to imagine that they would need heavy walking clothes for such a place. The man came back and handed Billy a folded piece of paper, which he put in his pocket.

He set off to the attic and within minutes was climbing in through the window. His entry had raised a small blizzard of dust and, through its swirling cloud, he saw Creecher lying asleep on the floor, tucked in to the slope of the roof.

Billy had rushed all the way there to warn the giant, but now he felt nervous about waking him. There was something so terrifying about that sleeping body. It took Billy right back to that first night. Again, there was no sign of life at all. He appeared, to all intents and purposes, a stone-cold corpse.

Billy took a nervous step forward and the floorboard creaked beneath his foot. By the dim light seeping in from the filthy window, he saw Creecher's dull yellow eye open. The giant breathed hard and then his whole body convulsed, as if sparked into life. Billy jumped back as the giant sat up and stared at him.

'Why are you here?' he growled.

'They're leaving London,' said Billy. 'Frankenstein and Clerval.'

Creecher was on his feet in a flash and lurched towards Billy, his arms outstretched. Billy shielded his face and stepped back.

'Whoa! I know where they're going,' he said. 'I ain't stupid. They're getting the coach to Windsor and then Oxford.' Creecher didn't need to know about the list of forwarding addresses yet. Billy would keep that information to himself for the time being. Never say more than you need to.

'Windsor?' said Creecher. 'Where is that?'

'I don't know, do I?' said Billy. 'I've never been out of London in my life, unless you count Southwark. West, I think. On the Thames.'

'Probably just as well,' said Creecher, with a sigh, handing Billy a news-sheet and pointing to a headline.

'*Giant spectre haunts London*,' quoted Billy and looked up at Creecher before reading the article to himself. Billy and Creecher's activities had not gone unnoticed, it seemed.

'We will wait until dark and then follow,' said Creecher, before walking back to the other side of the attic and sitting down.

'Oh no!' said Billy, shaking his head. 'You

might be going to Windsor, but I ain't. Find yourself some other Billy when you get there.'

'But I do not want to find another Billy,' said Creecher with a frown. 'I want this one.'

'Well, this one is a Londoner and he stays put.'

'I thought we were friends,' Creecher growled.

Billy stared at the giant, looking for a sign that he was joking, but his face was as grim as ever.

'You was about to throttle me a moment ago!' said Billy.

Creecher shrugged.

'Is your life so bad now?' he replied. 'What were you when I found you? A thief, and who knows what later – if you lived that long. What future did you have? Transportation, if you were lucky. The gallows more than likely.'

Billy could find nothing to argue with. It was true. For all that Creecher still unnerved and even terrified him, his life was better now. He didn't want to give that up. Even so . . .

'But I can't leave London,' said Billy plaintively.

'Why not?' asked Creecher, with another shrug.

'I don't know. It's just what I am. It's me. It's where I live.'

'I have no home,' said the giant. 'I belong nowhere . . .'

'Yeah, well, sorry. But I can't help that. I'm not leaving London.'

Billy took a deep breath and felt the dust coat his tongue. He walked to the window and looked across the rooftops towards the river. A fog was rolling in.

'Sorry,' he said, turning back to Creecher.

The giant did not reply at first.

'Perhaps you are scared to leave,' he said after a few moments.

'I'm not scared.'

Creecher looked up at him and then nodded sullenly.

'Well, I cannot make you come,' he said.

'No, you can't.'

An awkward silence ensued and Billy felt compelled to break it.

'Look, I'd better go. Good luck, eh?'

He held out his hand and after a moment the giant reached out and took it. The grip was not as firm as Billy had feared.

'Good luck to you also, mon ami,' said Creecher.

Billy climbed out of the window, expecting as he did so that Creecher's hand would grab him and wrench him back inside. But before he knew it, he was down in the alleyway and heading back towards his rooms in Soho Square.

There was the usual raucous traffic at Seven Dials but he was oblivious to it. Was this how it was going to end with the giant? They would just go their separate ways and that would be it?

Billy shook his head. He needed to think. What was life really going to be like on his own again? Without Creecher he would be back to his old pickpocketing ways, having to rely on whatever Gratz chose to give him for the trinkets he managed to steal. Without Creecher he would never earn enough to pay for his rooms or his clothes or the decent food he'd become accustomed to. He couldn't bear the idea of going back to the boy he had been.

Pickpocketing was a hard life. Some days Billy would take nothing at all. And besides, Creecher was right – it was only a matter of time before he got caught. Everyone got caught eventually.

It was also only a matter of time, too, before he ran into Skinner and the rest of Fletcher's old cronies. Billy might be able to talk his way out of trouble for a while by pretending the giant was still in London, but it wouldn't work for ever.

The more he thought, the slower his footsteps became. Creecher was right – he was scared to leave London. It was the unknown he dreaded most. He weighed his fear of Skinner against his fear of leaving London and found that the more he deliberated, the less it seemed to be about fear at all.

Billy realised that he actually *wanted* to go with Creecher. He did not know where it would all lead, but he knew that he needed to find out; he knew that he was not ready to let Creecher simply walk away and out of his life.

As soon as he arrived at his rooms in Soho Square, Billy packed a bag, settled his rent with his landlord and walked briskly back to the baker's. When he climbed into the attic, the giant was exactly where he had left him, as if waiting for Billy to return.

'All right,' said Billy, dropping his bag. 'Why not?'

'Good,' said Creecher with a grin. 'Then we must –'

'On one condition,' Billy interrupted.

'One condition?' growled Creecher.

'Yeah,' said Billy. 'I want to know who Frankenstein is and why we're following him. Otherwise you're on your own and I'll take my chances here.'

Creecher's frown deepened and Billy readied himself for an attack. But just as the giant seemed about to erupt in fury, he let out a long sigh and hung his head.

'Very well, my friend,' he said. 'You should know. You deserve to know. But I warn you, what you will hear will change your life for ever. Do you still want me to tell you?'

Billy nodded silently. There was a long pause.

'Frankenstein . . . made me,' said Creecher at last.

'Made you do what?' said Billy.

Creecher took a deep breath.

'No, my friend,' he said. 'Frankenstein . . . *made* me. He . . . *created* me.'

'You're saying he's your father?' said Billy, perplexed.

Creecher shook his head.

'No,' he replied. 'He made me. He formed me. With his own hands. He built me.'

Billy stared at him for a moment and then laughed drily.

'That's it, is it?' he said. 'That's the best you can come up with? Do you think I'm an idiot?'

'You asked for the truth –'

'Yes, the truth!' yelled Billy. 'Not a story. Not a joke!'

'It is no joke,' Creecher said.

'It's a riddle, then, is it?'

'No riddle. You have followed him. You have seen the work he does.'

'Yeah – so?'

'Do you not see it?' said Creecher. 'Frankenstein is my maker. I am his creature.'

'No!' shouted Billy, but without conviction, the word 'creature' echoing in his ears. Of course! Mr Creecher. What a fool he was.

'You know in your heart that it's true,' said the giant. 'You have always known that I am not as other men. Even I do not know what I am. Can I be human if I am built by human hands? Am I a machine? Am I –'

'Shut up!' Billy yelled.

'Wait! Billy!'

But he had already climbed out of the attic window and was scrabbling down the roof into the alley.

CHAPTER XVIII.

Billy ran without any real feel for direction. His running was purposeless save for a desire to put as much distance as he could between him and the giant.

He ran until his legs would take him no further and his lungs burned. He stood, doubled over and gasping for breath. It took a few moments for him to recover.

As he collected himself and looked around, Billy realised that he had run, instinctively, back to his old haunts. He was standing in front of the steps of a church, its columns crumbling, the paintwork cracked and peeling on the entrance door, which creaked back and forth in the breeze until a sudden gust slammed it shut. He needed to move on and quickly.

Billy turned off the street down a darkened alley that ran alongside the high-walled graveyard. He could barely see his own feet on the cobbles, but he would have known his way blindfolded.

He was halfway down when he heard footsteps behind him. Was he being followed? The end of the alleyway was in sight. Billy speeded up just as a shadowed figure stepped into his path. He was grabbed by the throat and pulled sideways.

'Well, well,' said Skinner, walking into the light from a window overhead. 'Don't hurt him, Tibbsy. He's one of us. You've come back to see us, Billy. Ain't that nice, boys? And look how smart he is. I do believe you've washed.'

Billy spat and tried to calm his breathing.

'You sound a bit out of breath there, Billy,' said Skinner. 'You want to look after yourself.'

Billy didn't reply but stood up straight, coughed and spat again.

'I'm not in the mood, Skinner,' he said.

'Is that right?' Skinner smirked, pulling a knife from his pocket. The grip round Billy's throat tightened.

'I've got no fight with you,' hissed Billy. 'If it's money you want, there's a purse in my pocket. Take it.'

Skinner nodded to one of the boys holding Billy and he rooted in Billy's coat pocket, found the purse and tossed it to Skinner.

'Thanks for the cash, Billy,' he said, walking

slowly towards him. 'But the fact is I just don't like you – never have.'

'Don't be stupid –' Billy began.

'What?' said Skinner, wide-eyed in mock fear. 'Is the nasty giant going to come and get me, then?'

Skinner looked around. The other boys chuckled.

'Well, where is he, then?' said Skinner, turning back to Billy. 'I don't see any sign . . .'

The boy holding Billy had stopped laughing and was staring in horror at something over Skinner's shoulder. Skinner turned to see Creecher standing behind him.

A strange sound emanated from his throat as Creecher grasped his neck and lifted him slowly from the ground. The other boys were already running, leaving Billy standing alone to watch Skinner's body dangle, twitching, from Creecher's noose-like grip. Skinner's face was turning a darker and darker shade of purple, his eyes bulging from their sockets.

'Let him go,' said Billy.

Creecher looked at him but did not release his hold on Skinner.

'Let him go!' shouted Billy.

Creecher loosed his grip and Skinner fell in a gasping heap on to the cobbles at the giant's feet.

Billy walked over to him and kicked him hard in the ribs.

'If I even see you again, I'm going to have him pull your innards out. Do you understand?'

Skinner coughed and gasped. Billy kicked him again.

'I said, do you understand?'

'Yes!' hissed Skinner.

Billy looked up at Creecher.

'What do you want?'

'I followed you,' said the giant.

'Why?'

'I was worried about you.'

'Yeah?' said Billy.

'Yes,' said Creecher. 'Is that so hard for you to believe?'

Billy shrugged. Creecher slowly turned and began to walk away. Billy stood watching him leave, and then called after him.

'Oi! Wait for me, you big lump.'

He trotted after the giant and they went back to the attic above the baker's. They sat down at opposite ends of the space and, for a while, neither of them said a word.

'How is it possible?' said Billy eventually. 'How can Frankenstein have built you? How can anyone do that?'

Creecher took a deep breath.

'I cannot tell you how he did it. All that I know of my creation I have gleaned from a journal Frankenstein left in his coat, which I took when I fled his laboratory. But he was clever enough not to detail his methods there, no doubt fearing that someone else might read it and reproduce his experiment.'

Billy rubbed his forehead with his fingertips.

'It can't be,' he said. 'No one has the power to do that. It's impossible.'

'And yet he has done it,' said Creecher.

'But don't you know anything about how he . . . made you?'

'I have learned a little of his methods since,' Creecher replied. 'And I have read as much as I can from the works he used in his studies. I do know that he used the marrow from human bones and tissue from various organs to build me. Using his scientific skills, combined with arcane knowledge he acquired from an early obsession with alchemy, he has gained the power to grow flesh and give it life.'

'Alchemy?' said Billy.

'You might call it magic,' said Creecher.

Billy remembered Gratz and the story of the Golem. Sorcery made more sense to Billy than science.

'In truth, what is now called science would once have been called magic,' continued Creecher. 'Maybe there is no difference.'

'I read as many works as I could lay my hands on, the better to understand how Frankenstein had arrived at my creation. I read the works of Jabir ibn Hayyan. I read Hermes Trismegistus and Paracelsus and Albertus Magnus and Nicholas Flamel, and found that for centuries alchemists have sought to master seemingly impossible forces.

'I had little interest in their search for a method of turning base metals to gold. It was their investigations into the life force itself that intrigued me. My eyes widened as I read of the elixir of life – a potion that would grant immortality – and of the creation of homunculi.'

'What the hell is that?' said Billy.

'Homunculi are men created to do the alchemist's bidding.'

'Like the Golem?'

'In a way,' said Creecher. 'But homunculus means "little man". They are smaller than a child. And no one knows if any alchemist has truly succeeded in creating a living being.'

'Until Frankenstein?'

Creecher nodded.

'I believe that Frankenstein's great discovery was in being able to bring life to his creation by harnessing the power of electricity.'

'How?' said Billy.

'It is the spark of life,' said Creecher. 'A man called Aldini came to this very city when you were a baby. He ran electricity through a dead dog, an ox's head – even a hanged man – making them twitch and cavort for the paying public.

'Frankenstein realised that these circus tricks could be so much more. Instead of bringing animation to the dead for a few seconds, he might bring real life to his own creation.'

Billy was still picturing the spasms and convulsions of the hanged man as Creecher continued.

'But for all his learning and powers, Frankenstein did not make the human being he had hoped for,' he said bitterly. 'Instead he built this monster you see before you. He brought me to life, but for what end? What is life without purpose?'

Billy was not sure what the purpose of his life was either, but kept his peace.

'So how did you meet Frankenstein?' he asked instead. 'I mean, how did you meet up after you'd run away?'

Creecher waved the question away.

'What does it matter? I met him and we talked and, though he clearly loathed being in my presence, he agreed to help me. He said that he needed to come to England to meet with some scientific minds that would assist him.'

'But how?' said Billy. 'Is he going to ... cure you?'

'I am not a disease,' said Creecher.

'Sorry.' Billy held up his hands. 'But why are you – we – following him? What is it that you want him to do? How is he going to help you?'

'He has promised to build me a companion,' said Creecher.

Billy was speechless for a moment.

'What do you mean?' he asked. 'Build another like you?'

'Yes,' said Creecher.

'But ... But why?'

'Because then I will not be alone in the world.'

'You're not alone,' said Billy. 'You've got me.'

Creecher smiled.

'That is good to hear. But it is companionship of another kind I want. Frankenstein has promised to build me a mate.'

'A woman?' said Billy, trying to calm the incredulity in his voice. 'So that's why he needs the bodies – the female bodies.'

Creecher nodded.

'He needs fresh organs to work with. He harvests them and stores them in hermetically sealed jars.

'If he builds me a mate, we will quit this world of men and go to the wilds of South America and live there in harmony with nature. The jungles of the Amazon will be our Eden. We have few needs and all will be met in our companionship.'

A procession of troubling images lumbered forward from the shadows of Billy's imagination and he tried in vain to banish them.

What on earth would a female version of Creecher look like? The monster that Billy imagined was worse than Creecher. Though he could not have said why, it somehow seemed even more of a crime against nature to construct a female.

As usual, Billy had the distinct impression that all these thoughts were visible to Creecher, who stared at him with an inscrutable impression, making Billy blush awkwardly and look away.

'I see you do not find the thought appealing,' said Creecher. 'Am I to be denied love, then?'

'I don't know,' Billy answered. 'What do I know about love? You're the one that reads all the books.'

He had never for one moment considered that the giant had any need or desire for love. Every time he felt that he was getting closer to understanding Creecher, he was shocked by some new revelation about the giant.

'Have you never loved before?' said Creecher.

Billy blushed and shook his head.

'No, never. You?'

Creecher shook his head.

'How could I?' he asked. 'What would be the point? No female born of woman would look on a man like me. She would have to be blind.'

Even then, thought Billy, *there's the size of you, the loose skin, the mortuary stink. It would take more than blindness to make you loveable.*

'If I could have a love and we could be together, I would want nothing more,' said Creecher with a childlike enthusiasm.

'But what if he builds this mate for you,' said Billy, 'and she doesn't love you? Supposing you weren't her type?'

Creecher laughed.

'She and I will be the only two of our kind in the world,' he replied. 'She will have the same yearning for acceptance that gnaws away at me. I will love her and she will love me back. There is no doubt about it.'

Billy wondered about this logic. He had never much considered love in his life. Romance was for rich people, not for the likes of him. But would this new Eve love Creecher's Adam simply because there was no other like her? Is that how love worked? He couldn't see what the fuss was about anyway. Who needed girls? Maybe Creecher would come to realise that, too, in time.

Billy was surprised at how resentful he suddenly felt towards this unmade creature. As strange as it was to accept, Creecher was the closest friend Billy had ever had. In truth, he was the only friend Billy had ever had. But all that would come to an end when she appeared on the scene. Billy wasn't going to the Amazon jungle. There was no Eden in store for him. What was the point of traipsing off to who-knew-where, only to be abandoned when Frankenstein had finished his second creature?

He knew that he ought to walk away now. But how could he just go back to being a ragged street thief in the knowledge of all that Creecher had told him? He would worry about the future when the future arrived.

'So?' said Creecher. 'Now that you know who I am, will you stay here – or will you come with me?'

Billy took a moment or two and then held out his hand. There were tears in Creecher's eyes as he took the hand in his and pulled Billy to him, hugging him.

'All right, all right,' said Billy. 'You trying to kill me?'

'Thank you, mon ami,' said the giant, letting him go. 'You will not regret it.'

Creecher clapped Billy on the shoulders and Billy felt a little overwhelmed by the giant's gratitude.

'I'm going to need some more money, though, before we go,' he said after a while.

Creecher smiled.

'Perhaps we will meet some generous dandies on our way to the coach?'

It was Billy's turn to smile.

'You never know,' he said. 'We just might.'

CHAPTER XIX.

Having liberated the purses and belongings from a couple of stout, ruddy-faced gentlemen farmers, Billy and Creecher made the journey to Clerkenwell and to Gratz's den for the last time before leaving London.

Creecher knew the way now and strode off, filling the alleyways with his enormous bulk. Billy was amazed at how quickly the giant had memorised the dense maze of London lanes. Creecher seemed to know them as well as Billy himself now, and he was happy to trust the giant's sense of direction and follow in his wake.

'The old man about?' said Billy as Gratz's nephew stepped out to meet them.

'Oh dear,' said the nephew. 'Oh dear me. I did send one of the lads looking for you, Billy . . .'

'What?' said Billy.

The nephew took a deep breath and puckered his lips as though suddenly tasting something sour.

'Uncle died,' he said. 'Last week.'

Billy could think of nothing to say. He turned to look at Creecher, who stared down at him from under his hat brim.

'Oh yeah?' growled Billy. 'Funeral, was there?'

'A very small one,' said the nephew. 'He didn't have a lot of friends.'

There was an awkward silence.

'We're leaving London,' said Billy, without looking at him.

'I'm sorry to hear it,' replied the nephew quietly.

'Are you?' snarled Billy.

'You've been good business,' said the nephew, with a smile.

'Yeah, well.' Billy could hear his voice getting more and more aggressive. 'I could get him to pull your stinking head off, you know.'

The nephew looked from Billy to Creecher and back again, his eyes flicking back and forth as he tried to weigh up who was the greater danger at that moment.

'I mean no one any harm,' he said. 'There's no need for violence.'

Billy cursed, but forced himself to calm a little.

'Good riddance,' he muttered. 'Good riddance to him. We're leaving London.'

'So you said,' the nephew replied. 'So you said.'

Billy kicked out at the counter and turned to Creecher, who stood in silence in the doorway.

'But when you come back –'

'Who says we're coming back?' Billy snapped.

'But *if* you come back,' said the nephew, with a smile, 'I would be honoured to carry on in business with you. Think about it.'

'Yeah,' said Billy with a sniff. 'We'll do that. Meantime, just give us a decent price on this stuff and we'll be on our way.'

Billy and Creecher began to unload their takings on to the battered and scratched wooden counter, and Gratz's nephew gave each thing his expert attention, his professional detachment being occasionally broken as he spotted a particularly choice item.

'Nice,' he said approvingly, as he totted up the value of the goods. 'Very nice. We're going to miss you, my friends. We shall miss you terribly.'

'Course you will,' muttered Billy.

'Don't be like that,' said the nephew. 'You have to know who your friends are in this game.'

Billy grabbed him by the collar.

'I ain't got no friends,' he said. 'Understand? Only him.' Billy indicated Creecher with a flick of his head. 'I spent my life trying to stay alive in this stinking town, but now I can do what I want, go where I like. I don't need you or your uncle. I'm done with feeding off scraps and sleeping in doorways.'

The nephew flinched as Billy let him go.

'You've certainly done well for yourself,' he said, taking the opportunity to move a little further away.

'You don't know what it's like,' said Billy. 'You and your poxy uncle. You don't know what it's like to have everyone despise you and look at you like you was dirt.'

'No,' said the nephew coldly. 'How could we?'

Billy nodded, not noticing his tone of voice or the bitter smile that accompanied it. He stood, agitated, flexing and clenching his hands.

'I have some more books for you, if you'd like,' said the nephew, turning to Creecher.

'How much?' said the giant.

'No, no. On the house. Call it a farewell gift.'

Billy cursed again and stormed outside into the night air. Creecher emerged after a few minutes, having closed the deal, a purse of coins in his hand. He stood and looked up at the sky, waiting for Billy to speak.

'I hated him,' said Billy, his face lined with the trails of tears. 'Gratz, I mean. Most of the time I hated him. Why the hell am I bothered that he's dead?'

'Because he was once all you had,' said the giant.

Creecher slowly, tentatively, reached out a hand and placed it on Billy's shoulder. Billy flinched but did not move away.

He stood for a moment, the storm of emotions gradually dying away. Then, taking a deep breath, he wiped his face on the back of his sleeve, took one last look at the rickety hovel they had just left and walked away, with Creecher a stride behind.

PART II.

CHAPTER XX.

Billy and Creecher made their way to the Strand as the lamps were being lit. The fog was as thick as sea-coal smoke and Billy was glad of it – it could only work in their favour.

Billy told the giant to hang back in the shadows while he went and had a word with the driver and bought their tickets – outside tickets. There was no way that Creecher could ride inside.

Just as the coach was about to move off, Billy whistled to Creecher, who moved with his usual silent swiftness to stand beside him. They climbed up on to the roof of the coach and grabbed the metal hoops provided, trying to get comfortable.

An old man cried out from the pavement below and someone yelled for him to hurry up. He had barely grabbed the side of the coach before the driver flicked the reins and they lurched forward. Creecher leaned over, grabbed the old man and pulled him up on to the roof.

He was panting and turned to thank Creecher, but his mouth seemed to lock open as he stared in awe at the giant. Billy chuckled to himself. He was sure the old chap would have thrown himself off had the coach not been moving.

The old man grabbed the hoops in his gnarled hands, white as bone. Having seen Creecher once, he seemed determined not to make the mistake again and hunched himself over, collar turned up against the cold.

'Where are you headed?' shouted Billy over the noise of the wheels, as the coach rumbled out of the courtyard and into the street.

'Windsor,' shouted the old man.

'Same as us!' shouted Billy in reply.

That seemed to exhaust the conversation. The old man hunched himself even more and closed his eyes. Billy looked at him with a kind of cold pity.

It was night-time now and they were heading away from the theatres and ballrooms of the city, along the Oxford Road. The great highwaymen and robbers of the past, like Jack Sheppard, had made their last journey down here, rolling along in the tumbril cart, the road thronged with people, making their way to the Hanging Tree at Tyburn. But no one had been hanged there for over forty years now.

Billy wondered if the old man had ever gone to Tyburn. That was the way to go: thousands of people standing at your feet as you gave your last dying speech and waved your fist at the justices of the peace and the marshal and all his men. To die a famous death – what Billy would not give for that!

More quickly than he could ever have imagined, they were plunged into a moonlit world of small houses and cottages, fields and copses. Billy had known that this strange smoke-free, building-less, open world existed, of course, but he had never even thought about it, much less seen it.

It was bitterly cold, and he muttered under his breath, cursing the giant. If it was not for him, Billy could have been inside the coach instead of stuck on the roof, freezing to death.

At one stop they were joined briefly by a younger man carrying a violin case. He took a moment to notice Creecher, but could not thereafter take his eyes from the giant and, when the stagecoach next stopped, he jumped off, even though Billy was sure he had intended to go further.

The cold was not the only hardship of travelling on the roof. Every jolt of every pothole went straight through to Billy's spine, and his arms were aching with the effort of stopping himself from falling off. He wondered at how well the old man held on, despite seemingly being asleep.

Creecher seemed unconcerned by the cold or the movement. His great form sat silhouetted against the night sky, as inscrutable and immovable as a statue, and Billy experienced a twinge of the old fear he had felt when he first met the giant.

But it was a brief moment only. Billy's dread had all but disappeared and been replaced by a sense of awe. Creecher was a wonder – a fearsome wonder, to be sure, but a wonder all the same.

Everything about the giant was extraordinary, and nothing more so than the story of his creation. But Billy had to know the rest of the story. It was a need, a compulsion. He was sure he had not heard the whole truth. And anyway, he was part of that story now.

By the time the stagecoach eventually arrived at Windsor, Billy's whole body felt numb with the cold and the vibration. He stretched and tried to get the blood flowing in his legs.

Creecher crouched a little and leapt from the roof of the coach, landing catlike, with barely a sound on the cobbles below. Billy shook his head in amazement as the giant melted into the shadows of the courtyard. Within seconds, even he would not have known Creecher was there.

The old man was still sitting. Billy tapped him on the arm.

'Come on, old fella,' he said. 'We're here. You don't want to miss your stop, do you?'

The old man did not move. Billy tapped him a bit harder, then grabbed his coat and shook him.

'Hey!' he called down to the driver. 'Come here. Quick!'

The driver gave Billy a long look, and then sauntered towards the coach and climbed on to the roof.

'I think he's dead,' Billy told him.

The driver felt the old man's hands and gave his face a couple of slaps.

'I think you're right,' he said matter-of-factly. 'George! Get up here. We got another dead 'un.'

Billy watched as the man called George climbed up beside the driver and the two of them forced the old man's bony hands to loosen their grip on the hoops. There was a crack as one of the fingers snapped.

'Hey,' Billy cried. 'Watch out!'

'Sorry, lad,' said the driver. 'It's got to be done. Can't very well leave him up here. It happens from time to time. Friend of yours, was he?'

'No,' said Billy.

'Do you know where he was heading?'

'Just Windsor.'

'Well,' said the driver. 'He's here. And it looks like he's here for good.'

'Maybe he has relatives,' said Billy.

'Maybe. Look, we'll check his pockets and see what's there. That's all we can do.'

Between them, the driver and his colleague carried the old man down. Billy followed and watched them as they disappeared into a stable block. Creecher was suddenly at his side.

'You are upset about the old man?' he asked.

'No,' said Billy, his voice catching a little. 'Why would I be upset? He's nothing to me.'

'And yet –'

'Look, I ain't upset,' said Billy, walking away. 'Shut up about it, won't you?'

He turned his back on Creecher and stared into the darkness ahead. The driver and the guard were coming out of the stables.

'Hey!' said Billy. 'Wait up.'

He took out his purse and offered the driver a handful of coins.

'Make sure he gets buried properly,' he said.

The driver took the money.

'That's uncommon decent of you. That's Christian, that is. I'll make sure the old man get's the best. Bless you.'

'All right, then,' said Billy, already turning away.

'But what if his family turn up?' said the driver. 'How will I get the money back to you?'

'It don't matter,' said Billy. 'You keep it.'

He returned to Creecher and they walked away from the lights of the inn and into the shadows.

'That was very kind of you,' said Creecher.

Billy shrugged.

'Yeah, well,' he muttered.

Billy took a deep breath. Tears were forming in his eyes and he was determined not to cry. He thought he would feel better after paying for the old man's funeral, but he didn't. The confusion and bitterness he had felt ever since he had heard of Gratz's death were still there. Creecher put a gentle hand on his shoulder.

'Kindness is not a weakness, mon ami,' said the giant quietly.

'Yes, it is,' said Billy.

CHAPTER XXI.

It was so quiet in Windsor in comparison to London. There was no way that Creecher could secrete himself in a place like that, even allowing for his ghost-like stealth. So Billy and the giant headed to the outskirts of town, where they found a suitable old barn for Creecher to stay in.

Billy made his way back to the coaching inn. It did not take long to find out the whereabouts of the Swiss travellers. They had, in fact, taken a cottage at the edge of the forest, not far from the barn in which Creecher resided.

Billy booked himself a room for the night. He may as well sleep in comfort – he was exhausted and his bones ached. But he was surprised to find that he could not get the old man from the coach out of his head. He kept picturing him there, hunched over, gripping the handles. He heard the snap of that finger and every time it made him flinch.

Billy was never going to grow old. That was no way to go, snuffed out like a candle. He was going to go out roaring if he had anything to do with it. What was the point of being alive if no one noticed when you died?

Billy thought of Creecher and wondered if the giant would ever grow old or ever die. Could you die if you were never truly alive? Would Creecher still be striding the Earth centuries from now, when everything Billy knew had turned to dust?

The bed was as lumpy as a patch of ploughed earth, but exhaustion won through and Billy slept soundly enough until the morning coach woke him as it rumbled out of the courtyard.

The route back to the barn was so different in the morning light. Although the sky was grey, the mist clung like cobwebs to the meadows and the lane Billy walked along. A farmer eyed him suspiciously, but he tipped his hat and walked on.

The lane curved through a stand of trees and, as Billy rounded the bend, he saw his way blocked by a herd of deer. They looked at him, each face a picture of alert concentration, each eye a fathomless black.

Billy froze in wonder. For a few seconds nothing moved except the twitching tails of the deer, and then they were off, bounding away across the meadow and out of sight.

Billy's heart raced with excitement. He grinned, exhilarated. He had never seen a deer in his life before; he did not even know what they were, and it took Creecher to name them from Billy's description.

Billy told the giant what he had discovered about the location of Frankenstein and Clerval's cottage. From the directions Billy had been given, it could only be a ten minute walk away through the forest, and so they set off.

Billy and Creecher looked out from the trees at the edge of the forest, the smell of damp earth and rotting leaves rising up from the ground. It was so dark where they stood that it was as if they stood in the night, and the cottage in the day. Even the thin sunlight that managed to seep through the clouds contrasted so sharply with the gloom of the wood that Billy had to squint into the relative brightness.

Within minutes of them watching, Clerval came out of the cottage, stretched and placed a knapsack on the ground beside the open door. Frankenstein emerged moments later and Billy could feel the giant flinch beside him, as if he was having to resist the urge to run towards Frankenstein.

The ever-cheerful Clerval slapped his friend on the back, picked up his pack and headed off. Frankenstein looked around him, and seemed to hesitate when he looked in their direction, but Billy knew there was no way he could see them. Could he sense Creecher? he wondered. But after a few seconds, Frankenstein set off after Clerval.

When both men had gone, Billy and Creecher walked over to the cottage. They peered in through the window, but there was little to see.

'Well, he's not working here, is he?' said Billy.

'No,' said Creecher sullenly. 'Does he think that I will wait for ever while he amuses himself, walking in the woods? Perhaps if I snapped Clerval's neck it might focus his thoughts.'

Billy winced at both the image and at the sudden change in Creecher's tone of voice.

'Still,' said Billy in an effort to placate him. 'the fellow at the inn says they're only here for a couple of days before heading on to Oxford. They've probably sent everything on.'

Creecher nodded grimly, still staring after the two men.

'When will he keep his promise to me?'

There was such a terrible longing in that voice, a black despair that Billy had never heard before. He was used to Creecher sounding angry, but this was something new. Billy reached out and touched Creecher's arm. When the giant turned there were tears in his eyes.

'Look,' said Billy, 'I know how annoying it must be –'

'Annoying? If only it was merely annoying.'

Billy said nothing, sure that whatever he said it would not make things better. He could see that Creecher was upset but felt powerless to help. It was Creecher himself who broke the silence.

'It is all I think about,' he said quietly. 'The idea that one day I will not be the only one of my kind. One day I will have someone to share my isolation with and we will each be everything to the other.'

The giant looked up into the forest canopy above their heads.

'But in my darker moments I think about what it will be like if Frankenstein does not fulfil his promise.' There was a note of desperation in his voice.

'He will,' said Billy. 'Of course he will.'

'I wish I could be so sure,' Creecher replied. 'What if something were to happen to him? What if a robber were to attack him and kill him? If he dies, my dream ends with him.'

'He's not going to die,' said Billy with all the comfort he could muster. But to himself, he had to admit that Creecher had a point.

'But if he did,' Creecher went on, 'I would be doomed to continue alone. I do not even know if I can die. Perhaps I will live on, for all eternity, alive and yet not quite alive, shunned and rejected.'

'Listen to yourself,' said Billy. 'I'm telling you – you need to stop reading all that gloomy poetry. It's turning you into a right misery.'

'But –'

'Frankenstein ain't going to die, and he is going to build you a mate,' said Billy. 'Course he is. You worry too much.'

He sat down on a fallen tree. After a few moments, Creecher joined him. Billy felt uncomfortable. He didn't know what to say. He struggled to remember what his mother might have said when he was a boy and feeling sad. He slapped the giant on the back.

'Everything will work out. You'll see.'

Creecher looked at him with a quizzical half-smile.

'It is unlike you to be so cheerful and optimistic.'

'I know,' Billy said with a chuckle. 'It must be the clean air or something.'

'All I want,' said Creecher, 'is to have another of my kind to spend my life with. Is that so wrong? If I stay among ordinary people I fear I will become the monster they all think me to be.'

Billy nodded and stifled a yawn.

'Yeah, well,' he said. 'Let's hope it all works out, eh?'

'But what if –'

'Look, I've said it'll be all right, haven't I?' said Billy. 'You don't have to go on and on.'

Creecher's face froze in a sullen frown and he stared off into the distance. Billy closed his eyes and sighed.

'Look, I'm sorry,' he said. 'It's just that –'

'Family is everything,' Creecher added. 'Without a family we are nothing. It is the centre of everything.'

Billy stared at him in disbelief.

'Family?' he said. 'You're planning to start a . . . a family?'

Creecher looked at him.

'But of course, mon ami,' he said.

That these two man-made giants might mate and produce children who would themselves go on to create a race of giants was an idea so unnatural it seemed impossible to contemplate.

'But how do you know that . . .' began Billy. 'I

mean, what if you can't ... you know ... ?'

'Then we will be content with each other,' said Creecher. 'But I see no reason why we will not be able to make children. Mere humans seem to have no difficulty –'

'Look,' said Billy suddenly, feeling sick, 'I've got to get going.'

'Very well,' the giant replied. 'If you –'

'I've got to go,' said Billy impatiently. 'Meet me at the inn tomorrow night and we'll coach it to Oxford.'

———— •◦• ————

It took Billy a while to get to sleep, but sleep he did, falling into a deep and formless void – or so it seemed at first. For slowly, as though his eyes were becoming accustomed to the dark, Billy began to discern recognisable shapes amid the gloom.

In this dreamworld it was still night-time, but there was a strange blue light washing the scene. He looked for the moon but could not find it. He was not in his room any more; he was back in the wood where he had left Creecher.

He was still struggling with this confusion when he saw that Creecher was standing near the fallen tree, and he called to him.

The giant turned round and it was then Billy saw that he was not alone. Though Creecher's figure obscured most of the view, Billy could see that whoever stood there was almost the same height.

'Creecher!' called Billy. 'Who is it? Who are you talking to?'

Creecher's teeth shone blue-white in the strange twilight and he turned back to the mystery figure, and Billy could hear them talking.

'Creecher!' called Billy.

Creecher began to walk towards Billy with the other person following behind. As they approached, the mysterious figure came into view and Billy was amazed to see that it was a woman. She was gigantic, like Creecher, and entirely naked.

'Children!' called the woman. 'Billy is awake! Come and meet him.'

Billy stared in horror as from out behind shrubs and trees came, one after another, a procession of gigantic children, each of them naked like their mother and formed like an infant, though they were very nearly Billy's height.

They moved with a horrible speed, clamber-ing over any obstacles that blocked their path and swarming towards Billy. He scrabbled back against a tree, cowering in fear as they slowed their movements and came to stand in a silent, inquisitive group around him.

They were all in silhouette. One of the children moved forward and into the blue light. His face was like Creecher's, pale and loose-skinned, his eyes deep-set, his mouth hard and lipless.

Billy gasped and jerked out of his nightmare, hitting his head on the bedside table.

'Owww!' he hissed. 'Damn it!'

He rubbed his head and tried his best to clear it of the image of those children, but with little success. They were still haunting his thoughts when he waited for Creecher at the coaching inn that evening.

CHAPTER XXII.

'**I**s that a bump on your head?' asked Creecher.

'A bump?' said Billy. 'Oh – yeah. I banged my head getting out of bed.'

Creecher chuckled and Billy blushed, leaving the giant to hang back in the shadows while he went to buy the tickets to Oxford.

Moments before the coach was due to set off, they strode across the courtyard with their bags and climbed on to the roof.

The driver and guard were engaged in furtive conversation. Billy frowned. He had been around dubious characters long enough to recognise them when he saw them. The guard, whose flattened, broken nose made his wide face oddly featureless, burst into laughter and slapped the driver on the back. The driver whistled to the horses and flicked the reins. The coach moved forward and they were off.

Billy and Creecher were alone on the roof this time, and each settled into his own world. Billy hunched his shoulders in a vain effort to hide his ears from the chill. Occasionally the raucous voices of the driver and guard would rise above the background rumble of the coach wheels and, every now and then, he would glance over at the black shape of Creecher, silhouetted against the blurred background. Billy wondered what went on in that mind of his.

Some miles into their journey, Billy noticed that the coach seemed to be picking up speed. The driver and his guard were passing a bottle between them and the driver whooped with delight as he flicked the reins and urged the horses on.

Billy got a better grip on the hoops and he saw that even Creecher was now looking concernedly at the trees hurtling past.

'Oi!' yelled Billy as a low branch whistled past his ear. 'Slow down!'

He was not sure that either the driver or the guard heard him, but neither took the least bit of notice if they did. Instead the pair cackled like witches, and the coach raced onward, heading downhill through a wood, gaining speed all the time.

As it rounded a bend, Billy felt his side of the coach rise. He looked over the edge and saw the wheel lifting from the ground.

'Slow down, you fool!' he yelled to the driver. 'You'll have us over!'

The guard threw him a wild look, his flat face looking like a carnival mask. He laughed as the driver gave another flick of the reins. This time the wheel began to float and the coach to tip.

Billy had a strange weightless feeling for a few seconds. He saw the driver panic and struggle to regain control, but it was too late. The coach leaned and fell on to its side.

The lane was banked and, fortunately, treeless at this point, otherwise it would have fallen flat on its side and even been crushed with the weight of those inside and the luggage on top.

Creecher and Billy were flung free on to the bank while the horses dragged the coach on two slanted wheels until the driver could get them to stop.

Billy shook his head and rubbed his neck, and gingerly got to his feet. Creecher was already standing and seemed as unharmed as if he had simply stepped from the coach.

Billy ran to help the guard get the people out of the coach, while the driver calmed the horses. The passengers were shaken but seemingly unharmed. They were forced to climb out of the door on to the side of the bank, and slide down to the ground. While Billy helped an old man out, the passengers all gathered on the other side of the lane, staring back at the coach.

'It's going to take an age to get that righted,' said the guard. 'We'll have to uncouple the horses and see if we can't drag it on to its wheels. Hopefully they ain't damaged – or the axle – otherwise we'll have to ride into town and fetch help.'

'And what are we supposed to do while you do that?' said the woman passenger. 'These woods are full of highwaymen and murderers.'

'Maybe if we all got round behind it and shoved,' a young soldier suggested.

'Hah!' said the old man. 'You may be able to shove. You can't expect me to do it – or the lady there.'

Suddenly there was a great creaking sound, and everyone turned to see the coach moving slowly towards them, until finally it landed back on all four wheels.

The lady began to applaud, and slowly everyone, including Billy, joined in. Creecher stood back and Billy could tell that he was bemused and touched, and a little embarrassed.

'Bravo!' said the lady. 'He is a Hercules.'

She walked forward with the lamp.

'Come on, sir,' she said. 'Don't be shy –' But she did not say anything else. She put her hand to her mouth in horror and staggered backwards. She screamed once – a sound so shocking in that dark and silent place that it seemed to rip through the air like a ragged blade. And then she dropped to the ground in a faint.

Her husband rushed to her side and stared at Creecher. Another passenger rushed forward and picked up the lamp she had dropped as she fell, and advanced on Creecher, who did not move an inch.

The others edged behind him as the light gradually illuminated the giant. He had removed his hat and scarf in his efforts with the coach and even Billy, who had seen him many times, shuddered at the face the lamp revealed, set against that gloomy place.

'Sweet mother of –'

'He's some kind of monster,' shouted the old man.

'A devil more like,' the guard muttered.

'I sought only to help,' said Creecher.

'He's French!' cried the driver.

'He ain't French,' said Billy.

'I ought to know that accent,' said the driver. 'I was at Waterloo, fighting them bastards.'

'He ain't –'

'Do something!' yelled another.

The guard walked forward with his blunderbuss and aimed it straight at Creecher.

'Hey!' shouted Billy, rushing forward and standing in front of Creecher. 'Why don't we all calm down a bit, eh?'

'He tried to kill my wife!'

'He never touched your wife!' Billy protested. 'And have you all forgotten it was him who set the coach straight? Without him you'd all still be stranded here.'

'It was the weight of him that probably turned us over,' said the driver, and everyone murmured their agreement.

'You brought the coach down, you lying bastard!' yelled Billy at the driver. 'I told you to slow down!'

'The lad's right,' said one of the passengers. 'You were driving too fast.'

Billy saw a flicker in the driver's eyes and, while the man was clearly never going to accept responsibility for the incident, it did seem to stop him in his tracks and calm him a little.

'Come on,' he said, turning to the passengers. 'Everyone back on board.'

'What about them?'

'Look,' said the driver. 'Do you want to get to Oxford, or do you want to stand here all night?'

After a small pause and some disgruntled muttering, the passengers returned to the coach. The guard, who had never once taken his eyes off Creecher, lowered his blunderbuss and followed them.

'Thanks,' Billy said to the driver.

'You'll have to make your own way from here,' he replied.

'What? You can't just leave us here in the middle of nowhere.'

'It ain't that far. But even if it was, there ain't no way you're coming back on that coach. Try it and Jack will blow your face off.'

A stream of the foulest abuse Billy could muster burst from his lips and outlived the rumble of the coach wheels as they died away in the distance. Eventually Billy stopped yelling and stood, head bowed. An owl hooted in the woods nearby.

'Come,' said Creecher.

'Shut up!' Billy snapped. 'Why do you have to be such a . . .'

He snarled and kicked a moss-covered branch and sent it tumbling into the darkness. Without the coachlights, the moon provided the only illumination to the scene.

'You see how it is for me,' said Creecher. 'I try to help and –'

'It's always about you, isn't it?' said Billy. 'Oh, poor me – I'm ugly and no one likes me. Boo hoo, boo hoo. Well, life ain't a bowl of cherries for the rest of us neither!'

'But you can live among them . . .'

Billy fumed for a few moments, unable to express his feelings. The truth was he had never felt part of 'them'. He had never belonged.

'Oh, yeah. I can get treated like filth,' he replied. 'I can starve or steal. I can hang. If you want someone to feel sorry for you, you've come to the wrong place.'

'Yet you would not see me shot, mon ami,' said Creecher.

'Look what is that "monnamee" thing you keep saying? It's getting on my nerves.'

'My friend,' said Creecher. 'It means my friend.'

'Ha!' Billy snorted. 'That's funny.'

He started to walk in the direction the coach
had taken, heading for the cover of the trees.
Creecher stood motionless for a few moments,
before following Billy into the moon shadows.

CHAPTER XXIII.

Billy and Creecher walked for a long time without speaking. The forest was dark and silent, save for the sound of their footfall and the occasional screech of an owl, or the frantic, rustling departure of some unseen creature in the undergrowth.

Branches clawed at Billy's face and fanged brambles caught on his clothes. Billy flapped them away angrily and looked up at the blue-black sky visible between the latticework of twigs high above his head.

Billy had led the way, but quickly found that it was easier to walk behind Creecher, in the path that the giant cleared. He scowled as he walked, staring malevolently into the huge black shadow ahead of him, blacker than the night.

They continued like that for some time, neither of them saying a word. The trudge of their feet on the bracken was the only sound, and its steady beat had a hypnotic and calming effect on Billy. Gradually his anger subsided. It was Creecher who spoke first.

'We should rest,' he said gently, turning to Billy. 'You should sleep.'

Billy could barely make out any features in the giant's face, save for the faint blue glow of a smile.

'I ain't tired,' said Billy, stifling a yawn, the last vestiges of grumpiness clinging to his voice.

'Just a few hours. You will feel better.'

Billy sighed. He did not have the energy to argue. He still felt angry with Creecher for their situation and angry with himself for getting mixed up in whatever it was that he was mixed up in. But there seemed little point in forcing an argument with Creecher. The last thing he wanted was to be left alone out there in the middle of a forest.

With a dexterity, skill and speed that amazed Billy, Creecher gathered enough dry material to start a fire with flints he took from his coat for the purpose. Seemingly within moments they were squatting in front of a warming blaze, the sparks taking flight, like fireflies, to follow the coiling blue smoke's journey towards the night sky.

'How come you know how to do that?' asked Billy, when he could no longer maintain his sulky silence.

'I lived for a long time in the forest,' Creecher said. 'I needed warmth as you need warmth.'

'How come you were in the forest, then?'

Creecher poked at the fire. Sparks flew around his head and his pallid face was lit by the yellow flames, making his eyes glow like hot coals.

'When I ran away from Frankenstein's laboratory,' he said, a terse tone of bitterness in his voice, 'I had to learn to live from the land.'

Creecher carried on gathering wood. Billy thought of how it had been when he had run away, so thankful to be away from the sweep, but so quickly aware that he might die on the streets, friendless and starving. The chill memory of it made him move closer to the fire's warmth.

He remembered another boy telling him about Gratz and how he would let you stay in the dry of his warehouse if you ran a few errands for him. It took Billy a day or two to realise what these errands were and, by that time, he was a thief.

'When I ran away, I had to find a living in the city,' said Billy. 'I suppose we both . . .'

Billy looked up to see Creecher walking off into the woods.

'Oi!' said Billy in a panic. 'You just going to leave me here?'

'I am going to fetch some food,' said Creecher. 'You must be hungry. Stay there. I won't be long.'

Billy hunched himself up, edging a little closer to the fire. The darkness seemed to have swallowed Creecher whole and there was no sign of the giant at all. There was only the sound of Billy's breathing and the flames' crackle and hiss.

Creecher seemed to be gone an age and Billy kept slipping into sleep, just managing at one point to stop himself falling face first into the fire. He was just relieving himself against a nearby tree when the giant appeared in the firelight, making him start. He carried an armful of what looked like rotten vegetables.

'What the hell is that?' asked Billy. 'I thought you'd gone for food.'

'This is food,' said Creecher.

'Don't look like it to me. I thought you was going to catch us a rabbit or something.'

'I've told you before,' said the giant, 'I do not eat flesh.'

Creecher gathered his bounty and began skewering it on sticks to put into the flames to cook. He tossed a white root towards Billy, who caught it and eyed it suspiciously.

'Eat,' said Creecher, biting into a similar one. 'They're good.'

'How do you know it's not poisonous?'

'It's not, believe me.'

Billy took a tentative bite and raised his eyebrows. Creecher smiled.

'Not bad,' said Billy.

And the rest of Creecher's assortment of roots, leaves, bulbs and berries were likewise surprisingly appetising. Billy sat back at the end, satisfied and full. Tiredness now overwhelmed him and, wrapping himself in his coat, he lay down.

His eyes grew heavy and Creecher's massive form began to melt and warp in the heat haze from the fire. The giant shimmered like a ghost as Billy's eyelids finally closed.

Billy woke just before daybreak as the canopy above him rang with the songs of a thousand birds. He blinked and tried to focus his eyes, looking up through the layers of leaves.

Sitting up he saw that the fire had died away to red embers and there was a sharp chill. He hugged himself and slapped his own face, trying to wake up. Then he realised there was no sign of Creecher.

Billy, city boy that he was, had a fearful dread of being left alone in the wood. But before he could decide what he was going to do about such a calamity, he saw Creecher striding soundlessly through the undergrowth towards him.

The moment that Creecher returned, the birdsong stopped. The effect was so startlingly sudden, it was as if Billy had instantaneously been struck deaf.

'What is it?' said Creecher, seeing the look on Billy's face.

'Nothing,' said Billy. 'I thought . . . Nothing.'

Creecher frowned and studied the boy's face.

'Come,' he said. 'I have found water.'

The giant led him to a stream meandering through the trees, opening out into a wide pool as black as oil.

Billy drank and the water was cold and caught in his throat, making him cough and then laugh. It tasted good. He splashed some on his face and put his whole head under, laughing again when he emerged, flicking water from his hair.

When he looked at Creecher, he saw the giant crouched over the pool, staring as though in a trance. He was staring at his own reflection.

There was a look of black despondency on his face.

'Hey!' called Billy. The giant took a moment to respond. 'We've got a bit of a problem, haven't we?'

'What is it?' said Creecher.

'Our bags are still on that coach,' said Billy. 'I can hardly follow Frankenstein dressed like a tramp, can I? We need money.'

Creecher sighed, as if these things were a tedious bore to him.

'What do you suggest, my friend?'

Billy smiled.

'I'm suggesting we do a spot of highway robbery!' he said gleefully.

Creecher frowned.

'Why do you take such pleasure in theft?'

'Why shouldn't I?' said Billy defensively. 'It strikes me that the whole world runs on theft of one kind or another. Anyway, I'm good at it.'

Creecher stared at Billy, making the boy shift uneasily.

'You hate the world, don't you?' said Creecher.

'Maybe I do at that,' said Billy. 'The world ain't exactly been no friend to me, has it? Besides, I don't see you wasting much love on the world, neither.'

Creecher's mouth twisted into a half-smile.

'True enough,' said the giant. 'We shall hate the world together, then.'

'It's a deal,' said Billy, shaking Creecher's hand.

CHAPTER XXIV.

Billy pulled the kerchief up over his nose and mouth and stepped out into the lane, holding his hand up.

'Stop there, gents,' he called. 'I'm going to have to ask for your purses and pocket watches.'

The carriage ground to a halt, the horses twitching nervously. There was a moment's pause while the two men in the carriage looked at each other. Then one pulled a pistol from his pocket and they both laughed.

'I don't see that happening, friend,' said the man with the pistol. 'And I'm going to need a good reason why I shouldn't blow your head off.'

Billy nodded.

'Fair enough,' he said.

Creecher strode out from the shadows alongside the carriage, grabbed the man's arm and snatched the pistol from him, hurling him to the ground.

'Is he a good enough reason for you?'

The two men stared at Creecher in terror and the horses snorted and pulled at the reins.

'Your valuables, gentlemen,' said Billy. 'NOW!'

The men fumbled in their pockets, throwing anything they found to Billy.

'Sure that's everything?' said Billy. 'Only, he's hungry and I promised him a snack. He's fond of liver. Human liver, that is.'

The driver whimpered and threw his bag, purse and watch at Billy's feet.

'Thank you, gentlemen,' said Billy with a bow. 'My colleague and I wish you a safe journey.'

As soon as his companion had scrabbled back into the carriage, the driver flicked the reins and they sped away down the lane. Billy had barely waited for them to disappear before he ripped his kerchief off and danced around.

'Ha!' he cried. 'Who'd have thought it? Me, a highwayman!'

Creecher seemed less than overwhelmed by the experience.

'Don't you ever get excited by anything?' said Billy, annoyed at having his enthusiasm so dampened.

'Not by robbery,' Creecher replied.

'Are you joking?' said Billy. 'I spent my life hearing tales of highwaymen. It don't get much more exciting. Shhh. Someone else is coming.'

The next person was a doctor on horseback. He had a pistol, but his horse was so terrified by Creecher's presence that it threw him to the ground before he could pull the trigger.

He did not have much of value on him, save for a pocket watch and a few coins, but Billy took the pistol before they sent him on his way.

The next arrival in the lane was a student and his father, making their way to Oxford. Despite the fact that neither of them showed the least interest in resisting, Billy made a great show of twirling his pistol, and almost shot the student's ear off when he accidentally fired it.

'No more pistols,' said Creecher, when the two men had disappeared after donating their purses, rings and watches. Before Billy could protest, the giant took the pistol from him and threw it far away across a hedge.

'Hey!' said Billy. 'Do you know how much they cost? We could have sold that! It ain't like you to be bothered about strangers getting damaged.'

'It's not them I'm worried about,' said Creecher. 'You're as likely to blast your own head off as shoot anyone else.'

Billy smiled. It was true. He had never fired a pistol before in his life.

'You have a go, then,' he said.

'What?'

'You do the talking for a change. You don't need a pistol, do you?'

Creecher's expression showed he wasn't keen on the idea.

'Go on,' said Billy. 'Or are you scared?'

Creecher raised an eyebrow and gave Billy a withering look.

'I am not scared.'

'Well, then,' said Billy. 'Next person who comes along.'

They did not have to wait long. A few minutes later, a portly gentlemen came cantering along the lane on a large white horse. Creecher stepped out in front of him.

'Stand and deliver!' said the giant.

The horse's eyes nearly popped out of its head in fright. It reared up, kicking out towards Creecher with its hooves, and then turned and galloped away, its rider just about managing to stay in the saddle.

'Stand and deliver?' said Billy, stepping out into the lane himself and looking at the horse and rider receding into the distance. 'No one says that.'

'But it is what highwaymen say,' said Creecher. 'I have read –'

'You and your books,' Billy sighed. 'You can't believe everything you read, you know.' He chuckled. 'Look at him go!'

Creecher joined in the chuckling and soon the two of them were howling with laughter.

When he had dried his eyes and come to his senses, Billy decided it was time to go. The traffic coming from Oxford would have been forewarned of their presence and it would only be a matter of time before someone called the marshal. So they left the lane and moved on under the cover of woodland, until they could see the spires and towers of the ancient university thrusting through the horizon.

They looked for somewhere for Creecher to stay and, just as at Windsor, a ruinous barn, partially overgrown and on the verge of collapse, seemed to provide a good hideout for the giant, who inspected it as though he were about to invest in a new property, nodding with approval as they emerged from its dark interior.

Billy headed into town and paid for a room at a cheap but respectable inn. He told the innkeeper that he was a secretary for a legal firm in London, bringing some important paperwork to Oxford.

When he mentioned that he had been the victim of a highway robbery but had managed to fight them off, the innkeeper was full of sympathy, and he received many hearty pats on the back from the customers in the bar. He enjoyed the lie.

Billy had put all their loot into the bag they stole from the doctor and, once in his room, he emptied the contents out on the floor to assess their value. It was a good haul.

He tested the bed, acknowledging its softness with a grateful grin, and headed back out into the street.

Billy found himself staring in amazement. London was a building site, with new terraces and squares going up every week. What was old seemed tumbledown and rotten, soot-crusted, unloved.

Here in Oxford the ancient buildings rose up all around in honey-coloured stone, bristling with spires and finials. It was like something from a fairy tale.

Billy lost no time in buying himself a new suit of clothes with the money they had taken in their highway robberies, and then he went on the slightly more hazardous expedition of searching for someone to exchange their stolen goods for cash.

He was nervous about such a venture in a foreign town, but it went smoothly enough. One of the college porters pointed the way for a few coins and, half an hour later, he was in the back room of a riverside public house, shaking hands on the deal and pocketing a purse full of cash.

With the forwarding addresses he'd been given in London, it did not take long to find Frankenstein and Clerval either. They had rented rooms near the library.

The two men were easier to follow here than in London. Oxford was a bustling town, but it was nothing like as busy as the city. Following them undetected without the cover of crowds, however, was a challenge.

The difference between the two men seemed marked now. Their excursions took a similar form to those in London, with a mix of sight-seeing, academic study and meetings. The difference was that this time it was only Frankenstein who had the meetings. Clerval's business interests had evidently been taken care of in London, as he was now a tourist and nothing more.

He and Frankenstein walked the streets, gazing up at the gateways of the hallowed colleges, and strolled along the river as punts glided by. They went to museums and galleries and then, as before, Frankenstein left his friend to go and pay visits on various learned gentlemen.

One afternoon, after a few days of following the two men around Oxford, Billy noticed that Frankenstein seemed particularly impatient, and Clerval sensed it, too, taking every opportunity to try to raise his friend's spirits.

Clerval was clearly oblivious to Frankenstein's work and no doubt put his friend's mood down to the troubled past that Creecher had alluded to, or to his friend's growing addiction to opium.

When Clerval made it clear that he wanted to visit the Ashmolean Museum, Frankenstein refused, miming a headache and pointing in the direction of their hotel. Good-natured Clerval naturally offered to forgo the visit, but Frankenstein insisted and they parted company.

But Frankenstein immediately veered from the course that would have taken him to the hotel and instead walked away from the centre of town until he came to an ivy-covered workshop. Billy waited for him to go inside and then crept stealthily closer.

As with Frankenstein's warehouse in London, there was no easy way of seeing in. The only windows were high up in the tall walls. Billy was not disappointed. He had no real wish to see what Frankenstein might be up to inside.

It seemed such an innocuous place, half covered in foliage. No one would have guessed the nature of what was going on there.

But as unsettling as he found Frankenstein's work, Billy felt compelled to know everything he could about the man and what he was doing. It had gone beyond a chore he performed for Creecher; a dark curiosity gnawed at him.

Billy stood transfixed, not wishing to go further, but just as unwilling to turn and walk away. A blackbird trilled in a nearby tree and shook him from his trance. He was about to leave when Frankenstein suddenly emerged from the door.

The scientist came out into the light like an animal from its lair. His face was pale and drawn and there were beads of sweat on his forehead. He fixed Billy with a fierce gaze that Billy found hard to hold.

'Who are you?' Frankenstein demanded, in a similar accent to Creecher's. 'What do you want here?'

'Nothing,' said Billy. 'I lost my way.'

Frankenstein looked unconvinced and started to walk towards him. Billy cursed himself for being so stupid. He turned and ran, with Frankenstein calling after him.

But now Frankenstein had seen him. He would have to be more careful.

CHAPTER XXV.

Billy walked back to Creecher's barn at dusk. He decided it might be best not to mention bumping into Frankenstein.

The light was swiftly draining away and the moon was already dimly glowing from behind the sooty clouds. Creecher stepped out in front of Billy, making him jump back with a cry.

'Can't you just cough or something,' said Billy, clutching his chest, 'so as I'd know you were there?'

'I'm sorry,' said Creecher. 'I did not mean to startle you.'

Billy took a deep breath.

'Yeah, well. No harm done. Frankenstein has a place down by the canal. He's back at work.'

Creecher nodded.

'It makes sense,' he said. 'This is a place of great learning. He will perhaps gain some knowledge that will help him in his work. I want to see this warehouse for myself.'

'What? I thought you didn't want him disturbed. If he –'

'I just need to see with my own eyes, mon ami,' Creecher broke in. 'I have waited so long.'

Billy sighed.

'Come on then,' he said.

They entered the streets of Oxford as night took full grip of the city. As they walked past a church, Billy called for Creecher to stop.

'Where are you going?' asked Creecher.

'Nature calls,' said Billy, climbing over the wall.

'In a graveyard? Have you no respect for the dead?'

'No, not especially,' Billy whispered from behind the wall. 'When you're dead, you're dead, ain't you? I don't think they'll mind . . . Hang on – what's going on over there?'

'What is it?' said Creecher, climbing the wall.

'Down!'

Creecher did not move. Billy grabbed hold of his arm and pulled him towards the tombstone he was sheltering behind.

'What is it?' Creecher asked again.

'Keep   your   voice   down,'   said   Billy. 'Resurrectionists.'

'I do not understand.'

'Bodysnatchers,' Billy explained.

The silence that followed this word seemed to last for an age. A flood of images raced through Billy's mind; the view of Frankenstein amid the bloody machinery of his work, the face of the hanged girl, the glint of yellow light that tripped along the saw's teeth.

He took another peek round the headstone. Two men stood a little way off, looking into an open grave, their forms lit by lantern glow from inside the pit. Billy could see the flickering shadows of a third man, who must have already climbed down to open the coffin.

He took a deep breath and motioned to Creecher to leave the graveyard. Then, rising silently and keeping low behind the headstones, he made his way to the gate. But when he turned round, expecting to see Creecher behind him, he saw instead the giant's silhouette against the blue-black sky.

'What are you doing?' Billy whispered, retracing his steps. 'Get down.'

'I'll be back,' Creecher replied, striding towards the resurrectionists without turning round.

Billy caught up with him just as one of the men spotted the giant and shouted to his colleagues. But a heartbeat later, Creecher had grabbed him, and Billy heard the snap of the man's neck and the crunch of broken skull as his body was tossed aside to hit a stone cross.

One of the other men hit Creecher a mighty blow across the shoulder with a shovel, but the giant shrugged it off without breaking his stride, pulled the shovel from his grip and swung it at the retreating figure. The blade smacked into the man's spine, making him howl in agony.

The howl did not last long, however, as Creecher was on him in a flash, picking him up and hurling him, face first, into the railings. The man fell and did not stir.

Billy saw the body of the buried corpse, lying like a discarded puppet, the shroud smeared with blood, its flesh pale and smooth as though it had never seen the light of day, like the worms that it would feed.

The only man left now was the one in the grave itself. Lamplight shone up, illuminating his face, and Billy could see fear and anger fighting for control.

The man pulled a pistol from the waistband of his trousers, cocked it and pointed it at Creecher.

'I'll send you back to hell, you devil!'

He fired. The flash lit the place for a split second, like a bolt of lightning. Creecher staggered backwards, put a hand to his shoulder and inspected the blood. Then he looked back at the man and smiled. Then he jumped into the grave.

Billy turned away and wished he didn't have to hear the man's last agonised sounds. When all was silent, he glanced back and saw the resurrectionist crumpled like a doll, his face rammed into the mud wall. Creecher was standing in the grave beside him, his head and shoulders visible above the edge. The lantern in the pit lit his features from below and cast a long, eerie shadow up the gravestone behind him.

There was something so horrible about the image that Billy took two steps back, and the effect was only made more disquieting as Creecher slowly heaved himself out to stand, beshadowed and backlit, by the open grave, as though resurrected at the Day of Judgement.

'Come on,' said Billy. 'That shot must have been heard. We shouldn't be found here.'

They left the churchyard and walked away towards the centre of town. Billy could not bring himself to look at the giant. The sight of him climbing out of that grave was still lodged in his mind.

'You are angry with me?' said Creecher.

'I'm fine,' Billy muttered.

'You feel sorry for them? For the grave-robbers.'

'No, I just . . . We could have just gone.'

'Those men rob the dead of their peace,' said Creecher. 'I hate them.'

'You're mad, you know that, don't you? Where do you think Frankenstein got his bodies from? How do you think he does that filthy work you seem so keen for him to do? How do you think he . . .' Billy tailed off.

Creecher scowled.

'Yes – I know,' he said after a few moments. 'You are right, of course. It is just that sometimes . . . sometimes I wish that I had never lived.'

He looked at Billy, his mournful eyes sparkling.

'It is mad, you are right. But I did not ask to be brought into being. These people – they and Frankenstein – have no right to do what they do. I need them and yet I hate them all the more for needing them. Does that make sense?'

'I don't know,' said Billy. 'Maybe.'

Creecher looked at the ground for a long time and then back at Billy. He wore the expression of a petulant child.

'I saw you get hit,' said Billy. 'Don't you feel pain?'

'Oh yes,' Creecher replied quietly. 'I feel pain. Sometimes it seems like it is all I feel.'

'Then how can you stand it?'

'Because I am also strong, mon ami.'

Creecher gave him a bitter smile and sat down and pulled his coat from his shoulder. His shirt was red with blood.

'Nasty,' said Billy.

'Yes, my friend. I bleed like any ordinary man. You have a knife?'

Billy nodded.

'Yeah. What of it?'

'The ball is in my shoulder,' said Creecher matter-of-factly. 'You must get it out.'

'What? I ain't doing that! You need a doctor or something.'

'I cannot go to a surgeon. Look at me. No – you must do it.'

Billy took a deep breath and closed his eyes tightly.

'Why did you have to tell me how sensitive you were?' he said, as he took his knife out. 'You could have said you didn't feel any pain.'

Creecher smiled at him.

'It will be fine, Billy,' he said. 'Quickly now.'

Billy gulped and leaned forward. The ball had hit the muscle of Creecher's shoulder and lodged there. He looked at the wound and swallowed hard. Although it bled like any wound, it looked more like a damaged piece of meat, as if it was a side of pork which had been struck instead of human flesh.

Billy put the tip of the blade into the wound and almost immediately he felt it touch the metal of the ball. Clenching his teeth so tightly he thought they might shatter, he slid the knife under the ball and jerked his wrist, flicking the ball out.

Creecher took a long breath and clicked his neck noisily. Then he shrugged his coat back over his shoulder.

'That ain't the end of it,' said Billy. 'Blood's going to get poisoned. That shoulder's going to rot, mark my words. I've seen it happen.'

Creecher shook his head and stood up.

'Not to me,' he said.

Billy frowned at the giant, who was already walking away.

'How come?' he asked, catching up.

'My body does not allow it,' Creecher replied flatly.

Billy raised an eyebrow.

'What? You're immune, are you?'

'I do not get infections of any kind.'

'But you must do,' said Billy. 'Everyone does.'
Creecher shook his head.

'Not me.'

'How come?'

'All things shun me,' said Creecher. 'Even disease. It is because of that I need a mate –'

'Shut up!' hissed Billy, putting his hands over his ears. He kicked out at a nearby wall, wincing as his toes hit the stone. 'This whole thing is crazy! Me. You. All of this. I'm risking my life with you around, and as soon as Frankenstein builds you your mate, you'll dump me, won't you? Won't you?'

'Billy –'

'I don't hear you denying it!'

Creecher reached out, but Billy stepped back.

'Perhaps I should get Frankenstein to build *me* a mate, eh?'

'We are friends,' said Creecher. 'That is also important to me.'

'For now,' Billy replied.

'But listen –'

'I don't want to hear it,' said Billy, and he walked away towards his lodging house.

CHAPTER XXVI.

Billy went to bed in a bad mood and woke with the selfsame scowl etched on his face the next morning. He got up and got dressed, and stomped outside into a day as gloomy as his mood.

He was cross with himself as much as anything else. What was he doing? What was he thinking of, leaving London to wander across England with this murderous giant?

Creecher's obsession made him dangerous company. He didn't care about Billy. All he cared about was getting his mate. Nothing else truly mattered. Billy had left London in the full knowledge that Creecher's whole purpose in being in this country was to ensure that Frankenstein kept his promise. It was not as if the giant had lied to him or tricked him.

Creecher wanted a mate and he wasn't going to rest until he had one. And then he was going to take her to the wilds of South America and that was that. They would raise a hideous pack of monsterlings and Billy would be forgotten about.

He couldn't help but be repulsed by the idea of that grotesque family. He thought he had accepted Creecher as a kind of human, but realised now that this acceptance could only go so far. A female version of the giant was bad enough, but the idea that they would breed more of their kind . . .

And Billy was going to get cast aside while these abominations created a whole race of monsters. The two things seem to merge in his mind – the pain of being discarded and his disgust at the notion of Creecher's monstrous progeny.

It was time for him to start looking out for himself again. Creecher was going his way and Billy needed to go another. He was alone. He had always been alone. Nothing had changed. Not really.

Yet he felt strangely affected by the mix of emotions rising up in him and, try as he might, he could not altogether ignore it. Billy had never felt important to anyone but his mother, and he had believed himself to be important to Creecher. He had believed that they were important to each other. He felt a wave of pain surge through him like a bolt of electricity.

As a distraction, he picked up a copy of the local paper someone had left on a bench. Leafing through it, something caught his eye. There was a report about highwaymen on the London road. He was in the paper! He was famous!

Billy read on excitedly, a grin across his face. But that grin soon disappeared as a thunderous scowl moved in to replace it.

'What?' growled Billy. 'It was me who did all the talking!'

Apart from a brief mention that he had an accomplice with him, the newspaper had devoted the whole piece to Creecher, telling its readers that the man was a giant with a London accent, who kissed all the ladies before he robbed them.

There weren't even any ladies! Billy thought angrily, screwing up the paper and tossing it on to the pavement, which was starting to spot with raindrops. He walked away down an alleyway, muttering to himself.

'Hey, you!' someone called from behind him. The voice was vaguely familiar.

When Billy looked round he saw the guard from the coach striding towards him with a group of men. Before he knew what was happening, he found himself surrounded and staring down the barrel of a cocked pistol.

'What's this?' said Billy, with as much bravado as he could muster. 'Leaving me in the road wasn't enough for you?'

'Where is he?' shouted the guard above the noise of the rain hammering against the cobbles. Billy could taste the gin on his breath.

'Who?'

The pistol was rammed forward, cracking against Billy's skull and making him wince.

'Don't play with me, boy!' hissed the guard.

Billy wiped away the blood that had begun to trickle between his eyebrows.

'I've been looking for you,' the guard went on. 'I thought you might show up and then, when I heard about the giant highwayman – well, I knew it must be you. I asked around and found out you'd been in the Blind Dog, looking for a fence.'

'What do you want?'

'I want your French friend,' snapped the guard. 'He lost me my job. He owes me some money, he does. And I aim to get it. So where is he?'

He pointed the pistol at Billy's face. His hand was shaking so much Billy was sure that he was going to squeeze the trigger, whether he meant to or not.

'All right, all right,' said Billy. 'The giant. Yeah. I know who you mean. But I don't know where he is, I swear.'

'Then that's bad luck for you.'

'Wait! *Wait!* All right. I'll tell you.'

The guard smiled and put the pistol down. He looked round at his comrades and grinned. He turned back to Billy and hit him hard in the stomach, making him double up in pain.

'Lie to me again and I'll kill you,' he snarled. 'Now take us to him.'

'Take you there?' said Billy.

'That's right. What? Do you think I'd just take your word for it?'

Billy was shoved back down the alleyway to where a cart was waiting in the road. The guard told him to get up at the front and the rest of the men climbed in the back.

As Billy took his seat he could see that the cart was full of chains and manacles.

'You're going to take us to him and you're going to persuade him to come quietly,' said the guard.

'I don't think so,' said Billy.

'I don't see that you've got much choice. Although I suppose we could just kill you here and take our chances with the giant . . .'

The guard sat alongside him and rested the barrel of his pistol in Billy's lap, leaning forward to whisper in his ear.

'The first time you play me false I'm going to blow your balls off.'

'Look, he's nothing to me,' said Billy. 'He made me go with him. You've seen what he's like. I couldn't do anything else.'

'Is that why you stood in the way when I was going to shoot him?' said the guard, as the driver flicked the reins. 'Now, which way?'

Billy nodded ahead.

'He's in a barn just out of town. But you ain't going to get those on him. Do you think he's going to let you? And he ain't going to be scared of that neither.' Billy looked down at the pistol.

'Let us worry about that, lad.'

In no time at all they were rumbling down the track that led towards the barn.

'He's going to kill all of you,' Billy said, his voice quivering with the motion of the cart. 'And then he's going to kill me for bringing you here.'

'Is that the place?' said the guard.

Billy nodded sullenly. His mouth felt dry, his palms clammy. He did not know what was going to happen in the next moments, but he was sure it was not going to be good. The driver pulled on the reins.

'Get out,' said the guard, shoving Billy in the ribs with the pistol.

When they had advanced a few yards towards the barn, he told Billy to stop and then pressed the pistol against the side of Billy's head.

'Call him out,' he hissed.

'Creecher!'

There was no response.

'Again!' said the guard.

'Creecher!' repeated Billy, more loudly this time.

Still nothing stirred. The guard twisted the barrel against Billy's scalp.

'Come out of there, you filthy troll – unless you want your little friend here to have his head blown off!' he shouted. 'Don't make me ask again!'

After a short pause, Creecher emerged from the barn. He had to stoop to get through the door and stood, head bowed, staring at the guard with cold fury in his shadowed eyes. There was a general groan of fear and wonder from the assembly.

'Finlay – get the chains.'

Creecher growled and clenched his hands into mighty fists and started towards the guard, who didn't even flinch.

'One step closer and I blow this boy's brains out.'

'Balls one minute, brains the next,' said Billy. 'Make your bleedin' mind up.'

'Shut up,' snarled the guard.

Creecher growled like an angry dog and Billy shut his eyes and waited for the pistol blast. But when he opened his eyes again, to his amazement, Creecher was standing still.

'Now you're going to let these fellows put some jewellery on your foul carcass and you ain't going to lift a finger to stop them. Cos if you do, this boy's meat – understood?'

Billy could not believe it when Creecher simply nodded in response. The men moved forward gingerly, but gained in confidence as, first, manacles were locked round the giant's ankles, and then his wrists. A great belt was tied around his middle and chains from his wrists and ankles were locked to loops along its length. Finally, a metal collar was placed around Creecher's neck and chains attached from loops on this to further loops on the belt.

All through the process, Creecher gazed directly at Billy and never once looked away.

'Excellent,' said the guard. 'Give him the drink.'

A man advanced towards Creecher, holding a small bottle. Creecher pulled back his thin black lips and bared his teeth in a snarl.

'Don't worry,' said the guard. 'It ain't poison.'

Creecher's snarl remained in place.

'Drink it!' hissed the guard.

The man with the bottle hesitated, but the guard nodded for him to carry on and, when he held the bottle to Creecher's lips, the giant allowed the liquid to be poured down. A moment later he blinked once and then shifted his weight, shaking his head.

'Just a little potion of my own devising,' said the guard. 'It will make you a little more obliging. Get him in the cart, men. Quick, quick. That's right, put the sacking over him.'

The guard let Billy go, shoving him to one side. He threw a purse at Billy's feet, where the coins it contained spilled on to the dirt. Billy wiped the blood from his forehead with the back of his hand and cursed.

'For your trouble,' said the guard, laughing as he climbed in next to the driver.

Billy looked up from the coins to see the cart rumbling away and Creecher staring out from under the sacking with a look of cold, murderous hatred.

He walked over to a tree stump and sat down. The rain had stopped, but he was soaking wet and cold. He hung his head and closed his eyes. He sat there for a long time.

Billy was free now. He could do what he liked. His life had been possessed by the giant for months, but now he was gone. Billy should never have become involved in his affairs in the first place. Creecher's struggle was his own business. Whatever happened to him and Frankenstein was none of Billy's concern. They could all rot for all he cared.

He was sick of hearing how badly Creecher had been treated. Because he was one of a kind, he thought that his pain was unique. But Billy knew all too well what it was like to be ignored, shunned and despised.

No – Billy should not feel bad about the giant. He ought to be happy: happy that he could do what he liked without fear of being throttled; happy that he was free again. And yet . . . Billy did not feel as happy as he thought he should. He was unable to shake off a growing sense of guilt, and it was not a feeling he was accustomed to.

This guilt made him angry. He had done nothing wrong, after all. Creecher could hardly expect him to let someone blow his brains out. He had had no choice.

But that thought only led inevitably to the memory of Creecher giving himself up. The giant had allowed himself to be taken to save Billy's life. He had gone willingly, without a struggle.

'I never asked you to!' shouted Billy to the wind. 'I don't owe you nothing!'

He shook his head. Why had Creecher done it? By the time the guard had shot Billy, the giant would have been on him, and Billy had no doubt at all that he would have killed any who had not the wit nor the wherewithal to escape. Creecher had put Billy's life ahead of his own.

But why? It didn't make sense. He had made it plain enough that all he cared about was Frankenstein building him a mate.

Billy returned to his lodgings, ignoring the disapproving looks he received from his landlord, and changed into dry clothes. He sat in front of his fire, staring into the flames. As his bones began to warm themselves, he became calmer.

He looked into the fire glow, into the blurred brightness of the flickering flames, and images from the past weeks shimmered before his eyes.

He seemed to see Creecher rise up and save him from Fletcher that first frosty night outside the bookshop. Then he looked again through the greasy window at Frankenstein in his blood-soaked laboratory, and saw Creecher rise once more from that open grave in the churchyard.

These spectres of the past and others danced before his eyes, but the one that returned again and again was the vision of Creecher being led away in chains.

'I don't owe you nothing,' said Billy quietly to himself.

CHAPTER XXVII.

Billy edged his way along the side of the stables. It had been easy enough to find. The guard was too cocky and drunk to imagine he had be followed from the coaching inn.

There was a half-moon, low in the sky. It gave Billy enough light to see where he was going without revealing his presence to anyone who might walk by.

As he approached the corner of the stables, strange noises sounded from a nearby copse. Billy had no idea what they were, but they made him jittery. The countryside seemed to be alive with squawking and barking and twittering.

He stepped behind the trunk of an ancient oak tree and felt his way cautiously round its massive girth, his hands rumbling over its cracked and weathered hide. Peering round, he saw a man sitting on a barrel outside the stable entrance, smoking a pipe, the red glow of it pulsing as he sucked.

Billy waited patiently until the man got up to answer a call of nature, before slipping silently into the darkness that lay between him and Creecher's prison.

The stables were pitch-black at first, until Billy's eyes grew a little accustomed and he saw that some light did seep through cracks in the shutters.

'Pssst. Creecher?' he whispered.

There was a bearlike moan in response.

'You ... come to ... gloat?' said Creecher slowly from the shadows. His speech was slurred. 'You ... who ... betrayed me.'

'I didn't betray you,' said Billy. 'Shhhh. What's the matter with you? You sound drunk.'

'Drugged,' Creecher replied. 'Why ... why ... are you ... here?'

'That's nice,' said Billy. 'I didn't have to come here, you know.'

'Then ... why have you?'

'Keep your voice down. I've come to get you out. After all, it was my fault – you being here. In a way.'

Creecher growled.

'He was going to blow my balls off!' hissed Billy. 'What was I expected to do?'

'You got ... your ... reward,' said Creecher.

'Look, I never asked for the money, but I wasn't about to give it back neither. I could have used it to get to London but I didn't. I came here. Now do you want my help or not?'

There was no response from Creecher and Billy took a deep breath and turned to walk away.

'Oui. Yes. I want your help. I am –'

'Shhh!' said Billy. 'There's someone coming.'

Billy scuttled clear of the building and hid outside, his eye pressed to a crack in the shutter. He saw two men enter the darkened ruin, like ink into filthy water.

'Are you asleep?' said a voice Billy recognised all too well. It was the guard from the coach.

Creecher made no response.

'No matter,' said the guard. 'No matter. We will soon go our separate ways, my giant friend. I am about to have a meeting with a learned gentleman with an interest in the natural sciences.'

The guard and his partner chuckled. Billy frowned. Frankenstein? Had Frankenstein discovered that Creecher was here? Creecher groaned.

'The gentleman concerned has a particular passion for anatomy. He's not as interested as I am in your sparkling wit. But he was most intrigued when I told him how big you were. I explained that you'd been ill for quite some time, and he said, were that illness to reach a fatal conclusion, he would buy your body in the interests of science. There now, you ugly piece of meat,' said the guard. 'You're going to make a contribution to mankind. You should be proud.'

Creecher stirred in his chains.

'Nothing to say?' said the guard. 'Never mind, never mind. Now drink this.'

'No,' said Creecher.

The guard sighed.

'Either you drink it or I take one of your eyes. It's a shame to damage the goods, but I think you'll still make a decent price.'

Billy heard Creecher moan, and it was clear that the guard had given him the potion.

'Good boy,' he said. 'That should keep you quiet for a few hours.'

'I thought we were going to see if that Swiss fellow wanted him,' said the other man.

Swiss fellow. Billy's ears pricked up at that. Was Frankenstein going to be offered his own creation?

'Nah,' said the guard. 'He only wants women, remember.'

'Well, I'm sure that can be arranged.' There was the sound of chuckling. 'But what about our gigantic friend here?'

'He ain't going anywhere, not until I decide what to do with him,' said the guard. 'Don't worry. Those chains would hold an elephant. Besides, that drug will knock him senseless. Come on – let's get a drink.'

The two men walked away and Billy left a long interval before going back to the stable door.

'Creecher!' he hissed. There was no response. 'Creecher!'

Billy entered the stables and felt his way over to where the giant sat draped in chains. The chains were certainly strong, but so confident were the men of Creecher's inability to break them that they had fixed them to the ring set into the stone-flagged floor with rudimentary padlocks.

'Creecher!' whispered Billy again. The giant still made no sound.

Billy opened the padlocks with ease. He had been able to pick more complex locks than this since he was eight or so. After loosening the locks from the ring on the floor, he traced them up to the manacles on Creecher's legs.

The locks on these were a little more testing, but Billy still had them open in a minute or two. After freeing Creecher's legs, he traced another set of chains up to manacles on his wrists, which were in turn attached to the metal yoke around his neck.

All the time he worked he kept saying Creecher's name. Billy's eyes had gradually become accustomed to the gloom, but it was still too dark to discern the giant's features. He was simply a great black shape, silent and motionless as a coal heap.

Finally, the last lock was picked and Billy could pull all the chains aside and fling them to the floor. As soon as he turned back to Creecher, an arm shot towards him and one of the giant's huge hands closed around his throat.

Billy gasped and struggled, beating the arm with all his might. It was only because the giant was drugged that he eventually loosed his grip, allowing Billy to scuttle quickly backwards out of reach.

'It's me, Billy, you madman!' Billy hissed, rubbing his throat.

'Bill-ly,' repeated the giant sleepily.

'Come on, we have to go. If they come back, we're both dead men.'

'Dead . . . men,' said Creecher.

'Oh God. Come on! You have to get up. You have to move.'

'Move.'

'Yes!' said Billy. 'Get up. Get up!'

Just as it seemed the giant was never going to move at all, Creecher slowly began to stand. Billy thought it best to get out of the stable, just in case his confusion returned and he decided to grab Billy again.

Billy stood in the track and watched the stable door, waiting for the giant to appear. The moon came out from behind clouds long enough to shed some dim light on the scene. Slowly Creecher shuffled out. He walked backwards at first, and then, as he reached the doorway, he turned and stared at Billy.

The effect was horrible in that light. The drugs had made the giant's face look even less animated than usual, his eyelids heavy, his gaunt head lolling. His arms hung limply at his sides.

Creecher looked at Billy as if trying to register who, or even what, he was. His head tilted and he peered into the gloom. Then he raised his arms and moaned plaintively, feeling the air between them. It was a pathetic gesture, as though he were a small child, confused and looking for reassurance. Swallowing his fear, Billy stepped forward and took the giant by the hand.

'Come on,' he said. 'You're all right. You're safe. You're with Billy now.'

'Bill-ly,' repeated the giant. 'Friend.'

'Yeah,' said Billy quietly. 'Friend.'

And he led the shuffling giant away along the dimly lit track.

They found refuge in a copse of trees on the outskirts of the town. Billy was worried that passers-by might hear Creecher's moaning as he tossed and turned in a drug-addled nightmare, shaking himself free of the opiate's grip.

The giant's jet-black hair only served to exaggerate the awful pallor of his skin. But studying Creecher's face for so long made Billy realise, for the first time, that there was nothing inherently ugly about the shape of it. In fact, though it took an effort of will to see it, the features were noble – handsome even. But the pleasing symmetry of Creecher's face was not enough to mask the horror that lay behind it.

While the giant writhed in his stupor, Billy forced himself to watch as the skin wrinkled and stretched over the barely concealed muscles of his face, as the thin black lips pulled back to reveal those brilliant white teeth and yellow-white gums, and as blood coursed visibly through a network of veins.

Could Frankenstein really have made Creecher? It seemed impossible. Yet Billy could see that Creecher was not human – or at least not wholly so. He was not simply the victim of disease or an accident of birth. He was some other kind of being entirely. He was something new, something unnatural.

But unnatural or not, Billy did sense humanity in Creecher. He was not some man-shaped thing. He had feelings and desires. He had a heart and, for all Billy knew, he had a soul as well.

CHAPTER XXVIII.

Creecher flailed about, fighting invisible demons, whimpering and crying – and, all that time, Billy stayed by his side, leaving him only when he slept soundly and then just to fetch water to feed the giant's raging thirst.

Often, Creecher would wake and immediately check for Billy's presence. As soon as he saw that the boy was there, he would fall asleep once more, calm and content.

Sometimes, when Billy was sure that the giant was fast asleep, he would creep close and lean his ear next to Creecher's mouth, fascinated by his breathless, deathlike slumber.

The only person Billy had ever looked after in his whole life was his mother when she had grown ill. But he had been too young to do anything but watch her die.

Now Creecher really did need him. And Billy had never felt needed before. It was a good feeling. It felt like nothing Billy had previously experienced.

He wondered if this was how Creecher had felt when he'd looked after Billy in the attic as Billy drifted in and out of his fever sleep.

Once Creecher was revived, Billy led the way and they left all signs of Oxford behind them, crossing fields and meadows and heading into open countryside. Creecher's movements were a little drunken at first and more than once he put an arm out for Billy to take. Eventually they ended up beside a canal.

'I wonder which way's north,' said Billy.

Creecher pointed along the canal.

'How do you know?'

Creecher shrugged.

'I just do,' he replied.

Billy sighed and shook his head.

'Look, there's a boat. Can you row?'

Creecher nodded. 'Yes, but –'

'Come on, then, before anyone sees.'

Creecher got into the boat and, after loosening the mooring rope and throwing it aboard, Billy climbed in after him. The giant began to row and the boat moved along the water as if powered by a steam engine.

'Woo-hoo,' cried Billy, waving at two children

who stood staring in disbelief on the towpath.

'Why do you ask which way is north?' asked Creecher as he rowed.

'Because that's where we need to go. We need to head north,' said Billy.

'Why?'

'Because that's where Frankenstein is headed. They're travelling to Scotland.'

'Scotland?' said Creecher.

'Yeah, they're going to somewhere called Matlock first and then Cumberland and –'

'How do you know all this?' growled Creecher.

Billy hesitated.

'The landlord of their rooms in London,' he said. 'He gave me their – what do you call it? – their itinerary, didn't he?'

Creecher's eyes narrowed.

'And were you ever going to tell me?' he asked.

'Probably not,' said Billy. 'I don't know. It just felt good to know something that you didn't. You weren't telling me anything back then.'

Creecher took a deep breath and smiled.

'No more secrets,' he said.

'Fine by me.'

There was a silence while the two of them adjusted to the new footing their relationship seemed to have gained itself. Creecher suggested they make camp, and they pulled up at the side of the canal, near a ruined church. They walked across a field that bulged with the remains of a deserted village, the foundations lying under a blanket of grass, like a sleeping army.

The church ruins provided shelter from a wind blowing in from the east. Billy helped Creecher gather some food, taking guidance from the giant on whether such and such a plant or berry was edible or not. Creecher made a fire and they sat down to eat the food they had gathered, Billy longing for some meat, but also proud that he had helped in the hunt.

'So,' said Billy. 'Are you ever going to tell me anything else?'

Creecher sat back.

'About what?'

'About you,' said Billy.

'What is it you want to know?' he asked.

Billy did not know where to start.

'Well, I don't know. Do you remember anything about how you . . . how you came to be alive?'

Creecher shook his head. 'Do you remember your birth?' he asked.

Billy saw his point.

'When I try to recall those first moments, my mind is awash with confusion,' said Creecher, frowning. 'It is a whirlwind of sensations, of light, of sound. I felt hunger and thirst, I felt cold and afraid, without really knowing what hunger, thirst, coldness or fear actually were.

'I discovered that I could move. My eyes were gradually able to focus and I could see my hands. I saw the fingers flex and then controlled the movement and became aware of that control.

'I had been lying on a table of some kind – a fact I only discovered when I moved and fell on to the stone floor. Pain was my next lesson.

'I lay there a few moments before, clumsily and shakily, I managed to get to my feet. A newborn child would have been immobile, but I seemed to have been born with an innate sense of how my body worked. I was more like the deer or the calf – able to walk, albeit unsteadily, within moments.

'But understand that I did not know what I was or where I was. I had jumped into existence. I looked about me but could not make any sense of what I saw.

'Using the furniture as support, I made my ungainly progress around the darkened room. But, of course, I had no knowledge at this time that darkness was not the norm.'

Billy shook his head, trying to imagine what it

must have been like to be the giant and take each step, not knowing what lay ahead.

'Then I saw a light,' continued Creecher. 'It was not bright, but it attracted me as though it were a diamond.

'I staggered towards its gleam and reached out a hand to touch it, but found my hand blocked by a barrier. I had no way of knowing, but what I saw was the moon, and the barrier was the glass of the window.'

Creecher smiled at the recollection of this foolishness and Billy was happy to join him.

'What happened next?' asked Billy.

'I saw an opening nearby – a doorway – and I walked through. The moonlight was brighter here and shone on to a stairwell.

'Over the fumes of the chemicals in the laboratory, my keen senses had detected another scent. And now that I stood away from the confusion of odours in the room, this scent came even more potently to my nostrils.

'Some instinct told me to follow this scent and, though my attempts at climbing my first staircase were comical, I found myself, at length, in front of another doorway. The door was open and revealed a very different type of a place to that in which I had awoken.

'The room was small and much more pleasant to my eyes, which had by now become so accustomed to the low light that I saw as clearly as if it had been day.

'I stepped into the room and was immediately struck by the texture of the rug beneath my bare feet. I smiled – and put my hand to my face, puzzled by this involuntary movement.

'In the centre of the room there was a tall structure whose purpose I could not begin to imagine, but, still following the scent which had brought me to this room, I walked forward.

'I stretched out my fingers and found that the structure gave way at my touch and was soft. I took some of this material in my hand and brought it closer to my face, the better to see it. I even put some small part of it in my mouth to test it, but it was dusty and only increased my sense of thirst and hunger.

'But this action had an unexpected result. The material I had grasped was the curtain that draped around a bed and, in pulling it apart, I now saw that there was a figure lying on the bed.

'He had hands as I had hands, and feet and legs as I had already seen that I possessed. Whatever I was, I must be some kin to this creature, and again my face was pulled into a smile as I gazed down at him, the moonlight tumbling through the open curtain and illuminating his sleeping face.

'Imagine my excitement at finding a companion! Tears sprang to my eyes and again I put my hand to my face in confusion.

'As I did so, the figure on the bed awoke and turned to face me. The look on his face is something I shall never forget and have no need to store inside my memory, for it is an expression I have seen many times since.'

Billy nodded. It was, no doubt, the expression he too had worn upon first seeing the ghastliness of Creecher's face, and he marvelled to himself that he now no longer felt that fear or repugnance when he looked at the giant. He saw a man. A friend.

'It was Frankenstein?' Billy said.

Creecher nodded.

'When I first looked down on him, his face seemed beautiful to me, and I hoped that I must look as he did.

'But the beauty of his face was shattered in an instant when he looked at me. His features distorted into a mask of horror. Even though I had experienced no contact with humans before, it was instantly clear to me that his expression carried all the emotions of terror and revulsion.

'I surprised myself by opening my mouth and making some primitive sounds as I reached out to him in a plea. But instead of greeting me as a fellow, he ran from me in panic, though I wished him no harm. I could not follow – he was far too quick for me and I stumbled through the house, suddenly aware of my nakedness.

'Something in me wanted to put as much distance as I could between me and the laboratory – a place which now filled me with an unspeakable loathing.

'I had seen that the man who had lain on the bed was wearing clothes, and I took some that I saw lying about, though they were comically small for my size, and took a coat from the hallway as I finally blundered out of the house and into the street.

'I was still not practised at using my eyes and unable to focus on distant objects. I seemed surrounded by a frightening collection of looming shapes.

'Though I did not know it at the time, this was Ingolstadt, the place of my birth – or, more properly, of my creation. My step quickened as my heartbeat raced, and I longed to rid myself of the walls and windows that seemed to close in around me on every side.

'I blundered into a horse – though, of course, I did not know what it was at that time – and made it skitter and whinny, and the driver saw me and shouted out in fright, striking out at me with his whip.

'My distress turned swiftly to anger and, had I not been in such a panic to quit that town, I would have pulled the man from his cart and dashed his head against the cobbles.'

'Where did you go?' asked Billy.

'Into the forest,' said Creecher. 'I felt instantly more at home there, among the trees and animals. The place was filled with scents and a musty perfume. I took myself to its heart and, covering myself with leaves, fell into an exhausted sleep.'

'It must have been terrible,' said Billy, 'not knowing what you were or what anything else was.'

'Yes,' said Creecher. 'It was terrible – to be lost and in need of comfort, like any newborn infant, and yet to be shunned and rejected by those creatures who appeared to my eyes to bear most similarity to me.'

'No wonder you were such a . . .' Billy's voice trailed away. Creecher smiled.

'Monster?' he suggested.

It was Billy's turn to smile.

'Yeah,' he said.

'How would you feel?' said Creecher. 'I did not even know how to feed myself. I had to try whatever I could and observe the animals and where they fed. I tried all manner of berries and leaves and roots. Some made my stomach twist and clench and others made me vomit.

'I had the experience of thirst without knowing how to quench it. My relief came only by accident. I saw a deer drinking from a brook and copied her. Oh – that first drink of cool water!'

'But how did you learn to speak and to read' asked Billy, 'if everyone took fright when they saw you?'

He could see that this was a particularly painful memory and did not press the giant as he sat there in silence for a few moments.

'At length, I came upon a cottage deep in the woods,' said Creecher eventually. 'It belonged to some French exiles. They had as a guest an Arabian woman, and as they taught her their language, so I learned by secret observation.

'Little by little I learned to read and to understand something of the world outside the woods. I learned of the cruelty of man to his fellow man, and it did not come as any great surprise.

'One day I had the opportunity to befriend the old man who lived at the cottage. He was blind and his disability immunised him from the fear he would no doubt have experienced on seeing me.

'I worked for him and took great pleasure in being able to help him. I felt like a secret friend to this family and I would have been a good friend to them had I been allowed . . .'

Creecher broke off from his tale and shook his head bitterly.

'But as soon as I was seen – by the man's son, on his return – then I was viciously beaten and chased from the cottage. I could have killed them all had I wanted, but I loved them. I felt worse now, for having known love and losing it, than I ever did in those hours of lonely despair.'

'But you must have met up with Frankenstein again,' said Billy, 'or you couldn't have followed him here. Did he come looking for you?'

'Hah!' said Creecher. 'No!'

'But how could he make you and then not even care what happened to you?'

'Did you not say that your own father left before you were born?' asked Creecher.

'That's hardly the same thing, is it?'

'Perhaps not, but Frankenstein is the only father I have. I met him on a mountaintop and made him promise to build me a mate.'

Creecher shrugged.

'And so here we are. Frankenstein does not want to do this thing, but he must. He wanted to forget about me. Perhaps he hoped that I would simply wander away and die in a ditch. But no – he does not get rid of me quite so easily.'

'What a bastard,' Billy muttered. 'What bastards, both of them – my father and Frankenstein!'

'Agreed,' said Creecher with a smile. 'But here we are – we struggle on without them!'

CHAPTER XXIX.

Billy stood for a few moments looking at the space at the canal where the boat should have been, stubbornly refusing to accept the inevitable conclusion.

'Damn it!'

'Did you not tie it up, mon ami?' said Creecher, as he wandered over.

'Me?' said Billy. 'I thought you'd tied it up!'

Creecher shrugged, and Billy cursed and kicked at the air in front of him.

'What are we going to do now?' he moaned.

'For now, we walk,' said Creecher, putting on his hat and setting off along the towpath.

The next address on the itinerary that Billy had been given showed that Frankenstein and Clerval were headed for Matlock, a spa town in Derbyshire. They were going to stay there a while before moving on to the lakes of Cumberland.

Billy had heard of these places, but only in the way that he had heard of Jerusalem or the moon. They were places mentioned by people in the crowds he worked in the winter season. They were places mentioned by the ever-growing stream of people who continually migrated to the capital from every corner of the country. How he and Creecher were going to get there was another matter.

After the incident with the coach to Oxford, Billy had decided that this form of transport was out of the question, and Creecher agreed. But they could hardly walk to Scotland.

Billy looked at the giant striding ahead of him. Creecher was still determined to get his mate, with all that implied. And yet something was different now and had been ever since Billy had seen Creecher through his drugged ordeal. The bond between them had been tightened.

Although Creecher's plan was the same, somehow it did not seem so set in stone now. Things change. Billy knew that as much as anyone. Who could tell where their adventure might lead?

Two layers of clouds hung above their heads: a high, pale layer, like a sheet of dusty muslin, and a lower layer of broken clouds, floating by, grey, like giant dustballs.

They walked all day under this filthy shroud, Creecher keeping parallel to the towpath, hidden among the trees, while Billy made his way alongside the canal, acknowledging the muttered greetings of the bargees and marvelling at the great horses who pulled the laden boats along.

Daylight faded and the world around them became, little by little, less distinct. Billy saw something ahead and whistled to Creecher who appeared moments later.

'Look,' said Billy. 'There's some sort of camp ahead.'

Creecher peered into the gloom and nodded.

'We can go back,' he said. 'There was a bridge. We could cross and go on the other side.'

'Look, I'm sick of walking,' said Billy wearily. 'I'm tired. And hungry. Maybe those people have got some food – real food, I mean.'

'You mean meat?'

'Yes, I do.'

Creecher took a deep breath and Billy waited for the inevitable growl, but none came. After a moment, the giant simply nodded his agreement. Billy could scarcely conceal his surprise, but thought it best to make nothing of it.

'Just stay out of sight, for now,' said Billy, and

he set off towards the camp before Creecher could change his mind.

And, as soon as he walked towards it, Billy could see that the camp was much larger than he had previously thought. He had set off with enthusiasm, but his step now slowed as he found himself wondering who these people were. The tents were plentiful enough to suggest a small army.

Billy stumbled over a tent peg and cursed under his breath. But it was at precisely that moment that the smell of cooking reached his nostrils, and a smile curved across his face for the first time in a while.

He could now detect smoke rising up over a large tent in front of him, and he set off with renewed vigour. Skirting the tent, he saw a considerable amount of people gathered round two large fires.

Intimidating though the large numbers were, Billy felt he'd come too far to turn back and strode forward as purposefully as he could. He was about to announce his arrival, when the smoke drifted his way, catching in his throat and temporarily blinding him.

Billy coughed and spluttered as he wiped the tears away from his stinging eyes. He was all too aware of the laughter that was breaking out around him. *Still*, he thought, *better laughter than anger*.

'I'm travelling north,' said Billy. 'I thought you might have food. I don't mean no harm.'

Billy blinked and tried to focus on the faces in the firelight, and it was only then that he saw the true nature of the people who were gathered around the fire.

There was a man – or, at least, he assumed it was a man – who had hair all over his face, as though he were a dog. Another man supported himself on his arms, having no legs at all. A man no bigger than a child stood next to two identical women who, Billy saw to his amazement, appeared to be joined at the hip.

'What . . . ? Where . . . ?' stammered Billy.

A man nearby laughed heartily and slapped him on the back, making him start.

'Calm yourself, friend,' he said. 'You are in no danger, I assure you. We are not as fearsome as some of us look. Chaney – stop scowling at the poor boy. You look like a dog who's lost his bone.'

The speaker was a tall, slender man with long hair, a small pointed beard and thin moustache. His face was wide and handsome and his broad smile revealed a row of the whitest teeth Billy had ever seen.

'Allow me to introduce myself,' he said. 'Mr Browning at your service, proprietor of this theatre of the grotesque, and these fine fellows are my merry band of strolling players.'

Billy became aware that the various conversations around the fire were dying out, one by one, and all faces were beginning to turn in one direction. Billy joined them.

Creecher was walking towards the fire. Evening was upon them now. The light had been leached from the scene and the sky above was darkening, the effect exaggerated by the fire's golden blaze. And out of this surrounding gloom came the giant.

There was a great stepping back and adjustment as he materialised from the darkness. A path cleared in front and around him, and he walked slowly forward, looking this way and that as the crowd formed its collective gasp.

'This is my – my travelling companion,' Billy said. 'He won't do you no harm.'

Billy could see the fear in the eyes of even these bizarre creatures. But, to his surprise, Browning did not back away. He walked towards Creecher, holding out both hands, as if the giant were a long-lost brother.

'Magnificent!' he said in admiration. 'Absolutely magnificent!'

Creecher seemed as taken aback by this reaction as Billy.

'Come,' said Browning. 'Join us, my friend. Eat. I swear you won't taste better rabbit anywhere.'

'He doesn't eat meat,' said Billy.

'All tastes are catered for here, my friends,' Browning replied. 'Chang there is a Buddhist and seems to eat nothing but rice and roots. Chang, get some rice for my friend here.'

'Look,' said Billy suspiciously. 'No offence, but who the hell are you people?'

'Ha! None taken, dear fellow. We are, collectively, Browning's Carnival of Freaks.'

'Carnival of Freaks?'

Browning laughed.

'That's right, my boy. We are a travelling brotherhood of the bizarre, a company of curios, a – well, you get the idea.'

Billy looked at Creecher, who was staring down at a midget, who had wandered over to have a closer look.

'But you must travel with us, my friends,' Browning cried.

'I don't know,' said Billy. 'We tend to travel light and go as we please.'

Browning nodded.

'And how has that been for you?' he asked, looking at Creecher. 'No offence, young fellow, but
surely your friend here attracts a bit of attention.'

Billy looked at Creecher and nodded.

'A bit, yeah,' he said. 'But nothing we can't
handle.'

'But why handle it at all? Come with us. We
are all freaks in this carnival. Another one won't
matter.'

'What about me?' asked Billy.

'You look like a boy who could turn his hand to
most things,' Browning replied. 'What work have
you done?'

Billy rubbed his face and sniffed.

'Bit of this, bit of that,' he mumbled.

Browning laughed.

'No one cares what you were before you walked
into camp. You could be a thief or a killer, for all
we care, just so long as you do what's asked while
you're here. You'll get a roof over your head –
albeit a canvas one – and all the food you want.
What do you say?'

Billy looked at Creecher, and he could see that
the giant was thinking the same thing: Browning
was right. A travelling freak show was the best
place to hide as they went north. It made perfect
sense.

'All right,' said Billy.

'Oui,' said Creecher.

'Excellent!' said Browning, clapping his hands together and walking away. 'Excellent!'

CHAPTER XXX.

The camp woke early. Billy and Creecher had been well fed the night before. Billy had eaten rabbit stew until his stomach hurt, and he wondered at how someone as huge as Creecher could get by on a bowl of rice and vegetables.

But already Billy was hungry again, and he joined a small crowd gathered round the fire for a bowl of porridge. He looked at the mix of carnival freaks and workers and, in the harsh morning light, Browning's words came back to him: 'You could be a thief or a killer . . .' They looked like a set of escapees from Newgate and Bedlam.

Added to which, Billy could scarcely understand a word the carnival workers said. He was familiar with the slang of London – the thief's cant and the flash talk – but this was something else altogether.

Seeing Billy's confusion, one of the men told him it was a special slang used only by the fairground workers, a mix of English slang and some foreign words, mainly Italian. He told Billy he would pick it up soon enough.

After breakfast, the freak show began to pack up. Billy had imagined that this would be a disorganised affair, given the nature of the performers and the workers, but far from it.

Every person seemed to know what was required, and Billy was soon struggling to keep up with the barrage of orders that was being fired at him from right and left.

The tents were taken down with military efficiency and divided into all their various elements with practised ease. The canvas was folded, the rigging wound and boxed. All the trappings of the camp were dismantled into smaller and smaller pieces and then stored in marked crates and barrels.

Billy broke off from what he was doing to look about at the swirl of bodies around him. At first glance it seemed chaotic, but Billy could see that everyone had their allotted task and went about it with good-humoured efficiency. There was an endless stream of talk and calling and whistling and laughing and cursing.

Creecher walked past, carrying a crate that would have taken two men all their effort to

drag. Browning stood nearby, gazing in admiration. He turned to Billy and grinned like a little
boy. The grin was infectious and Billy joined in.
He had never imagined being able to take pride
in knowing Creecher, as he did now.

Where were they supposed to take all this
equipment, Billy wondered, and how did they
carry it from one place to the next? Surely they
must need dozens of wagons to haul it – but he
looked around and could see none.

Browning walked by and slapped him on the
shoulder, smiling at the confused expression on
Billy's face.

'It's a wonderful sight, isn't it?' he said. 'No
matter how many times I see the carnival up stakes
and move on, it never fails to move me. I think it is
why I do this, you know. It is the idea of always
moving, of never having to remain in one spot.'

'But where are the wagons?' said Billy.

'Wagons?' Browning repeated. 'Wagons? My
boy – this is the nineteenth century. We can do
better than wagons!'

Browning grabbed his arm and pulled him in
the same direction as many of the most heavily
laden carnival men were heading. They walked
through a gap in a stand of poplar trees and were
instantly on the towpath of the canal.

Billy could not help but whistle appreciatively. Moored along the canal, stretching away into the distance, was a row of narrowboats, all richly decorated with *Browning's Carnival of Freaks* written on the side.

'These canals link all the great and growing cities,' said Browning. 'We will travel north this summer and be back down in London for the autumn. They are not the fastest way to travel, but they can take the heaviest load you could wish to put aboard.

'These canals are like blood vessels, lad – veins and arteries that we move through like a drug.'

'A drug?' said Billy.

'Oh yes,' Browning replied. 'We are like opium to those people of the mills and manufactories. Their lives are soulless, mechanical, and we give them magic and wonder. We let them escape the dull treadmill for an hour or two. We give them visions that would astound the most ardent of opium eaters, my young friend.'

Browning walked on to oversee the loading. Soon all that remained was to hitch up the horses and loose the great mooring ropes. On Browning's command, the flotilla of narrowboats slowly moved on, huge horses, decorated with black plumes, pulling them through the inky waters.

At regular intervals, Billy would see groups of people standing and staring on the towpath or on the opposite bank. Browning was clever enough to keep the most valuable of his exhibits out of view, while making sure there were enough sights to arouse wonder among any onlookers.

Billy sat astride the roof ridge of one of the narrowboats, looking towards the prow and Creecher. The giant was sitting with his back towards him, his collar pulled up and his head bowed over a book, so that all Billy – or anyone else – could see of him was his hat.

Creecher seemed to be blocking everything out, curling up into his own world. Billy had thought he might find some sense of companionship among these other outcasts, but the giant seemed incapable of socialising. Apart from Billy, he seemed to have no need of friendship. It was as if he had given up on humankind – of whatever sort – and was determined to hold out for the mate that Frankenstein would build him.

Billy, on the other hand, was surprised at how accepting the carnival freaks were of Creecher. Apart from the initial appreciative stares when he first arrived, they barely glanced at him. It was as if there was an unspoken code that, among each other, no one would have to suffer unwanted attention.

If anything, the carnival folk stared at Billy more, suspicious, perhaps, of a stranger and his relative normality. He felt the freak here.

The boats were queuing up at a lock gate. Billy took the opportunity to stretch his legs and Creecher stood alongside him. Browning walked towards them, with Bradbury, the tattooed man, at his side.

'I'm not sure I like these people getting a free glimpse of you, Mr Creecher,' Bradbury said, pointing to the lock-keeper and his family, who were staring in awe from a safe distance.

'No matter, Bradbury – it's all publicity,' said Browning, with a chuckle. 'Now, what are we going to call you, my friend?'

'What do you mean?' asked Creecher.

'Oh, but you have to have a stage name!' said Browning. 'It's crucial! No one would pay to see Bradbury, here, without us putting up a sign saying "The Illustrated Man". Do you see?'

Browning turned away, looking up at the sky as though he might find inspiration there. Billy glanced at Creecher, who raised an eyebrow suspiciously. Billy grinned.

'Of course!' cried Browning, making Billy jump. 'The French Ogre!'

Browning wrote the words in the air and stood back in admiration, viewing the imagined board in front of him.

'But he's Swiss,' Billy pointed out.

Browning waved the objection away.

'No, no, no,' he said. 'Swiss Ogre does not work at all. Take it from me – "The French Ogre" is perfect. Perfect!'

Browning walked away to instruct the sign-writer. Billy watched him go and then looked at Creecher.

'Ogre,' repeated the giant, looking down at himself.

'It's just a name,' said Billy. 'Don't take it personal.'

But Billy could see that the name rankled the giant as he returned to his book.

CHAPTER XXXI.

The carnival was assembled in a field at the edge of a town Billy had never heard of. He had been so intent on the tasks allotted to him that he was taken by surprise when he finally turned round and saw the scale of it.

A huge tent stood in the centre, long trailing flags fluttered gaily and noisily from the poles that supported it. Around that were satellite tents and stalls.

'It's quite something, isn't it?' said Browning, walking up beside him.

'It is,' Billy agreed. 'I mean, I've seen plenty of fairs in London, but putting up something this big so quickly – it's amazing.'

Browning patted him on the shoulder.

'I've taken this carnival to some of the greatest cities in Europe,' he said. 'When the season is over here, we will head south across France and then work our way through Italy. You could come with us, my friend. You and the giant would be very welcome.'

Billy shook his head.

'Nah. Thanks for the offer and everything, but he's got a particular need to head north.'

'And you?'

'Me?' said Billy. 'Something tells me you wouldn't be interested in me without him.'

Browning grinned.

'You may have a point,' he said.

Billy laughed.

'Thanks for not trying to lie, anyway.'

Browning put his thumbs into his waistcoat pocket and sat down on a barrel.

'So why are you travelling with the giant?' he asked. 'You make an odd couple.'

Billy laughed again at that.

'Once it was because I was scared of him,' he replied. 'Now it's because I want to. It's like I've started a story and I want to see how it ends. You know what I mean?'

'I do,' said Browning. 'But stories don't always end well, you know.'

Billy nodded.

'I'll have to take that chance,' he said. 'How about you? How did you come to be travelling with a load of freaks?'

Browning's smile disappeared.

'Freaks is a word we do not use with each other, Billy. It is a stage name – like "The French Ogre". We are all strange, my friend. These people are simply strange in an obvious way.'

Billy shifted uncomfortably, annoyed with himself for having made a bad impression so soon. But Browning assured him that no offence had been taken.

'Well, then,' said Billy. 'How come you are running this carnival of . . . obviously strange people?'

Browning roared with laughter and slapped Billy heartily on the back. He repeated Billy's words to Bradbury as he walked by, but the tattooed man didn't seem to find the remark as hilarious as Browning did.

'I used to be a painter,' said Browning. 'I trained at the Royal Academy under a compatriot of your friend – a Swiss painter called Fuseli. You know his work, perhaps?'

Billy shook his head.

'You must know *The Nightmare*,' said Browning. 'It's incredibly famous. A woman lies on a bed, as if thrown there. A wild-eyed horse leans in through the bed curtains, while a grotesque imp sits on her chest. Wonderful – quite wonderful.'

Billy raised an eyebrow.

'I'll have to take your word for it,' he said.

'But these painters nowadays,' Browning went on. 'They wander about the countryside painting waterfalls and mountains. Nature – pah! Who wants to look at the natural when you can have the supernatural? Eh? Eh?'

Billy smiled and shrugged.

'But, in truth, I was not going to be the great painter I hoped to be. My father was rich and my mother soft-hearted. It was a combination that meant I was indulged in my interests.

'I travelled Europe, sketching and writing awful poetry. Then I met Bradbury and my life changed.'

'Bradbury?' said Billy, wondering how the dour tattooed man could change anyone's life.

'I rescued him from a spot of bother in Venice,' said Browning. 'He was accused of murder, but I had been a witness. Bradbury had certainly killed the man, but it was self-defence.

'I managed to save him from the hangman's noose and paid his fine. I asked him where he was staying, assuming, from his American accent and tattoos, he was a sailor. But I was surprised to learn that, although he had been a sailor, a series of misfortunes had led to him being part of a freak show.

'The owner of that freak show was a vile character,' Browning continued. 'He treated those poor creatures as though he were running a menagerie. And even then – no keeper of animals would have been so cruel.

'I resolved there and then to create my own freak show, but one in which those whose gifts were being exhibited were shown respect and humanity.

'I had found my vocation. I bought the freak show from him and it came to form the core of this great enterprise. We few travelled through Europe, through the Ottoman Empire, Egypt and India, collecting companions as we went. The results, you see around –'

Browning's long speech was cut short by a bout of coughing. He pulled a white silk handkerchief from his pocket and put it to his mouth. Billy saw the flecks of blood on it as he wiped his lips and put it back in his pocket.

'This northern air doesn't agree with me,' Browning said, with another cough. 'You must excuse me.'

CHAPTER XXXII.

It took another couple of hours for the carnival to ready itself for paying visitors. The tents had yet to be decorated and hung with signs and images that hinted at the treasures within, without telling too much.

A great deal of effort was put into deciding how to present Creecher to best effect. Browning and Bradbury were in discussion for some time before they hit upon the idea of having a circular tent, devoid of all imagery, with only the words *The French Ogre* emblazoned across it.

'The visitors will do a much better job of telling their friends what he looks like than we could ever do in a painting,' Browning reasoned.

Inside the tent would be a large, round cage that appeared to be substantial but was, in actual fact, mainly constructed of painted wood. Creecher would sit inside the cage in chains.

After his experience in Oxford, the giant took a lot of persuasion to agree to this staging. Browning said that the chains were vital to the effect, that no one was going to believe that he was dangerous unless he was chained.

He showed Creecher again and again that the chains were not real and that he could open the manacles himself should he so wish. In the end, the giant consented, though with little enthusiasm.

While Creecher's cage was being constructed, the other exhibits had to be brought out and arranged in the various tents. The carnival performers were getting into their costumes and taking up their positions. Slowly but surely, the whole place was being transformed.

It was twilight now. Browning had explained to Billy that the carnival was 'a dream' – 'a fever dream', Bradbury had interjected – and night was needed as a backdrop. Even though Billy had seen the performers all day and had grown used to them – or, at least, had been able to stop himself staring – it all seemed very different now that torchlight was taking over from daylight.

'Have a look round before the crowds arrive,' said Browning, with evident pride. 'If there is a greater show on earth, I'd like to see it!'

So Billy wandered around, from stall to stall, tent to tent. There was Chaney, 'The Wolf Man', and Kafka, 'The Human Beetle'. A large tank of water decorated with sea shells and corals contained Agnes, 'The Mermaid' – a woman who appeared to have a long fish's tail instead of legs. Her flesh looked soft and pale and she floated in the cloudy liquid like a drowned body, her long red hair draped like seaweed over her naked torso. Billy started, dry-mouthed.

Lily and Milly, the conjoined twins, walked by.

'Good evening, Billy,' they said together.

'Evening, ladies,' said Billy with a nod. 'You're looking very fine.'

Lily and Milly looked at each other, a hand clasped to each mouth, then they blushed and hurried away, giggling.

Billy entered a large tent with a banner over the entrance saying *Browning's World of Wonders*, which Browning had already told him contained some of the curios he had collected at great expense during the course of his travels.

One large glass tank held a two-headed sheep, both faces carrying the same forlorn expression. A three-headed dog stared ferociously from another large tank.

There was one jar in particular that caught

Billy's attention, containing a strange figure. It had the proportions of a small child, but with strangely adult features. Besides which, it was too small even for a child, being only about a foot tall. The label read: *Homunculus*.

Billy remembered Creecher saying that word. *Homunculus*. It was what alchemists were trying to make.

There did not seem to be much connection between this sad, little pickled figure and Creecher's giant form. Billy leaned in for a closer look and the eyes of the homunculus opened. He stepped back, startled. Looking again, the eyes were shut once more, but there was something about that thing that made Billy's fresh creep. He left the tent without turning back.

He immediately walked into a tall, beautiful woman dressed in a tightly-waisted red silk dress. Coiled around her long neck and narrow shoulders was a very large snake.

'I don't think we've met,' purred the woman.

'No,' said Billy, his gaze shifting between the woman and the snake.

'My name is Lamia,' she said, with a crooked smile.

'Oh.'

The woman smiled, and a tongue flicked out between her lips – the same kind of darting, forked tongue that flicked out of the snake's mouth. Lamia grinned, revealing a sharp pair of fangs, before walking away towards her tent.

'Stay away from her if you've any sense,' said Bradbury, who was standing nearby. 'She's Eve and the serpent combined.'

Billy had no plans to go anywhere near her or her snake if he could possibly help it. He turned to face Bradbury, who was staring at him with his usual look of contempt.

'You don't like me much, do you?' said Billy.

'No,' Bradbury replied matter-of-factly. 'Nor your friend.'

'Well, Browning seems very keen, so . . .' Billy left it at that and began to walk away. Bradbury grabbed him by the arm.

'Things change,' he growled. 'I can smell trouble a mile off.'

'The giant's all right,' said Billy.

'What makes you think I'm talking about him?'

Billy stared into Bradbury's face, but the swirling patterns of his tattoos seemed to move and he could not hold his gaze. He shrugged Bradbury's hand away and walked off without looking back.

The carnival had opened its gates to paying customers and the whole area was seething with people, gawking and staring, giggling and squealing.

Billy decided to go and check on Creecher. He nodded to the man on the entrance and walked in. The tent was packed.

It was hard to get a clear view with so many people in front of him, but even from that distance, and with all the obstruction, Billy could see the unmistakeable form of Creecher, sitting inside the cage.

Browning had placed low lanterns around the outside, so that Creecher was lit from below, hurling a giant shadow up on the canvas above. Browning knew his business: even though Billy had travelled with the giant for months, he felt a shudder go through him at the sight.

The crowd was excitable and noisy, perhaps knowing that silence would invest the scene with even greater dread. A man banged the bar of Creecher's cage until one of Browning's men came and stopped him. Browning himself stepped forward, carrying a bright lantern.

'Behold!' he cried theatrically. 'The French Ogre!'

He nodded to Creecher, who stood up and walked forward, chains clanking. The whole crowd took several steps back, gasping as the full horror of the giant became apparent in the lantern light.

Creecher let out a low growling moan. Browning had told him that he must not talk, that the horror would be greater if he was a shambling mute. A woman at the front fainted and had to be carried out. The remaining crowd listened in awed silence as Browning recounted the wholly fictitious history of the French Ogre.

Creecher shuffled back into the shadows and the show was over. The crowd left, looking nervously over their shoulders as they did so. Browning clapped his hands and almost danced a jig. Everyone agreed it had been a great success.

But Billy noticed that Creecher himself did not join this celebration. The giant sat sullenly alone for some time after the show was over, brooding darkly in the shadows.

CHAPTER XXXIII.

Over the next few weeks, Browning's Carnival of Freaks made its steady way along the arterial waterways of the Midlands. Town after town came to see 'The French Ogre' and went on their way, unnerved and horrified, satisfied that their money had been well spent, eager to tell their workmates and families of the wonders they had seen.

Creecher's fame spread along the canals, through the mills and mines, factories and foundries, and the expectation of his arrival became ever more heightened as they moved north.

Crowds of people would greet the narrowboats before they had even arrived at the town in question, eager to catch a glimpse of the giant – something Browning was just as eager, now, to avoid, and Creecher was forced to sit under a tarpaulin.

Billy could not tell what the giant made of this attention. Most of the time while they travelled he would sit alone under cover, reading his books, ignoring all around him.

But, at other times, Billy thought he detected a kind of vanity developing in Creecher. There seemed to be a haughtiness in him sometimes – as though he enjoyed his new-found celebrity status. Browning was only too pleased to encourage the giant to think of himself in such terms. He told them several times that, in all his days taking carnivals across Europe, he had never seen the degree of interest and excitement that Creecher had generated.

But Creecher made it very clear that they would not be staying. The carnival was simply a means to an end, and it was that end – the pursuit of Frankenstein – that remained uppermost in his thoughts.

At every mention of the inevitable time of their departure, Browning would become more and more animated on this subject and offer greater rewards to induce them to stay. But the more enthusiastic Browning was, the more sullen and silent Creecher became in response.

Billy had wondered if the giant might be tempted to take him up on the offer. After all, was this not the best chance he had of belonging

somewhere? Was not his best chance at normality here among the abnormal?

But Billy realised that, in truth, Creecher
did not consider himself a freak – and the other
freaks knew it. Their earlier acceptance of the
giant had turned to a kind of cold indiffer-
ence. Increasingly, Billy and the giant found
themselves on the outer edges of the camp,
neither able to fit in. Then one night, everything
changed.

They had arrived at Manchester as dusk fell.
Billy had heard of the city but had never really
had an image of the place, and he was startled by
its sheer scale, its wide, straight streets and alien
architecture.

It was a very different crowd than they had
experienced thus far, too. Maybe Creecher's fame
was starting to work against him: perhaps the
audience now felt that he had to do something
more than they had expected. Maybe the giant
could not be as astonishing as his publicity.

Whatever the reason, there was a hostility to
the crowd. Billy could feel the tension and it
made him nervous. He could see that Browning
felt it, too.

When it came to showtime, as usual, Browning
stepped forward and lit up the giant's cage with

a lantern. And, as usual, the crowd took a step back when they saw the full horror of Creecher – the size of him, the full ghastly look of him.

But when Creecher returned to the back of the cage and the relative gloom, there was a momentary pause before the crowd stepped forward again – though not as close as before.

'He's just a man in a costume,' shouted someone at the back.

'Yeah,' said another. 'It's a trick!'

Within seconds, the whole tent was shouting that Creecher was a fake and that they wanted their money back. Browning tried to calm the crowd but he was jostled and pushed, and would have fallen had Bradbury not stepped in.

'Friends!' shouted Browning. 'Friends! I assure you, there are no tricks or fakes at this carnival!'

A small mop-haired boy approached the cage with a long stick and began to poke Creecher with it. Someone in the audience pointed him out and everyone turned from Browning to watch this new entertainment.

Creecher endured these attentions in silence, turning only once to glare at the boy. But the boy took this as an invitation to continue his assault with even greater vigour.

A ripple of laughter broke out. The rest of the crowd soon joined in. Billy looked at Browning. This was certainly not expected and, for the first time, he saw a troubled look break out across the carnival owner's face.

'For God's sake,' he muttered to Bradbury. 'He's an ogre. He's meant to terrify people, not make them laugh.'

But then, almost on cue, Creecher turned on the boy and snatched his stick, pulling it into the cage with one hand, while trying to grab the boy with the other. The boy's parents just managed to pull their son away, before the giant's hands reached his throat.

Creecher roared with anger and stood up, lurching forward, shaking his chains, pulling them off and throwing them down on the floor of the cage.

As soon as the crowd saw that he was free, they rushed for the exit, screaming and shouting, knocking each other over in their haste to escape. Browning watched them go, grinning.

'Excellent,' he said, turning to Billy. 'What a performance! Shaking free of the chains was a stroke of genius. We must get the big fellow to do that in every show.'

But Billy had seen that look on Creecher's face

before. That was no performance. The boy – and
Browning – had had a lucky escape. It was time
to leave.

———◆◆◆———

Creecher, of course, did not argue when Billy
suggested that they should make the rest of the
journey on their own, but Browning put up less
resistance than Billy had thought he might.
Perhaps he, too, had realised just how close they
had come to a terrible incident.

Browning knew a man who was taking narrowboats north and who, for a fee, would take Billy
and Creecher with him. He even took care of the
money himself, saying it was the least he could
do. Although Billy had been given a small wage
along with all the other crew, Creecher had been
happy to accept just food and a steady supply
of books and journals, a selection of which he
carried with him now.

'I hope you find what you're looking for on your
travels north, my friend,' said Browning, shaking
Creecher's hand. 'But if not, then perhaps you will
return to the carnival.' But it was said with little
conviction. They all knew that this was the end.

With that, they were off. Lily and Milly called

their farewells and waved excitedly as Billy walked away. Creecher grinned and Billy blushed. He looked back to see Bradbury's painted face scowling at him. There would be no fond farewells from him.

Frankenstein and Clerval had been headed for Matlock, but there was no need to follow them there. If they'd stuck to the itinerary, then they would already be on their way to Keswick in Cumberland, where they apparently intended to stay for some weeks.

Billy and Creecher walked through the wide streets of Manchester towards the meeting point with the bargeman. Creecher wore his long coat with the collar pulled up, and his wide-brimmed hat shaded his face. Striking cotton workers stood about in sullen groups. They looked pale and tired. The few that noticed Creecher gazed in wonder, tugging at their neighbour's coat sleeves to point after them. But Billy and Creecher had already slipped into the shadows and disappeared, like dreams at dawn.

'Lord have mercy!' said the bargeman, when he saw Creecher.

'It's all right,' said Billy. 'It's all make-up. We didn't have time to change.'

'Hah!' said the bargeman, holding his chest.

'Thank God for that. Frightened the life out of me. But he's huge, though.'

'Not really,' Billy replied. 'It's all special boots and so on. Tricks of the trade.'

The bargeman nodded and leaned forward to get a better look at Creecher's face, grimacing as he did so and pulling back almost immediately.

'We'll stay out of your way in the hold,' said Billy. 'You won't even know we're here.'

PART III.

CHAPTER XXXIV.

It was June now. It had been months since they had left Oxford. It was warmer, particularly at night, but the skies were still mainly overcast and glowering. Billy wondered again if Creecher carried this weather with him.

They had travelled north along the Leeds and Liverpool Canal and then onwards up the Lancaster Canal until they reached the end of its course. Navvies laboured noisily to forge a new canal route to Kendal.

Through a combination of walking and riding in the back of wagons and carts when they could, Billy and Creecher continued their journey into the high country of Westmorland and Cumberland.

Creecher would read to Billy whenever they stopped to make camp: one night it might be a novel of high adventure, another a long and mournful poem. Billy preferred adventure, but knowing how much Creecher enjoyed his poetry, he listened to whatever the giant was reading with equal attention.

The wide, open spaces seemed to allow Creecher room to be the giant he was. These northern folk were suspicious of all outsiders, and yet they appeared to acccpt Creecher as just another example of how strange the world beyond their boundaries could be. Or most of them did, at least.

Creecher still had the power to terrify and unnerve at close quarters and in daylight, but they tended to restrict their travels to the night, dusk and dawn, when he possessed the ability to melt into the shadows.

They had thought to break their journey with bouts of highway robbery, but realised it would be impossible as the country became more wild and open. There were simply not enough people to rob, and those few they had stopped had little or nothing to steal.

So they had taken instead to asking for rides. Initially they offered to pay, but very quickly they discovered that no payment was expected.

Billy would sit up front with the driver if there was room, and Creecher would go in the back, where his size was less obvious. It was from one such wagon that they now alighted.

Billy thanked the driver as he and Creecher jumped down. The driver waved back and flicked the reins, encouraging the horses in the direction of the town which nestled in the valley below at the foot of a long hill, down which the rough road precipitously snaked.

'Could we not have gone a bit further?' asked Billy.

'That is not our destination,' said Creecher, who was already climbing over a drystone wall and striding off into the bracken. 'You heard the driver – Keswick is this way. And Frankenstein is in Keswick.'

'I know. But he also said it's miles away. We could have picked up another wagon.'

'Too small a town,' Creecher replied. 'Too many people.'

Billy knew the giant was right. There would be no way of hiding Creecher in a town that size. In such a confined space, he would only horrify and alarm.

Billy struggled to keep up with Creecher as he strode up the hill. He marvelled at how light-footed the giant appeared, despite his great size. He was like some animal which had been long out of its true environment and now delighted in being able to roam freely.

'It is good to be in hill country,' he called over his shoulder, as Billy bounded after him. 'The air smells better here.'

And he was right – though Billy would have liked to have more of that air in his lungs. He panted and gasped and his muscles burned.

But now Billy shared Creecher's urge to get to the summit and, after a brief rest, he set off again with renewed vigour, challenging himself to keep pace with the giant – a challenge he almost met.

He clambered over the final crag as ravens croaked above him, flipping and tumbling like acrobatic shadows. The summit was a kind of flattened plateau, studded with wind-polished boulders, as though hammered home by a god.

Creecher stood ahead of him, resting one dusty boot on a boulder and staring off into the distance. Billy walked tentatively forward. He felt a reverence here, a sense of awe he had never felt in a church – though, to be fair, he had only ever entered a church to pick pockets.

A mist moved in the valleys, the peaks of hills bursting through here and there like islands in a swirling sea of cloud. Billy had never seen anything like it in his life.

'It's beautiful,' he said.

'Yes,' Creecher replied. 'It is.'

And, all at once, Billy realised that he had never said the word 'beautiful' in his life before. It was a word that had lain unused in his mind, like a family heirloom – too ostentatious ever to be sullied by the likes of him.

He said the word again, quietly this time, only to himself, savouring the syllables as though they were an untried delicacy.

Billy and Creecher could have been the only two living creatures in the world, or so it felt to Billy. It was as if they stood at the dawn of a new world, a world as yet unformed, brimming with limitless possibilities.

Creecher turned to Billy and smiled. For once, Billy did not find the effect disturbing. He didn't know whether he was simply getting used to Creecher, or whether this landscape had produced a more human expression from the giant. But in that moment he didn't care. He looked out across the mist and whooped with joy. A buzzard soared up above them and mewed plaintively, as though in response.

Billy and Creecher clambered over a crag and down through drifts of scree, slipping and sliding as the shards of slate stone moved under their feet. They continued through bracken and rowan and mountain ash until they arrived at a cleft in the hillside, into which a stream had worn its way through layers of ancient rock, smoothing them like gemstones.

They were both hot from walking and stank like the hold of a fishing boat, so when a deep pool presented itself, Billy, without a moment's hesitation, stripped off and jumped in.

The cold water slapped his bare flesh and made him yelp, but he sank into its embrace, letting the chill waters wash over him.

He emerged, gasping, to see Creecher finish disrobing and preparing to join him. The sight of the giant's naked flesh was startling, and it was then that Billy noticed what had troubled him all those months ago when he had first seen Creecher's bare torso. He had no navel.

Of course, thought Billy. What need did he have for that scar of birth, when he had not been born in that sense? No umbilical cord had been cut at his entry into the world.

Even though he had accepted the facts of Creecher's origins many weeks before, the sight of that smooth stomach, with its translucent flesh, brought a chill to Billy that the coldness of the water could not entirely be blamed for. As Creecher lowered himself slowly into the pool, Billy was overwhelmed by the surety that he did not want to share those dark waters with the giant.

He climbed out and tried not to make eye contact with Creecher, so that he might not know if his eagerness to leave had been noticed.

Instead, he looked at himself in the black water. Was that really him? His shoulders were broad where they had once drooped. He raised a hand to his arm as though it belonged to someone else, and marvelled at the firm muscles that met his touch.

The pale and sickly, thin and spindly Billy that worked the streets of London had metamorphosed into another, stronger version. Months on the road had changed him. He had seen little of the sun those last months, yet still his face was a healthier shade than it had ever been, and it had broadened like his shoulders. It was not a handsome face especially, but it was a long way from ugly.

Billy looked around for the giant, but Creecher was nowhere to be seen and the surface of the water was as untroubled as a sheet of glass.

It was some moments before Billy caught sight of him. He was at the bottom of the pool, curled up on the stones like an unborn babe. His eyes were open and there was a look of utter tranquillity on his face.

All at once, he snapped out of his trance, floated to the surface and climbed out, coils of his long black hair hanging down his wet and colourless back like leeches, while the all too visible veins pulsed beneath his pallid flesh.

They sat a while and dried their bodies in the warm breeze, then got dressed and walked on. Billy's hair was long now too; the wet locks fell about his face and he tossed them back behind his ears.

As they traversed a ridge, the mist began to break up, and Billy was amazed at how quickly it disappeared, revealing the landscape below. To see so far and to see such expanse of open land, with only the merest hint of human life here and there, tucked in among the humpbacked hills – the sheer scale of it had a vertiginous effect on Billy.

How can people live like that? he thought. *How can they live with such silence and separation?* He needed the heartbeat throb of a city. Or at least he had always assumed he did.

They found their way on to a sheep drover's track and Billy was struggling to keep up with Creecher again. The giant said that they should find a place to rest and pointed to a barn on the other side of a high stone wall. As soon as there was a break, they passed through and went inside.

The barn was cool and dark. There was a pile of hay at one end, and Billy and Creecher settled themselves down. Within moments, they were both asleep.

CHAPTER XXXV.

Billy dreamed he was back in the chimney again, looking up at the tiny circle of light above. It seemed so far away. He wished he could float up and out of the chimney, like smoke.

Then he felt something grab his ankle. He kicked at it, but the grip just got stronger. Then there was a tug. Then another. Then Billy was yanked down in a cloud of soot.

The sweep dragged him out of the fireplace, banging his head against the marble surround, and hurled him down in front of the hearth.

'You come when I call!' he shouted, hitting Billy across the side of the face with the back of his hand.

Billy snatched up a poker and held it up in defence, but the sweep was too quick for him, twisting his arm so that he dropped it. Then he grabbed Billy by the scruff of the neck and lifted him to his feet.

'Try and hit me, would you?' he said. 'Me, who feeds you and puts a roof over your head? Why, you little . . .'

The sweep thumped Billy in the stomach, making him double up and collapse to his knees, gasping.

'This ain't the half of what you're going to get when we're out of here, I can tell you that for nothing,' growled the sweep.

'What's going on here?' said a voice behind Billy. He turned, wincing, to see a manservant watching from the doorway.

'None of your affair,' the sweep snapped.

'Don't adopt that tone with me!'

'He works for me and I'll do as I like! It ain't no concern of yours.'

'You should be ashamed of yourself. He's nothing but a boy.' The manservant stepped forward. 'I'd like to see you try and hit me, you coward.'

'Think I'm scared of you?' said the sweep, squaring up to him.

Billy saw his chance and bolted past both men, into the hall and out of the front door, which slammed behind him – and the noise woke him, or at least the echo of the noise in the real world. Billy tried to rouse himself. There was someone

there – a figure standing silhouetted in the doorway of the barn, too small to be Creecher.

'My eyes ain't as good as they was,' said the
figure. 'And this thing in't exactly accurate, but
I'll hit something if I pulls the trigger.'

'Don't do that,' said Billy quickly. Creecher sat
up beside him. 'We meant no harm. We're just
travelling through and looking for somewhere
dry to spend the night.'

The farmer squinted at Creecher and then back
at Billy.

'Where you headed?'

'Scotland.'

'Scotland?' said the old man with a whistle.
'That's a long way off.'

'Well, Keswick first,' said Billy.

'Keswick. Just down the valley, lad.'

Billy cautiously got to his feet and dusted
himself off.

'We'll be on our way, then.'

'You looking for work?'

'No, not real—' began Billy.

'What kind of work?' Creecher interrupted
him.

'Son went off to the army. Got himself killed.
Left me here on my own,' said the farmer. 'There's
a wall needs fixing for starters. Help me with that

and I'll give you a place to stay and food as well.
I ain't much of a cook, but you won't go hungry.'

'We'll help you with your wall,' said Creecher.

Billy nodded, understanding that this place
gave them a good base from which to look for
Frankenstein.

'All right, then,' the old man replied, finally
putting the gun down and walking out of the
barn. After a moment, Billy and Creecher
followed him.

'Name's Thwaite,' said the old man.

'I'm Billy,' said Billy. 'And this here's Creecher.'

'This is my farm,' Thwaite explained. 'Black
Crag Farm. I owns all the land hereabouts.
Thwaites have done for centuries. Thwaite bones
in the burial ground. Thwaite blood in the earth.
Do things my way and we'll get along fine.'

Billy could not decide whether the old man
really was as short-sighted as he claimed to be,
or whether he simply chose not to see the giant
for what he was, for he made no comment on
Creecher's appearance.

He certainly seemed to see well enough to
correct any mistakes Billy was making as they
got to work on the wall.

'Use a nice, big, flat one there,' said Thwaite.
'No – not that one. A *big* one! That's it, that's it!'

Having satisfied himself that they had the hang of it, the old man left Billy and Creecher to get on.

They laboured on either side of the wall. It was hard work, even for Creecher, and before long they were both stripped to the waist, Creecher's translucent anatomy still unnerving to see.

But Billy found himself enjoying it. His muscles had been honed by weeks of hard graft on the carnival, but this was skilful work, and satisfying.

The sun gradually moved across the fellside, and it was a relief when the shadow of a great oak nearby fell across them as they worked. Birds flitted among the branches and took flight. Billy watched their tiny shapes fly away across the valley and out of sight.

How different this life was to the frantic pace of London, or the drudgery of the cotton mills. Was this how men were supposed to live? thought Billy. Was this their natural state?

It felt natural: hard work and open air. Maybe this was what he had always craved but never known it. It felt good to have the sun on his back. Even the ache in his muscles seemed right, somehow. He felt alive – alive in a different way.

It was late by the time they finished and Billy slumped down against a stone gatepost, tired and sore. The light of evening was making the stones glow, and Billy looked at the new wall with unexpected satisfaction. He gazed down at his blistered hands and then back at the wall. Creecher stood nearby, smiling.

'You look proud,' he said.

'You know, I think I am,' Billy replied, surprised by the thought.

But he did feel proud. Billy had never made anything in his life and here he was looking at something that might still be there centuries after he was dead and gone. He hoped it would. It would probably be the only thing to show he'd ever walked this Earth. Not that anyone would know he'd built it.

The old man wandered up the field with the slow, deliberate tread of a hill farmer, trailing his long shadow across the grass like a cloak.

'That's a good job,' he said. 'That's a good wall for a first wall.'

Billy beamed with pride and glanced at Creecher, who also looked fairly pleased with himself. Thwaite patted the wall as he might the flank of a horse.

'That's not bad at all.'

Billy patted the wall himself and then patted Creecher on the back. The giant grinned.

'Are you in a hurry to get to Scotland?' said the old man. 'Only I've got more work if you want it.'

Billy looked at Creecher, and Creecher nodded.

'I suppose we could stay a while longer,' Billy replied. 'We couldn't say how long, though.'

'That's good enough,' said the old man. 'I can't say how long I'll be around neither.'

That evening, back in the farmhouse, Creecher read them poems from a book called *Lyrical Ballads*. Billy found the poems hard going mostly, but he was gripped by one of them – 'The Rime of the Ancient Mariner'.

Old Thwaite had already fallen asleep, but Billy leaned towards Creecher, eyes wide and alert, hanging on his every word. When he reached the section where the dead crew rise up and sail the ship, Creecher's voice seemed to change:

> *'The loud wind never reached the ship,*
> *Yet now the ship moved on!*
> *Beneath the lightning and the Moon*
> *The dead men gave a groan.*

They groaned; they stirred, they all uprose,
Nor spake, nor moved their eyes;
It had been strange, even in a dream,
To have seen those dead men rise.

The helmsman steered, the ship moved on;
Yet never a breeze up-blew;
The mariners all 'gan work the ropes,
Where they were wont to do:
They raised their limbs like lifeless tools –
We were a ghastly crew.

The body of my brother's son
Stood by me, knee to knee:
The body and I pulled at one rope,
But he said naught to me.'

With those words, Creecher came to a halt, staring at the page, the muscles in his face twitching. Suddenly he slammed the book shut, waking Thwaite, who sat up blinking and saying how much he'd enjoyed the poems.

'That's all for tonight,' said Creecher. 'I'm tired.'

And with that, he got up and strode out of the cottage.

CHAPTER XXXVI.

It was clear that following Frankenstein and Clerval would be more difficult here in Cumberland. So much had happened since Billy had last seen them that the whole notion of pursuing the men had almost been expunged from his mind. The memory of Frankenstein and the body in the warehouse seemed like a distant dream.

Billy found the two men easily enough. The rooms they had rented were near the centre of town. He watched them leave and set off on a walk. Frankenstein looked relaxed and cheerful, as though his travels north had calmed him. He certainly had nothing of the furtiveness he had displayed in London or Oxford. He and Clerval were tourists once again, it seemed – tourists and nothing more.

Billy restricted himself to keeping track of them while they were in Keswick, where there were enough people and enough places to hide him. Once the men left for one of their country-side walks, he did not usually attempt to pursue them and returned, instead, to help Creecher with work around the farm.

But one particular day, there being little farm work to do, Billy decided to give the men a healthy head start, before setting off after them.

Soon the relative clamour of Keswick was behind them and they were heading out into the wide, open land beyond. Billy had assumed the men were going hillwalking, but rather than aiming for the fells, they came instead to a kind of low, flat-topped mound. A ring of massive upright stones stood on this natural plinth, surrounded all about by hills – hills which the clouds had darkened as if by design, allowing the bright-lit stones to stand out with even greater drama.

Billy hid in the lee of a hedge, bees buzzing among the bramble flowers. Frankenstein and Clerval spent a great deal of time marvelling at the huge lichen-covered stones, but it was not until they had moved on that Billy looked at them for himself.

'Some say they are giants,' said a voice behind him.

Billy turned to see a girl standing nearby. She was beautiful. Her face was pale and almost luminous in the strange light. She wore a dress of deep blue and her eyes were grey and glinted like pools of pure water from the shadow of her bonnet. She giggled at Billy's lack of response.

'Sorry, miss,' he said, flustered. 'I wasn't expecting to see anyone. Especially not a pretty . . .'

The girl giggled again.

'I beg your pardon, sir,' she said. 'But to whom do I have the pleasure of speaking?'

'Clerval,' he replied, suddenly conscious of how ugly and low-born his own name seemed. 'William Clerval.'

'What brings you to Cumberland, Mr Clerval?' she asked.

'Oh, I'm travelling with a friend – we're heading for Scotland. I'm from London.'

He could not take his eyes from this girl. It was as if the whole world had slid away, leaving only her face, her beautiful face.

'There were two other gentlemen from London here just a few days ago,' said the girl. 'They were poets. It was so exciting. I never thought to meet a real poet. I begged them to read us something they had written, but they were too shy, I think.'

'We mustn't keep the gentleman from whatever it is he is doing,' said another girl, stepping
forward.

Billy had not noticed her till now. He frowned.
The girl frowned back. A buzzard wheeled overhead, mewing plaintively.

'Florence,' said the first girl. 'Don't be so
impolite.'

'It's time we were getting back to the house,
Jane,' she replied. 'Your mother will be worried.'

The two girls turned and began to walk away.

'Jane,' mumbled Billy quietly to himself. He
liked it. Then he called after her hurriedly, 'I
write poetry myself.'

'Well, that *is* a coincidence,' said the girl called
Florence, without looking round.

Billy frowned at her again.

'I came to the stones for some, you know . . .'

'Inspiration?' Jane suggested, stopping and
turning back to face him.

'That's it.'

Florence sighed loudly.

'I do have to go, I'm afraid, Mr Clerval,' said
Jane. 'It was nice meeting you.'

A slight breeze caught a few loose strands of
her hair and blew them across her face. She lifted
a gloved hand to push them away.

'Perhaps I could walk some way with you?' said Billy, approaching slowly.

Jane smiled and nodded.

'But the stones . . . ?' said Florence.

'I don't think they're going anywhere,' Billy replied frostily.

Florence put her arm in Jane's and they set off along the path that ran beside the hedge Billy had hidden behind. Billy did his best to ignore Florence, but in no time at all they came to a gate and stopped.

'Is this where you live?' asked Billy, noticing the house for the first time.

'It is.'

'Jane, really,' said Florence.

Jane opened the white gate, which creaked a little at her touch, and stepped through under an arch of climbing yellow roses. The scent was thick and heady.

'Well, goodbye, Mr Clerval,' she said, smiling.

'Yes,' said Florence. 'Goodbye.'

Florence slammed the gate shut and a cascade of yellow petals rained down. Billy stood and watched Jane walk away and, as she approached the door of the cottage, he called out.

'Wait!'

The girls turned round, a look of surprise on Jane's face, one of annoyance on Florence's. The breeze caught Jane's hair again and it rippled across her face. She brushed it patiently aside and looked at Billy expectantly.

'Can I see you again?' asked Billy.

The wayward coils of hair sprung free from her fingertips. Billy was held in a grip firmer than Creecher's Herculean grasp.

'You may, if you're passing,' she replied. 'I'm not going anywhere.'

And, with that, Jane disappeared through the door, shepherded away by Florence, and Billy was left alone with the bees and the buzz of his thoughts.

He tapped his fingers on the gate and walked back towards the stones. The clouds had moved on and the effect was now reversed, with the stones standing out dark against the hills now bathed in golden light.

The change was startling. The shadowed stones seemed ominous now, less like benign figures than mourners at a funeral, or sinister witnesses to a crime, as if they had gathered to watch some terrible event long ago and been frozen there.

CHAPTER XXXVII.

When Billy closed his eyes, he saw Jane's face smiling at him. When he opened his eyes, he seemed to hear her voice whispering to him from the brook or the wind in the bracken.

He wondered what his mind had been filled with before it had become fixed on this girl – and then realised that it had been filled with Creecher and Frankenstein.

Billy looked at the giant. He was sitting with his back against the wall they had built on their arrival, reading a book as usual.

'Have you got any poetry I can borrow?' Billy asked.

Creecher looked up and peered at him.

'I just fancied reading some,' said Billy.

'Truly?'

'Yeah . . . What? You think I can't understand it or something? I'm not stupid you –'

'Calm down, my friend,' said Creecher. 'I never

said you were stupid. What sort of poetry?'

'I don't know. Not too gloomy.'

Creecher picked up a book and handed it to Billy.

'Have a look at this,' he said. 'It's new. It does not quite –'

'Thanks,' Billy replied, opening it up and scanning the page. 'That's perfect. It goes on a bit, but the first bit ought to do it.'

'Perfect?' said Creecher, peering at him. 'In what way?'

'Look, it doesn't matter,' said Billy. 'Can I borrow it?'

'Of course. I'm glad you like it, but –'

Billy never heard the rest. He headed for the farmhouse to ask Thwaite for a piece of paper and a pen. Then he sat at the kitchen table, carefully transcribing the poem, with the old man watching silently as he did so. It had been a long time since he had written anything, and it took him quite a while.

When he had finished and the ink was dry, Billy folded the paper and put it in his pocket. He stood up and went to the doorway, looking out at Creecher sitting where he'd left him.

From that distance, and with no human to compare him with, he could almost have been mistaken for any other man. Almost. Thwaite came out from the house and stood alongside Billy.

'Can I ask you something?' asked Billy.

'You can ask,' said the old man. 'I can't promise I'll know the answer.'

Billy smiled and looked back towards Creecher.

'Something troubles me,' he said.

'And what's that?'

'Why aren't you bothered by Creecher?'

'Why aren't you?' said the old man.

Billy smiled. It was a fair point.

'I'm used to him. But when I first saw him . . . Well, let's just say he has quite an effect on most people. But not you. Why not?'

The old man took a deep breath.

'I do not question the ways of God,' he said.

Billy peered at him.

'I'm sorry, sir. I don't understand.'

Thwaite smiled.

'I think you do,' he said, with a grin.

'No, sir,' said Billy. 'I don't.'

Thwaite scratched his stubbled chin and looked hard at Billy.

'All right,' he replied. 'If it be His will that I tell, then tell I shall. I prayed for help and He sent me two angels.'

Billy laughed at the thought but saw immediately that the old man had not been joking.

'You think that Creecher is an angel?' he asked incredulously.

'Well, he ain't human, is he?' said the old man. 'Any fool can see that.'

Billy raised an eyebrow. He could hardly disagree. 'But what about me?' said Billy. 'Don't I look human?'

Thwaite looked Billy up and down for a long time.

'Possibly,' he replied eventually. 'But I reckon there's probably all kinds of angels.' And he headed out into the fields.

Billy walked over to Creecher, who glanced up from his book as he approached. His skin seemed to shimmer coldly in the shadow of the wall. He looked like he came from another world all right, though Billy would not have guessed at heaven.

'The old man thinks you're an angel,' he said, sitting down next to the giant.

'Maybe I am,' said Creecher matter-of-factly.

'Yeah – and maybe you're not.'

Creecher frowned.

'Are you angry?' he asked.

'Yes,' said Billy. 'No – I don't know. I like old Thwaite.'

'I like him, too.'

'Then let's stay here.'

'I cannot,' said Creecher, in a tone of finality.

'Because you have to follow Frankenstein,' Billy sighed with exasperation.

'Yes.'

'Let him go. He doesn't want you. He hates you. He thinks you're a monster. Why do you follow him about like a dog?'

'He has promised to help me.'

'But we could have a new life here,' said Billy.

'You perhaps,' Creecher replied.

'Look where we are. There's no one for miles around. You could live here and read your books and –'

'I need more than that,' said Creecher, getting up and snapping his book shut.

The giant walked away, heading up to the fell top without saying another word.

———◆◆◆———

The next day, Billy stood in the shadow of the clock tower in the centre of Keswick, watching Frankenstein and Clerval amble round the town. Billy had the distinct impression that Frankenstein's work in England was drawing to a conclusion.

Frankenstein had rented a small warehouse at the edge of town, but it seemed more of a store-room than a workplace. He had visited it once, but only briefly. Soon he would no doubt move on, and Billy and Creecher would have to move on, too, in pursuit.

Each time Billy dwelt on this, Jane's face would appear, smiling, beautiful.

The two men disappeared inside a shop, and Billy took the opportunity to pull out his copy of the poem and read it through again. He had just reached the end, when the two men emerged once again.

They were laughing as they stepped out into the sunshine, but no sooner had Clerval started to walk away than Frankenstein stopped and turned to peer suspiciously in Billy's direction, making him jump back into a doorway.

Frankenstein's casual manner was a facade as always. Underneath that thin veneer he had the same old look of a hunted man.

'He knows he's being followed. I'm sure of it,' said Billy, when he saw Creecher later that day. The giant nodded.

'He knows I'm here,' said Creecher. 'I told him that I would be with him when his work was complete. In any event, we are bound together, he and I.'

'How do you mean?'

Creecher grinned.

'He used his blood in my construction. We are bound together. I can sense him – smell him.'

'You can smell him?'

'Oh, yes,' said Creecher. 'Always.'

Billy screwed up his face. The more he learned of the giant's creation, the more unsettling he found it. The idea that Frankenstein had used his own bodily fluids in the process was somehow revolting.

'So in a way, we are family, he and I,' Creecher continued. 'We have the same blood in our veins.'

'Yeah,' said Billy, eager to move on. 'But if you have this bond, why do you need me to track him? You could just stay nearby and move when he moves.'

Creecher took a deep breath.

'Do you know how lonely I have been, Billy? Knowing that any person I tried to speak to would cry out in horror at best, and try to kill me at worst. To mankind, I am what Browning said I was – an ogre, a monster from fairy stories and nightmares.

'But Fate brought us together, Billy. Against all the odds, I had at last made contact with a person who seemed able to tolerate me long enough to see that there was more than horror there.

'In truth, I could have tracked Frankenstein without you, but I would never have learned so much of his actions as I have through you. I should have had to hide away in some dark corner of London until I sensed that he was leaving and then follow his scent wherever it took me. I would have found him just as well, but I would not have found you or our friendship.'

'Shut up,' said Billy, smiling. 'You're reading too many of those novels of yours. You're beginning to sound like a woman.'

Creecher chuckled. A great burst of sunshine washed across the fellside and eventually over Creecher and Billy, too, warming the colours all around them and making everything glow as though lit from inside. The effect was startling and Billy felt his heart flutter giddily for a moment.

'If I'd always lived here ...' he began, but he seemed unable to finish the sentence.

Creecher looked down at him.

'You think you would have been a different person?' said the giant.

'Maybe,' Billy replied.

His mind was suddenly flooded with images

of his life in London, and it had the speeded-up, black jitteriness of a nightmare. Had he woken from a dream? Was this the real world, and the past just an illusion? Or was this the dream? Would he wake at any moment and find himself back in the baker's attic?

'I'm going to go for a walk,' said Billy.

He told himself his walk was aimless, but it wasn't true, and before long he was walking past the great stone circle and on towards the little cottage, with its gate and arch of roses.

Billy looked in through the window. The scene was bathed in an amber glow from the fire. There was a woman sitting in a wooden chair, sewing – a woman Billy guessed must be Jane's mother.

Florence was reading a book and Jane approached her from behind, placing her hands over her eyes until she called out in mock anger and Jane left off, laughing brightly. Billy grinned.

He remembered the scene in Great Russell Street with the family there and had a repeat of the selfsame yearning. *This is what Creecher must have felt as he stared in at the cottage in the woods*, thought Billy.

Billy had a sudden vision of himself sitting in just such a cottage, basking in a golden glow.

Jane came wandering through from the kitchen, carrying a huge pie, steam rising from the crust. A child – no, children – came running and laughing as she placed it on the table. She smiled at Billy, her face a picture of joy and contentment, and Billy smiled at the dream and was filled with a sense of loss when it dissolved.

He walked back to Black Crag Farm, his heart aching, as darkness fell across the landscape and the clouds parted and a million stars pierced the limitless blackness of the night.

CHAPTER XXXVIII.

There seemed little point in pursuing Frankenstein and Clerval around Keswick again so, the following day, Billy worked with Creecher, clearing rocks from a field near the farm. Afterwards, he washed and smartened himself up and headed over to the stones. He found Jane sitting in the garden, reading. He had to walk past several times before she noticed him.

'Mr Clerval,' she called. 'What a nice surprise.'

'I was just passing,' said Billy from across the fence.

'Mother, this is Mr Clerval, whom I was speaking of.'

The older woman Billy had seen through the window came out from behind a tree and smiled at him. Billy lifted his hat.

'I'm very pleased to meet you, Mrs . . . ?'

'Cartwright,' said Jane's mother. 'Clerval is an unusual name. Is it French?'

'Swiss, ma'am,' he replied.

'Well, don't stand there all day, young man. Come round and have a cold glass of lemonade. Florence!' she called into the cottage. 'Get Mr Clerval a lemonade.'

Billy came through the gate in time to return Florence's scowl at the window with a warm smile.

'Are you staying locally, Mr Clerval?' asked Jane's mother, as he sat down.

'Yes, ma'am,' he replied. 'I'm staying with a friend at Black Crag Farm. We're helping Mr Thwaite with some jobs about the place in return for our board and lodgings.'

'You certainly look like a strong young fellow, doesn't he, Jane?' said Mrs Cartwright.

'Mother, really. You're embarrassing Mr Clerval.'

'Oh, Mr Clerval seems fairly unembarrassable to me,' Florence remarked, putting a jug of lemonade on the table.

'You're from London?' asked Mrs Cartwright.

'Yes, ma'am. How did you guess?'

'Oh, we get a lot of people now,' said Florence, sitting down. 'They come up from London for the scenery, you know. They wander about for a bit until they get some mud on their shoes, or it starts to rain, and then they go.'

'I'm headed for Scotland,' Billy went on. 'Me and . . . my friend. He has an arrangement to go to Scotland and I said I'd accompany him.'

'Scotland is very wild, they say,' said Mrs Cartwright. 'And the people there don't take kindly to strangers.'

'How soon will you go?' Jane asked.

Billy looked off towards Black Crag Farm.

'I don't know,' he said. 'Soon, maybe.'

'Oh,' said Jane, brushing the creases from her dress.

After some short polite conversation, Mrs Cartwright left them to return to her pruning. They talked for a while longer. Billy felt tongue-tied and clumsy and could think of little to say. He was happy to listen to Jane. He felt both nervous and relaxed in her company. It was an intoxicating combination.

'Jane,' said her mother, coming over. Billy had forgotten she was there. 'Shall we go for a stroll among the stones? The evening light is rather wonderful.'

'Of course, Mother,' Jane replied. 'If you would like to. Will you join us, Mr Clerval?'

'Perhaps Mr Clerval will read us some of his poetry?' said Florence, giving Billy a withering look.

'Oh, I don't think –' began Jane.

'Oh, would you, Mr Clerval?' Mrs Cartwright enthused. 'Jane does so love poetry.'

Florence grinned wickedly.

'Very well,' said Billy. 'I did bring one with me. It's not very long and I've only just written it, so don't expect too much, will you?'

'Oh, I'm sure it will be lovely,' Mrs Cartwright replied.

The group left the garden and wandered over to the stones. Mrs Cartwright sat down on one near the centre of the circle, with Jane alongside her. Florence stood behind them, clearly looking forward to what she hoped would be Billy's embarrassment.

Billy took out the piece of paper, unfolded it, coughed twice, licked his lips and began.

'*A thing of beauty is a joy for ever*,' he said, in a quiet, faltering voice.

'What's that?' said Jane's mother. 'Speak up. I can't hear you.'

Florence giggled, until Jane flicked her with her fan and shushed her.

'*A thing of beauty is a joy for ever*,' repeated Jane. 'I like that. Is there more?'

'It's only a start, you know,' said Billy. 'I mean, I haven't really worked it all out yet.'

'Even so,' she said.

Billy licked his lips and looked nervously about him, before clearing his throat and speaking more loudly:

'A thing of beauty is a joy for ever:
Its loveliness increases; it will never
Pass into nothingness; but still will keep
A bower quiet for us, and a sleep
Full of sweet dreams, and health, and quiet
*   breathing.*
Therefore, on every morrow, are we
*   wreathing*
A flowery band to bind us to the earth,
Spite of despondence, of the inhuman dearth
Of noble natures, of the gloomy days,
Of all the unhealthy and o'er-darkened
*   ways*
Made for our searching: yes, in spite of all,
Some shape of beauty moves away the pall
From our dark spirits. Such the sun, the moon,
Trees old and young, sprouting a shady boon
For simple sheep; and such are daffodils
With the green world they live in; and clear
*   rills*
That for themselves a cooling covert make
'Gainst the hot season; the mid forest brake,

Rich with a sprinkling of fair musk-rose
   blooms:
And such too is the grandeur of the dooms
We have imagined for the mighty dead;
All lovely tales that we have heard or read:
An endless fountain of immortal drink,
Pouring unto us from the heaven's brink.'

Billy had been nervous when he began, but had gained in confidence as he spoke. He had not been able to make eye contact with Jane, though, and as he turned to her now, he saw her eyes filled with tears.

'Oh, Mr Clerval,' she said. 'That was beautiful. Beautiful. You should publish your work.'

'Oh, I don't know about that.'

'Is that the end, then?' said Mrs Cartwright. 'Oh. Well done, well done.' She clapped her hands vigorously.

'Florence,' she said, getting to her feet. 'I need to stretch my legs. Will you take a turn with me across the field?'

'Of course, Aunt,' said Florence. 'Jane?'

'Jane should rest,' said Mrs Cartwright. 'She can stay with our poet.'

Billy smiled and Jane blushed a little. Even Florence's mood seemed to have improved.

'It was a lovely poem,' she said, as she walked away.

When they had disappeared from view, Billy sat down next to Jane.

'Say those lines again, will you?' she said.

'Which lines?' Billy asked, taking the hands that she stretched out towards him.

'The ones about quiet breathing,' she replied.

Billy had to fight the urge to embrace her. Instead he leaned forward and spoke softly into her ear again:

> *'But still will keep*
> *A bower quiet for us, and a sleep*
> *Full of sweet dreams, and health, and quiet*
> *   breathing.'*

Jane pulled her face back and looked into Billy's eyes. They sparkled with tears and seemed like shimmering, depthless pools. Billy felt as if he might fall headlong into them.

'Have you lived here all your life?' he asked, pulling back a little.

'Oh, no,' said Jane. 'We are only renting. We come from Manchester.'

She cast a quick glance across the field in the direction of her mother.

'We came here for reasons of health,' she went on. 'The clean air and so on. The doctors thought it might be beneficial.'

Billy nodded.

'We passed through Manchester on the way here,' he said. 'It seemed an awful place – all those ugly, giant mills and warehouses. The people there looked so beaten down. You must have been glad to leave.'

'Glad?' said Jane incredulously. 'Not at all. Manchester is a fine place and my father owns one of those mills, I'll have you know. The people there are happy to have work.'

'They didn't look very happy.'

Jane shook her head and sighed.

'What would those people be doing otherwise? Living in hovels and tending some tiny plot of land? It's progress, Mr Clerval. We can't all stay in cottages in the countryside. Men like my father are helping to change the world . . .'

But Billy was not really listening any more. He was simply watching the movement of her lips. She was so beautiful, he thought. So beautiful.

'But I'm talking too much,' said Jane. 'Mama says that women should not speak about such things, but I believe that we are –'

Something caught Jane's eye behind Billy's head and she gasped, staring in horror. It was at that moment that Florence arrived, with Jane's mother a pace behind.

'What is it, Jane?' asked Florence, seeing her face.

'The stones,' she said. 'I saw one of them move.'

'Jane, my dear,' said Mrs Cartwright, putting an arm round her daughter. 'Now you know that they cannot move. You're overtired. If Mr Clerval will excuse us . . .'

'Of course,' said Billy, looking at Jane. 'Are you sure you're all right?'

'You must forgive me,' said Jane. 'I have a weak and silly heart.'

'Nonsense,' he replied. 'You have the best of hearts.'

Jane smiled weakly at him as Florence and her mother led her away. Billy turned back to the stones, frowning. He walked to their centre and looked from one to the next. Then he set off for old Thwaite's farm.

It was dark by the time he got back. He found Creecher standing in the moonlight, looking down the valley. The giant seemed vague and transient in that light – as though he were constructed of shadows and moonbeams.

'You were at the stone circle,' said Billy.

'Was I?' said Creecher, turning round.

'Yes. Why are you spying on me?'

'Why are you meeting people in secret?'

'You don't own me,' Billy snapped. 'I can do what I like.'

'Then why keep it a secret?' said Creecher tersely.

'Look, I'm sorry I didn't tell you about her,' Billy replied. 'I was going to, honest.'

Creecher scowled.

'*Honest*,' insisted Billy. 'I just wanted to get to know her a bit, that's all. I just wanted something of my own, something that wasn't about you and Frankenstein. It's always about you and Frankenstein. I've got my own life, you know.'

'She enjoyed your poetry,' said the giant coldly.

Billy winced and blushed.

'Yeah, well. They like that sort of thing, don't they? Girls, I mean.'

'You have not told her about me?' Creecher asked.

'Of course not,' said Billy.

'Or Frankenstein?'

'No,' said Billy. 'I'm hardly going to tell her that I'm walking the length of Britain with a man-made giant, am I? Or that we're tracking the man that made it, because he's going to build another one.'

Creecher stared at Billy, and the intensity of his gaze made Billy squirm. He searched through the words he had just spoken, trying to discover the cause for the sudden drop in temperature.

'*It?*' Creecher said eventually.

'What?' asked Billy, but he knew he'd made a terrible mistake.

'You said, "the man that made *it*". Is that how you see me? Am I a thing? Even after all that we have been through together?'

'No,' pleaded Billy. 'God, it was just a slip of the tongue, that's all.'

But Creecher was not going to be so easily placated. He walked away and leaned against the wall they had made when they first arrived. An owl shrieked in the copse of trees behind the barn.

'Damn it!' said Billy to himself.

Creecher had melted into the shadows of the wall by the time Billy walked after him. He stood at the giant's feet.

'Maybe that is how I used to see you. But not now. Don't be a fool.'

Creecher turned to face him, his eyes flashing in the darkness, and Billy took a step back, worried that the word 'fool' had been too much.

'I came all the way up here to help you,' he went on. 'To help you find some happiness. Why can't you let me be happy?'

'You helped me because you were scared of me,' snarled Creecher, 'and then because of what I might do for you.'

'At first, maybe.'

Creecher snorted derisively.

'You ain't going to make me feel guilty,' said Billy. 'It's not like you helped me out of the goodness of your heart neither. You only helped me because you needed me to follow Frankenstein.'

'Pah!' said Creecher. 'I have never needed you.'

Billy was caught by surprise at how much those words stung him. He stared at the giant for a long time before replying.

'Well, then,' he said coolly. 'There ain't no problem, is there?'

'This girl,' Creecher growled, 'do you love her?'

'No!' said Billy. 'Of course not. I don't know. Maybe.'

Creecher got to his feet and walked out into the moonbeams. Billy followed him and grabbed his arm.

'Why are you so angry with me?'

The giant refused to turn round.

'Look, I didn't understand before. About why you wanted a mate. I couldn't see why I wasn't enough for you.'

'But you do now?' said Creecher quietly.

'Yeah,' Billy replied. 'Maybe I do.'

Creecher muttered something under his breath.

'I won't tell her anything about you or Frankenstein,' said Billy. 'Why would I? I just want to be with her.'

'And me?' Creecher asked, turning to face him. 'What about me?'

'Don't say that,' said Billy. 'It ain't fair! What was going to happen to me when Frankenstein built your mate? You'd have forgotten about me in a heartbeat.'

Creecher looked at the ground and then walked away, gradually dissolving into the darkness.

'Yeah!' shouted Billy. 'You've got no answer to that, have you? Have you?'

———————◆———————

The following day, after he had finished his work on the farm, Billy walked to the stone circle again. His argument with Creecher was still clinging to his mind when he woke, but very quickly he felt lighter, as if a weight had been lifted from him.

He was glad those things had been said. They needed to be said. It had to end somewhere – they both knew that. Why not end it here, where Billy had a chance of happiness? Creecher could look after himself.

Billy gathered wild flowers as he went, smiling to himself at what his old cohorts back in London would have made of such behaviour. When he reached the circle he saw Jane taking the air nearby, but he lost his nerve and hid behind one of the stones as she approached.

Peeping out, he saw that she was looking another way, and he quickly sneaked out to place the flowers on an altarlike stone, before scuttling back behind one of the monoliths.

He watched Jane walk this way and that. She was singing a song to herself in a clear, quiet voice, and Billy began to fear that she would never see his gift.

But, all at once, she turned, making him jump back out of sight. A few moments later, when he peered out, she was standing holding the posy in her pale hands and smiling – a sweet, puzzled expression on her face.

'Thank you,' she said, without turning round.

Had she seen him? Billy did not know. He only knew that the moment would be ruined, somehow, by the awkwardness of any meeting that would follow it. So he stayed where he was.

The next time he looked, Jane was walking towards the cottage gate. Billy sank back against the stone and laughed. He felt a little foolish, but even that felt good.

Everything felt good.

CHAPTER XXXIX.

Billy spent the next morning digging out an old tree stump, while Creecher helped Thwaite replace a roof beam in the house. He and Creecher had barely spoken since their argument about Jane.

It was hard work. A group of sheep came to a safe distance and watched him, staring with their long, silly faces. Billy shooed them away and they bolted, bounding down the hill as though pursued by wolves.

Billy looked down across the distant fells and saw the scattered farmhouses dotted across them. Maybe one day he would live in one of those cottages with Jane.

They would have some sheep and tend the land. Billy would work in the field until dusk, then come home to his wife and sit by the fire with his children, and tell them how he once knew a terrifying giant and how they became friends . . .

As Billy returned to the farmhouse, he saw Creecher resting in the shade of the barn, reading.

'If I wanted to stay a bit longer,' he said to the old man, 'would that be all right with you?'

'How much longer?' asked Thwaite.

'For good maybe,' said Billy.

'Just you?' The old man looked over towards Creecher.

'Just me.'

'What about the big fellow?'

'He's got to go to Scotland,' said Billy.

The old man winked and tapped the side of his nose.

'Scotland, is it?' he said. He nodded and sucked on his pipe.

Billy half opened his mouth to assure old Thwaite that Creecher really was bound for Scotland and not heaven, but thought better of it. Scotland, heaven, hell – what difference did it make? Creecher was going, that was all that mattered.

'So I can stay?' said Billy.

'Aye – of course you can, lad,' he said. 'Stay as long as you like.'

Billy walked over to the little cottage by the stones when he had finished his work and had washed. Every rock and leaf seemed to have its own particular significance now that he thought he might live here permanently. He noticed new things at every stride. It was as if his senses had been heightened.

He saw dragonflies flitting past, using the path as their guide. He noticed the new bracken fronds rising up and curling open. He heard a skylark twittering above him, a lamb bleating down the valley. He saw quartz crystals twinkling on a distant crag and slate shards, watered by a nearby spring, shining in the sunlight.

Glistening fragments of the poems Creecher had read out over the past months came back to him, tumbling one over another until Billy was no longer sure whether he was remembering or inventing.

'I was just passing,' he said as Florence opened the door of the cottage. 'I wondered if I might call on Miss Cartwright.'

'I'm sorry,' replied Florence coldly. 'She cannot see you today, Mr Clerval.'

She was already closing the door.

'I was only planning to stay a few min—'

'I'm sorry, Mr Clerval,' said Florence, and she shut the door.

Billy frowned and raised his hand to knock again, but paused midway. There was no hurry. He just needed to get Jane away from this frosty witch, and there would be ample opportunity to do that. *'Stay as long as you like,'* the old man had said. He had all the time in the world.

Billy decided to walk into Keswick. He would buy Jane a present. He still had some money left. Girls liked gifts. He was sure of it.

But Billy had never bought a present in his life. He had no idea where to start looking and, after walking round in circles for ten minutes, he stood staring confusedly at passers by.

He saw two women enter a dressmaker's shop, but Billy knew he could never go into a place like that. He stood outside a jeweller's, but could not work up the nerve to ask the price of any of the items he looked at in the window.

He would have found it far easier to steal the jewellery, but he felt uncomfortable with the idea of giving Jane something he had stolen. He wanted to make a new start with her. His whole life was about to begin again. It was as if a great fog had lifted and he could see clearly at last.

Suddenly it came to him: a book. That was what he would buy her. But what book? He did not want to buy her poetry. That would confuse things. He hoped that now he had got to know Jane, he might let the whole idea of his being a poet gently die away.

A novel, that was the thing. Women loved novels. And women loved Jane Austen, didn't they? He would buy her a Jane Austen novel – the one that Creecher had been reading when they were in the attic, back in London. What was it called? *Permission*? No – *Persuasion*. Perfect.

Billy knew he had seen a bookshop at the end of the alleyway leading down to Frankenstein's warehouse, and so he set off, whistling a song his mother used to sing.

He paid for the book and had it wrapped in lemon-coloured tissue paper and tied with sky-blue twine. And, all the time, Jane's smiling face flashed across his mind like sunlight on water.

When he stepped out of the shop, he looked down the alleyway. He walked towards the warehouse and stood staring at the ivy-covered building, wondering where the story would end, but content to let it go on without him.

He was just turning away when he thought of Clerval. Borrowing the man's name had made

Billy think of him more and more in the past few days.

He had always liked Frankenstein's friend, and somehow he felt a bond with him. He sympathised with Clerval, for he, too, was a victim. Through no fault of his own, his fate, like Billy's, had become entwined with those of Frankenstein and his creation. Billy wondered if he did not have a duty to warn him.

Then there was a loud thud and everything went black.

CHAPTER XL.

Billy took some time to come round. Different levels of consciousness seemed to wash over him like waves, each one leaving him more awake than before, his blurred vision slowly focusing, the echoing sounds in his ears gradually sharpening.

The more awake he felt, the more the pain in his head kicked in, and he groaned and winced as he tried, unsuccessfully, to sit up.

He was lying on a raised surface. He couldn't move his arms or legs and slowly realised he was tied down. He blinked again and shapes began to materialise out of the dimly lit gloom.

'Ah,' said a voice. 'You're awake.'

Billy looked towards the sound and saw a figure with his back to him. He knew where he was and who the figure was before Frankenstein had even turned round.

'What were you doing here?'

'Nothing,' said Billy, struggling to break free of his bonds. 'Let me go. You've got no right.'

He began to yell until Frankenstein clamped a hand over his mouth. In his other hand, Frankenstein held a knife with a long, sharp blade.

'If you shout once more, I will have to cut out your tongue,' he said calmly. 'Now, you either talk to me, or never speak again.'

Billy closed his mouth and Frankenstein removed his hand.

'All right, I was just looking for something to pinch,' said Billy. 'Turn me over to the Justice of the Peace if you want.'

'I've seen you before,' said Frankenstein.

'I don't think so.'

'Yes. You were at the warehouse in Oxford. And I think I saw you before that in London – at the British Museum. But you were a ragged urchin then. Why are you following me?'

'I'm not following you,' said Billy. 'I've never seen you before in my life.'

'Stop this silliness at once.' Frankenstein leaned towards Billy's face with the knife. 'It is very tiresome.'

Billy nodded.

'All right,' he said. 'What of it? I ain't done nothing wrong. I'm English, mate. This is my country – I can do what I like.'

'Is that so? I thought that even in this wonderful country there were laws to govern its people.'

'None that says I can't walk in the same direction as you, Frankenstein.'

Frankenstein grabbed Billy's face and Billy was surprised at how repelled he was by the touch of those hands.

'You know my name?' said Frankenstein. 'How do you know my name?'

Billy made no reply but stared sullenly into Frankenstein's eyes.

'Answer me!'

'I know what you've done,' said Billy, tiring of Frankenstein's voice. 'I know what you are.'

'What do you know?'

'I know everything.'

Frankenstein snorted.

'Then you are a lucky fellow, my young friend.'

'Don't talk to me like I'm a fool. Creecher told me all –'

'What's that?' said Frankenstein. 'Who are you talking about?'

'Creecher,' Billy replied. 'It's what I call him. I thought it was his name. But he was saying "creature", wasn't he? *Your* creature!'

Frankenstein smiled. There was a wildness to his eyes that Billy had never seen before.

'The thing of which you speak – it is a monster. A foul and hellish monster!'

'And whose fault is that?' said Billy. 'No one asked you to bring some great giant to life! You ain't God!'

Frankenstein smiled.

'God! How quaint. Even scum like you turn to God at their end. I have no need for God.'

'It's wrong!' shouted Billy. 'It's wrong to think you can just make something and then turn your back on it.'

'Come now,' said Frankenstein. 'Do fathers not do this every day? Has God not done that with his own creatures? Am I so very different? And with more reason. The thing I made is a foul horror.'

'But what if you'd been kind to him?' asked Billy. 'He can't help the way he looks. You made him that way.'

Frankenstein shook his head.

'You sound a lot like him,' he said. 'He has obviously worked his spell on you, and I suppose, in some ways, you must be a remarkable young man to accept such a creature as a friend. But I wonder if he has told you the whole truth.'

'About what?'

'Has he told you anything of his life before he came to England?'

'Yeah. He told me all about you, for a start.'

Frankenstein smiled.

'Did he now?' he replied. 'And did he, I wonder, also tell you that he is a child killer?'

'What?' said Billy, startled.

'Ah.' Frankenstein smiled bitterly. 'So he did not tell you all of the truth, I see. Yes! He murdered my brother. Poor William! Strangled him. A small, defenceless boy.'

'No!' said Billy. 'I don't believe you.' But as he said it, he remembered the giant's hands around his neck. The pain in his head returned with even more force.

'But you know it's true, don't you? You cannot have been with him so long without seeing his murderous rage?' Frankenstein peered at Billy and seemed to read something in his eyes. 'My God – you've seen him kill, haven't you?'

Billy did not reply but looked away.

'Is that it? Did he kill for you? Is that why you travel with him?' Frankenstein leaned closer. 'He is a monster, an evil monster. He killed my little brother for no other reason than he bore the same name as me.'

'No!' shouted Billy. 'You're lying.'

'Why would I lie?'

Billy tried to blink away the tears that sprang to his eyes.

'And as if that were not bad enough,' continued Frankenstein, 'he deliberately placed the blame with poor Justine – poor innocent Justine – who hanged for his crime. The monster placed the boy's locket on her sleeping body to incriminate her. He is a murderer and a coward.'

'And whose fault is all that?' said Billy. 'Who built him? It's your blood in his veins!'

'Can a father be responsible for every action of his son? How could I know that I would make a monster?'

'Then why are you planning to build him a mate?'

'What choice do I have?' Frankenstein replied, a wild desperation in his eyes. 'If I do not do as he says, he will exact his revenge. He will kill my family, my friend Clerval, my own Elizabeth, whom I am to marry: everyone who is dear to me.'

He turned away and leaned on a nearby bench.

'Besides,' he said, 'I was moved by his request. I did have some responsibility to him, after all. And he promised that he would leave Europe once and for all and never bother mankind again.'

When Frankenstein turned back to face Billy, there were tears in his eyes. The small knife had been replaced by a much larger one.

Billy shut his eyes.

'Oh God . . .'

But instead of cutting Billy's throat, Frankenstein cut the ropes that tied him to the table, and he slid off, panting with fear.

'I should report you to someone,' said Billy. 'I should get you arrested.'

Frankenstein grabbed his arm.

'If you do anything to prevent me from building his mate, that monster will kill you. Whatever friendship you imagine you have with him, do not think to test it in this way. If I told him that killing you would speed the process of building his mate, he would do it in a heartbeat, you can count on that.'

'No!' said Billy. 'He wouldn't kill me.'

Frankenstein grinned.

'Truly? You are quite sure of that?'

Billy's heart fluttered.

'He wouldn't kill me!' he repeated quietly. 'I know it. He's my friend.'

Frankenstein merely smiled and shook his head. He let go of Billy's arm.

'Look at what you've done!' said Billy, moving away from him. 'Don't you feel guilty or nothing? Look at the lives you've ruined. You make me sick!'

Frankenstein was calm now, his voice quiet. 'Have you ever lost anyone you loved?' he asked.

Billy did not respond.

'Have you ever seen someone die?' continued Frankenstein. 'Have you ever seen someone you love fade away, never to return?'

'Yes!' Billy replied. 'My mother. What's that got to do with anything?'

'I saw my mother die also,' said Frankenstein. 'My beloved mother. I vowed then that I would seek to conquer death – and I have!'

'You haven't conquered death! You haven't even conquered life! All you've done is make a monster!'

'I did what I did with the best of motives,' said Frankenstein. 'And I regret nothing!'

He leaned towards Billy.

'Tell me, if you could have saved your mother's life by killing another, would you have done it?'

'And did you save your mother from death, then?' Billy answered, avoiding the question.

'No. But my work may help others. I have succeeded where the great have failed. I have created the first in a race of immortals!'

'Immortal *monsters*,' Billy corrected him. 'What good is that to the rest of us? We're all going to die and Creecher and his mate are going to live for ever. They're going to breed. They'll take over the world. You're insane.'

Frankenstein waved Billy's protests away.

'Soon I will leave for Scotland,' he said, opening the door to the warehouse. 'I need only one more item to complete my work. Do nothing to stop me, or the monster will destroy everything you hold dear, and then – then he will come for you.'

CHAPTER XLI.

Billy searched the farm for the giant but found only the old man. He looked up and saw Creecher silhouetted on the ridge where he often went to sit and read. Billy climbed up after him.

Believing there could be good inside a monster like Creecher had made Billy believe there might be good inside him, too. But now that belief had been shattered by a lie. Creecher was a child killer. He was just a monster, after all.

'You lying freak!' yelled Billy, trying to focus his tear-smeared vision.

He searched for a weapon and saw a rock near his foot. He picked it up and, without further hesitation, hurled it at the giant. It struck him on the forehead and he groaned and took a step backwards.

Creecher put one of his great hands to his head and then held it in front of his face, staring at the blood now smeared across his fingers.

'It was you who killed that boy in Swissland, wasn't it?' Billy shouted at him. 'To think I ever listened to you . . .'

'What is this?' said the giant. 'Why do you suddenly say these things?'

'Frankenstein told me!'

'Frankenstein?' snarled Creecher. 'Why have you spoken to him? I forbade you –'

'What does that matter?' Billy cut across him. 'Did you murder his brother or not?'

Creecher did not reply. Billy put his hands to his face.

'It's true, ain't it? Frankenstein was telling the truth!'

'You believe his –'

'Don't!' shouted Billy. 'Don't you lie to me again.'

Creecher stood in silence, the blood already drying on his face. He lowered his head and looked at Billy from under his eyebrows.

'There is not a single day goes by that I do not regret that boy's death, or the death of Justine,' said Creecher. 'I was a child myself in age. I . . .'

The giant opened his mouth to speak again, but the words would not come.

'Why?' said Billy. 'Why would you do something like that?'

'The boy stumbled upon me by accident,' said Creecher, after a moment. 'I had no idea who he was.' He looked at Billy. 'I had a notion that I might take him away and make him my companion . . .'

Billy closed his eyes and shook his head. Is that what Creecher had done with Billy? Taken him away to be his companion? Tears dripped down his cheeks.

'So what did he do then?' asked Billy. 'What did he do to annoy you?'

Creecher's face twitched a little before he spoke.

'He struggled,' said the giant. 'He called out and I tried to quiet him by putting my hand over his mouth. He called me an ogre.'

'What? You killed him because he called you an ogre?'

'No!' yelled Creecher. 'I killed him because he told me that he was a Frankenstein! And when I killed him I clapped my hands in triumph because I realised that I had power, too. Frankenstein could give life, but I could take it away!'

'And the girl?' said Billy coldly, into the echo of these words. 'What was her crime?'

Now tears sprang to Creecher's eyes and he put his hands to his face.

'None,' he murmured. 'I found her by accident and saw her sleeping in a barn. She had been searching for the boy and was trapped outside the city when Geneva's gates were locked that evening.

'She was so lovely. But her loveliness only served to make me all the more conscious of my own ugliness. I placed the locket I had snatched from the boy's neck in the folds of her dress.'

'Why?' said Billy.

'Because I knew that she could never look at me the way I looked at her. I was filled with a hatred of all mankind – at the happiness that was denied to me. And don't tell me that you do not share that hatred, Billy.'

'Maybe I did once. But this ain't about me. You always want to shift the blame to someone else, don't you? It's always someone else's fault. You murdered that little boy and then you killed the girl, just as if you had put those big fat hands round her neck as well.'

Billy felt tired all of a sudden. His head still ached from where Frankenstein had knocked him unconscious. His eyelids felt heavy.

'I should stop the both of you,' he added quietly. 'The idea that he's going to make another one of you – another ugly rotten ogre!'

'Don't,' said Creecher, shaking his head.

'What the hell will she look like? I mean, you're bad enough. But a giant sow? It's disgusting. It's . . . But wait – maybe Frankenstein has learned some new tricks while he's been here. Maybe he'll build something that looks human this time. Maybe she'll be beautiful! What will you do then, you big freak? She's not going to be interested in you then, is she?'

Creecher marched forward, his eyes blazing, his arms outstretched.

'Stop calling me a freak!'

'That's right!' Billy cried. 'Come on! Kill me! That's what you want to do, isn't it? That's what you would have done when I wasn't any use any more.'

Creecher pulled up short and put his hands to his face.

'No!' he shouted. 'We were friends!'

'We were never friends!' yelled Billy. 'We were just two freaks walking in the same direction! But no more! You're on your own. I'm staying here.'

'But –'

'No, I don't want to hear it. If you're going to kill me, then get on with it. Otherwise go away and leave me alone.'

The giant grabbed Billy by the collar and lifted him off his feet.

'What will a boy like you do in a place like this?' He tossed Billy to the ground. 'You will not last a day.'

'That's my problem,' said Billy, through his tears. 'I don't need to have a woman built for me. I've got a real girl. A girl who loves me.'

Creecher snorted.

'She doesn't love *you*!' he sneered. 'She loves the boy you pretend to be. She loves a poet, not a thief.'

'I'll be a better man for her,' said Billy. 'She will make me better.'

Creecher took a step forward and towered over him, blocking out the sky and standing like the night in human form.

'Treasure her, then,' he growled. 'Because if you try to prevent Frankenstein from completing his work in any way, I will crush her pretty head, and those of her mother and her friend, before I come for you.'

With that, Creecher turned on his heels and strode away across the hilltops until he disappeared from sight, merging with the dark clouds that seemed to sink to greet him.

Old Thwaite made no comment about the giant's departure. He seemed to accept it with the same fatalism that he accepted their arrival.

In the days that followed, Billy caught the odd glimpse of Creecher on the hills above the farm. He seemed to have become part of the fells now, haunting the crags like some giant of old, more myth than man.

But Creecher made no attempt to speak to Billy, and Billy had no urge to climb to meet him. He waited for the time when he would look to the hilltops and not find the giant there, and know that he and Frankenstein had finally gone north and out of his life.

Billy had wanted to visit Jane, but the giant's words still rankled with him. *She doesn't love you. She loves the boy you pretend to be.*

It took him days to work up the courage to visit again, but when he arrived at the cottage he was told by her mother that she could not see him that day.

Could not, or would not, thought Billy, as he walked forlornly back to the farm. Had Jane already guessed that he was not who he seemed? Had Florence guessed and poisoned her against him?

He suffered three sleepless nights worrying

about all this, and then, on the fourth day, when he returned from mending a wall in one of the top fields, the old man gave him a letter.

'Lady come with this after you'd gone,' he said, eyeing Billy suspiciously. 'Asked for Mr Clerval. Hadn't a clue who she was talking about, and then I figured it must be you.'

The old man fixed him with a stare that Billy could not hold, waiting for an explanation that Billy was not going to give.

'Yes,' said Billy. 'Thanks.'

He walked to the barn, opened the letter and read it. It was written in a neat but faltering hand, the pen pressed so lightly on the paper that the ink had scarcely left a stain in places.

'*Dear Mr Clerval,*' it said.

'*Thank you so much for reading your poem. It was a moment that I will treasure always. A thing of beauty is indeed a joy for ever. I do so wish we had been given more time to get to know each other, but sadly it was not to be. I hope you have a safe journey to Scotland and a happy life thereafter. Yours truly, Jane Cartwright.*'

Billy smiled, slightly puzzled. As if he would have left without saying farewell! How pleased Jane would be when she discovered that he was not, in fact, leaving at all. They would have all the time together that they wanted. 'A moment that I will treasure always,' she'd said. There was something special between them. He knew it.

CHAPTER XLII.

Billy rehearsed what he was going to say over and over again as he walked towards Jane's cottage the next day. He set off intending to tell her the whole truth about his life, excluding only those parts that involved Creecher and Frankenstein – and those only to ensure Jane's safety. Billy was going to prove Creecher wrong. Jane could love him for who he really was.

But even as Billy told himself that this must be the way to go, he was troubled by doubts. It might be too much for her to take. What good would it serve to present to her the whole novel of his life in one short story?

Would it not be better to ease her gently into a greater knowledge of his shortcomings *after* he had won her affections? That was not a lie. It was the truth in chapters.

He had been certain that he was going to admit that he was not really a poet, but she had quoted the poem in her letter. Perhaps it was best that he draw a line under everything that had happened before and start again.

'I'd like to speak to Miss ... Jane,' said Billy, when Florence came to the door. She looked even more dour than normal, her face wan and her eyes red-rimmed.

'I'm afraid that –'

'Look, I just want to see her,' he said quickly, determined not to let this gatekeeper prevent him. 'Tell Jane that –'

'She's dead,' said Florence.

'What?'

'Jane. Jane is dead.' Tears welled up and rolled down her cheeks.

'She can't be ...'

Florence began to sob. Billy grabbed her by both arms and shook her.

'You're lying,' he growled.

Florence stared, wide-eyed, recoiling from him in horror. Billy let her go and she tried to shut the door. He put his foot in the way to prevent her.

'What is the meaning of this?' said Mrs Cartwright, coming to the door. 'Mr Clerval?'

Billy did not reply. He stared past Jane's mother and saw a coffin on the table beyond the kitchen and the hall.

'No!' he shouted, banging the door with his fist and almost knocking it off its hinges. 'No! Why did you have to die, you . . . you . . . ?'

'Please,' said Mrs Cartwright, trembling. 'This is not right, sir. Show some respect.'

'When?' said Billy, stepping backwards. 'How?'

'Last night. She had a weak heart,' sobbed Florence. 'She told you so herself. We were here for peace and quiet. But her heart . . .'

Florence could say no more and Mrs Cartwright put her arm round her and hugged her. Billy stared past them both to the coffin, his eyes burning.

'I would ask you to leave now, sir,' said Mrs Cartwright.

'Don't worry,' he replied coldly. 'I'm going.'

Billy turned and left, heading towards the stone circle. He clenched his teeth together so hard they felt as though they would crack under the strain.

He strode forward to the largest of the stones and punched it with his right hand. Then he punched with his left. Then right and left and right and left, until his knuckles were bleeding and he could stand it no more.

CHAPTER XLIII.

Billy stood on a hilltop, watching Jane's funeral far below. He had barely slept those past couple of days, and his face was drawn and pallid. His heart ached and a drowsy numbness pained his senses. The mourners were few and tiny, like little black beetles.

Billy walked back along the fell tops, sunlight beaming from between the clouds, lighting swathes of bracken and crag. A clap of thunder sounded in the distance and then another, louder this time. The long lake below was as black as pitch, until the wind scratched a thousand ragged waves across its surface.

A twilight fell across the fells and a pulse of lightning lit up quartz veins and the wet scree, where spring water seeped out like a weeping wound.

Rain fell and Billy strode ever higher, reaching a ridge that shelved away steeply on either side. He walked its ragged knife edge, willing the lightning to strike him or the gusting wind to push him off. But the more he walked, the calmer the air around him became.

The storm was moving. The sky was clearing and, one by one, the pin-sharp points of starlight punctured the blackness above.

When, at last, he reached the highest point, Billy slumped, overcome by exhaustion, against the summit cairn. On those cold stones, encased in darkness, he howled out his pain until the tears would come no more.

———◆———

Billy sat in the barn before first light, head bowed, staring at his feet. He could not have felt more ruined if he had been struck by lightning on the fell top. He felt like his soul had been blasted and splintered.

The barn suddenly grew darker and Billy looked up to see Creecher blocking the doorway.

'What do you want?' he asked.

'Your hands ...' said Creecher, noticing the scabs and bruises.

'What do you want?' repeated Billy.

'I did not think we should part on such terms,' said the giant. 'I had wondered, now that you had calmed a little, if you might still accompany me to Scotland. I know that –'

'It's over,' Billy said. 'Between us. It's over. I ain't going anywhere with you.'

Creecher nodded.

'Then I wish you well, mon ami. Whatever you think of me. I hope that you and the girl will –'

'She's dead,' said Billy.

'What?'

'She's dead and you killed her.'

'I never touched her,' Creecher protested.

Billy turned on him, eyes wild.

'You don't have to touch anyone!' he shouted. 'You're like a disease, a curse! She saw you that day at the stones and her poor heart . . . Look at you. You shouldn't even exist. I wish you didn't!'

Creecher hung his head for a while, before speaking again.

'I loved you, Billy,' he said. 'I could not have loved a brother more than I loved you.'

'Well, I never loved you!' Billy yelled. 'Not once! Not for one single second!'

He looked Creecher up and down with an expression of disgust.

'How could anyone love you?' he asked.

Creecher half opened his mouth to speak, then slowly turned round. Billy did not watch him walk away but when he did finally look in that direction, the giant was gone. This time Billy could sense that he was gone for ever.

Old Thwaite was in the kitchen, sitting in his chair by the range, fixing a boot. He looked up as Billy walked in and nodded.

'I'm leaving,' said Billy.

The old man stared at him for a while and then back down at his boot.

'Aye,' he said. 'Well, you take care of yourself.'

Billy stood looking at the old man, not knowing what to do. He felt as though he ought to mark his parting in some way, but he did not know how.

'Thanks for everything,' he said eventually.

'Aye,' said the old man, without looking up.

Billy went to the barn and gathered his meagre possessions and put them in his bag. He found a large purse of coins that Creecher must have left, and he took what he needed from it, leaving the rest for the old man.

He paused in the doorway and looked out at the view; a view he had thought he loved. But it did not move him now.

Billy walked into Keswick and booked himself on the night coach to Manchester. Maybe he would try to work the narrowboats on the way back to London.

He ate a meal of chops and gravy in the coaching inn and, after washing it down with a beer, began to feel a little guilty that he had not paid his respects to Jane. He still felt angry with her for dying on him. For once in his life he had dared to look ahead, but the sunlit future he had glimpsed was no longer there; it had been robbed from him.

Checking that he had time, Billy set off through the dimly lit streets and headed towards the church, which lay on the outskirts of the town, surrounded by its graveyard.

The church gate was locked, but he jumped the wall with ease. It was very dark. The church was a silhouette of deeper blackness against the blue-black night, a crescent moon smiling crookedly behind the spire.

Billy lit the lantern he had hired from the inn. He kept low, with the light close to his body. He didn't want to draw attention to himself.

It was a small churchyard and it did not take him long to work out where Jane must be buried. But when he reached the spot, he was confused to see a fresh grave, open, newly dug.

He walked on, but returned, sure that he had the right place. He checked the gravestone. There, next to the gaping pit, were the words *'Jane Cartwright, beloved daughter'* newly inscribed into the slate. Then he looked into the blackness of the grave.

Holding the lantern over it, Billy could see the coffin at the bottom. The lid had been prised off and then hurriedly replaced. He could see the gap.

'No!' he muttered.

He slid down into the grave pit, taking the lantern with him. He held his breath and pulled open the lid.

There was Jane, pale and beautiful, her long hair loose and flowing round her face. Her white shroud was torn and her chest ripped open. Where her heart would have been, there was now a gaping hole, lolling open like a fool's mouth.

'Noooooo!' screamed Billy.

He staggered back, slipping in the mud and almost falling into the coffin. The lid rattled under his feet as he scrabbled to try to get out. Frankenstein's words came back like an echo – *'I only need one more item and then we can go.'* He'd taken her heart! He'd taken her heart for Creecher's mate!

'You evil bastard!' yelled Billy.

His voice travelled in the darkness and, nearby, doors began to open. Billy struggled again and again to climb out of the pit, his clothes getting covered in mud. He just managed to throw himself over the edge as the sexton arrived at the gate with his keys.

Within seconds, the cry of 'Grave-robbers!' went up, and a group of men tumbled out of a nearby tavern and ran to the sexton's cries.

Others began to arrive and they pointed at Billy, who had dropped the lantern as he made his getaway over the churchyard wall. With angry shouts, they were soon chasing him down the street.

His route away from town was blocked and so he was forced to run back into the centre, where more and more people were being alerted to the crime at the churchyard. There was no way for Billy to stop or explain. He was a dead man if he did not escape.

He ran on without looking round. He could hear the crowd shouting and their hobnails clattering on the cobbles behind him – hobnails that he had no doubt would trample him if they ever caught up.

He turned into an alleyway but it was a dead end. There was a door to his right and, without time to pause or think, he tried the handle and it opened.

There was a man standing in the hallway with a look of complete surprise, and Billy rushed forward, shoving him over. The man fell backwards and Billy leapt over him, heading for the back door as the first of his pursuers reached the front of the house.

Billy pelted through the garden and vaulted the fence into another alleyway that headed downhill, back towards the river.

He could hear that the crowd was on his heels once more, some having gone through the stranger's house, the bulk having gone round. A sideways glance told him that he was going to get cut off if he didn't change his route.

Billy was out of sight of the crowd just long enough to leap behind another fence, where he huddled down and stayed put, listening to the running footsteps pass and fade.

When it was all clear, he ran and hid under a bridge. The crowd were milling about above. The light from their torches and lanterns glittered in the river. Billy could even hear some of them talking about what they would do to him when they found him.

But they didn't find him. Billy stayed shivering under the bridge until even the most determined of the mob had accepted that their quarry must have escaped. Then he slunk away into the night.

CHAPTER XLIV.

Billy became aware of a skylark twittering above his head. It seemed to be the only living thing for miles around and the only sound apart from his own shallow breathing. He had escaped from Keswick in the early hours of the morning and was now walking the drover's track to Ambleside.

Billy was struck by how ridiculous the skylark looked. He had to squint to see it against the blue brightness. And the more he looked and squinted the more ridiculous and hateful the bird became. He wished he had a slingshot to bring it down.

'Hey! What have you got to be so cheerful about?' he called out. 'Why's your heart so full? Look at you, up there, all high and mighty. Go on! Keep flying!'

He picked up a stone and hurled it skyward. 'Soar off into the blue! Sing somewhere I can't hear you! Get off into the sun and burn, why don't you?'

The bird fluttered away. Billy felt exhausted all of a sudden. He pressed his fingers into his eyes, the tips shoving the eyeballs back into the sockets. The pressure made him lightheaded; stars twinkled in the blackness.

When he finally took his hands away and blinked into the daylight, the scene was blurred, as though he were looking through the bottom of a greasy glass.

He took a deep breath and closed his eyes again. A terrible darkness came upon him and he felt like he was being punched and pummelled by a dozen unseen demons. He had to open his eyes again to convince himself that he was alone.

His vision had returned and, if anything, he seemed to see with a sharper clarity than ever before – as if some filter had been taken away. He was overcome with a sense that he now saw the world as it was, stark and without hope.

He shook his head as if to rid himself of any residual fog from his days of delusion. Creecher, Jane – they were a dream and nothing more. He saw that now. He had been asleep. Now he was awake.

London. That was where he belonged. He would seek out old Gratz's nephew. He was a tricky cove but a useful one. What was his name? Fagin. That was it.

As he walked along the lane, Billy's gait seemed to change. He was bigger now. All that walking and heavy work had done wonders. For the first time he felt the new power that seemed to course through his body.

He stretched his neck and thrust out his jaw, setting his face against the world as a sailor might against a hurricane. His arms, heavier now and tipped with meaty fists, swung in rhythm with a walk that had become, by degrees, a swagger.

He turned his nose up at the scents all around as a dandy might baulk at the cesspool's stink. This landscape was poisoned now.

Billy saw a piece of wood leaning against a wall and picked it up. It was dry but still heavy. There seemed to be no rot.

He felt the weight of it and smiled. This would be his souvenir of the place. A little whittling here and there and he would have a decent walking stick come club. Better than a pistol any day.

Billy continued on his way. The lane curved away from him now as it fell downhill towards a hamlet, whose slate roofs he saw ahead.

Two young men stood talking next to an open gate. They quietened as Billy walked towards them and one of them muttered something as he passed. Billy stopped and turned round, retracing his steps.

'What was that?' said Billy.

The man who had muttered did not reply, but looked at his friend and smiled. They were both a good foot taller than Billy and several years older.

'I asked you a question.'

'He don't mean no harm, friend,' said the other man. 'Pay no heed.'

The man who had spoken muttered something else Billy could not catch and then spat on the grass at the foot of the wall.

Billy took a deep breath and looked away. A cloud shadow slid down the fellside towards the valley floor and the light dropped. His grip on the wood tightened. He turned back to the two men and shook his head slowly. Then he swung the club and struck the nearest of them a mighty blow to the side of his head.

The man dropped to the ground, his legs buckling under him, his head hitting the earth with a thud. The second man made half a move towards Billy, but one look into his eyes seemed to make him think again. Cursing, he ran away as fast as he could.

The man at Billy's feet groaned and reached a hand out towards him. Blood was already streaming from a black wound at his temple, red rivulets running down his cheek and neck and filling his ear.

Billy looked down at him. He felt no remorse, no pity. He felt only disgust and anger. Raising the stick above his head, he hit the man again – and saw the face of the sweep looking back – and again – and saw Fletcher – and again – Frankenstein this time – and then one final, mighty blow cracked down on Creecher's broken, bleeding face.

Billy stood there panting in the horrible silence that followed. He turned the stick about. The handle was now a foul thing, filthy with gore, and he went to the brook nearby and washed it and cleaned his hands and doused his face.

People would come before long. He set off up the channel carved by the brook, staying low among the birch and rowan and bracken. In minutes he had rounded the crag and stood on the fell top.

He did not look back for fear of being seen. He must make the most of his head start and cross the hills to the neighbouring valley.

Billy clambered up scree and bracken-covered fellsides, and up over purple granite crags, rarely stopping, barely acknowledging his aching muscles and blistered feet. He stood atop a rock-strewn ridge, the clouds so close he felt he could pull them down and hold them to his filthy face like a damp rag.

A lake lay below: a vast pewter platter, burnished here and there by intermittent sunlight that permeated weakly through the clouds above.

Weeks ago he would have looked on the sight with awe and wonder, but now he gazed in cold contempt at a landscape he had grown to hate. Finally, he spotted a town ahead and made for it, as an exhausted swimmer makes for dry land.

———◆———

Billy swaggered into the courtyard of the coaching inn. He could see the wariness in people's faces as he approached, and revelled in it. A woman pulled her boy nearer to her and Billy smiled and doffed his hat.

'What name is that, sir?' asked the man at the booking office.

'Sikes,' he replied. 'Billy – No, Bill ... Bill Sikes.'

And with that he boarded the coach and settled into his seat. At last, he was going home. As the driver flicked his reins, he closed his eyes and instantly his thoughts turned to Creecher. Where was he now?

Billy pictured the giant striding through a slightly wilder version of Cumbria – he had no real idea what Scotland looked like. He imagined him skulking in whatever cover he could find, haunting the two travellers every step of their journey.

He wondered what would become of the giant without his help. He would certainly find life more difficult. Billy hoped so, anyway. He wanted Creecher to feel the loss of his friendship. That was all the punishment Billy could mete out.

Would Frankenstein ever build the giant his mate and, if he did, what then? If they loved, it would be Jane's heart beating in the breast of that unnatural ogress. Billy's own heart flinched at that realisation and, though his mind refused to return to the thought, something in his soul had been irrevocably damaged by it.

Billy took a deep breath. Just thinking about Creecher and Frankenstein made his blood boil. He needed to cut that part of himself away and leave it behind, along with so much of his life.

That weaker, whining Billy was dead. The new Billy was never going to be beaten or bullied or bossed about by anyone ever again.

Billy thought expectantly of the great black, stinking ants' nest that was London. That was where he belonged. He was a creature of the streets, not the fields. The city held no fears for him now. He would deal with Skinner if he had to. He did not need Creecher any more.

Billy opened his eyes and looked out of the carriage window. A heavy mist lay like a filthy fleece in the bottom of the valley. He closed his eyes once more as the coach rattled down the steep road to be swallowed up in its awful blankness.

READ ON FOR THESE
TERRIFYINGLY TERRIFIC EXTRAS:

- **Inspiration and Sources**
- **Who was the Real Frankenstein?**
- **Chris Priestley's Top Five Monster Movies**
- **Reading Guide**

INSPIRATION AND SOURCES

My fascination with Mary Shelley's creation began when I first saw Boris Karloff turn to face the camera in the 1932 movie of *Frankenstein*. Much as I still love that movie and Karloff's performance in it, my enthusiasm only increased when I eventually read the book and discovered a very different creature.

Frankenstein was first published (anonymously) on 1 January 1818 by Lackington, Hughes, Harding, Mavor & Jones of Finsbury Square in London – where Billy first meets Creecher. Mary was just nineteen years old.

Four years earlier, the pregnant, unmarried Mary Godwin had run away with the (married) radical poet, Percy Bysshe Shelley. She would use many of the sights she saw on their travels as settings for *Frankenstein*.

The idea came to her at the Villa Diodati, a house on the shores of Lake Geneva in Switzerland, rented by the 'mad, bad and dangerous to know' poet Lord Byron, in the cold and rainy summer of 1816.

Mary's half-sister, Claire Clairmont, who was nineteen and pregnant with Byron's daughter, and Byron's doctor, John Polidori, were also in the party. With thunderstorms raging outside, they came up with the idea of a ghost story competition.

Mary had a nightmare that would later become the basis of the novel and two of the most famous characters of all time: the arrogant scientist, Victor Frankenstein, and his terrifying and tragic creature. Mary described the dream in the preface to the 1831 edition:

I saw – with shut eyes, but acute mental vision – I saw the pale student of unhallowed arts kneeling beside the thing he had put together. I saw the hideous phantasm of a man stretched out, and then, on the working of some powerful engine, show signs of life and stir with an uneasy, half-vital motion.

Mary and Shelley were both part of the Romantic Movement, which also included the Lake Poets Samuel Taylor Coleridge and William Wordsworth (who was still living in the Lake District at the time of Billy's visit), and painters such as Constable and Turner.

Mary and Shelley were also very political. Shelley had been sent down from Oxford for atheism and he was spied on by government agents for his radical views. These were troubled times and there were many riots and disturbances in the years preceding *Frankenstein*'s publication. The leaders of the riots were often hanged when caught.

Following the suicide in 1816 of Shelley's first wife, Harriet – she drowned herself in the Serpentine in London's Hyde Park – he and Mary returned to England and married. In 1818 they (and Claire Clairmont) stayed in London in a house in Great Russell Street, near to the old British Museum (in the now demolished Montagu House), before leaving for Italy, hoping to join their old friend, Lord Byron.

Mary's children, William and Clara, both died in Italy and Shelley himself drowned in a boating accident in 1822 in the Bay of Spezia. Shelley's body was cremated on the beach and his heart snatched from the funeral pyre. Mary kept it for the rest of her life, wrapped in a copy of Shelley's 'Adonais' – his poem written on the death of John Keats.

In 1823 – without Mary's permission – *Frankenstein* was turned into a successful play (given the very Jane-Austen-like title of

Presumption). The play departs from the book in many aspects – most significantly, the intelligent, articulate creature of the novel becomes a shambling mute.

Many movies have been made of the book, the first being a silent by Edison Studios as early as 1910. The most famous is the 1932 James Whale version, starring Boris Karloff as the creature and Colin Clive as Frankenstein.

The Romantic poet, John Keats, and his friend Charles Brown, went on a tour of northern England and Scotland in the summer of 1818, stopping off at the Castlerigg stone circle near Keswick on their way – a few days before Billy arrived. Keats didn't seem very impressed and passed this description into his poem 'Hyperion':

Scarce images of life, one here, one there,
Lay vast and edgeways; like a dismal cirque
Of Druid stones, upon a forlorn moor

Keats' 'Endymion' (which Billy passes off as his own work) was published in 1818 but was panned by the critics. Keats was diagnosed with consumption (tuberculosis) – a disease that had already killed his brother Tom – and he moved to Italy in the hope that the climate might help him. He died in 1821 and was buried in the Protestant Cemetery in Rome, in a grave not far from where Shelley's ashes were eventually laid to rest.

Victor Frankenstein and Henry Clerval continued their journey north after leaving the Lake District. If you want to know what happened next, then you will have to read Mary Shelley's *Frankenstein* ...

———•◆•———

Charles Dickens was five years old when *Frankenstein* was published and had been living in London since he was three. His father was in a debtor's prison and, as a boy, Dickens worked ten hours a day pasting labels to cans of shoe polish to help his family.

Oliver Twist – about a boy who is born in a workhouse and is eventually rescued from a life among the thieves of London (thieves that included Bill Sikes and Fagin) – was Dickens' second novel, published in monthly instalments from February 1837, a few months before Queen Victoria came to the throne. If you want to know what became of Billy Sikes, then you will have to read *Oliver Twist* ...

WHO WAS THE REAL FRANKENSTEIN?

There are so many misconceptions about *Frankenstein*. It is a book that everyone knows and yet few people seem to have actually read. There are many screen adaptations and yet almost none of them are true to their source. Everyone recognises an image of Frankenstein when they see it – although what they are recognising is not Frankenstein at all but his creature. So who – or what – was the 'real' Frankenstein?

Well, firstly, the Victor Frankenstein of Mary Shelley's novel was not a doctor. There is no 'Doctor Frankenstein' other than in the movies. Or Baron Frankenstein for that matter. He was not a surgeon. He was not a medical student of any kind. Mary describes him as a 'student of the unhallowed arts'. His passion was alchemy and his discovery of science at university was only of interest insofar as it could further his aim of finding the secret of life itself.

Frankenstein travelled to England in his search for greater knowledge because he knew, as Mary Shelley did, that England was at the forefront of scientific and medical innovation at the beginning of the nineteenth century. And it is in England that my book, *Mister Creecher*, imagines a meeting between Frankenstein's monster and a teenage thief called Billy.

The Romantics were more interested in science than one might at first think. Shelley was fascinated by electricity and had experimented with voltaic batteries. He and Byron were discussing galvanism and speculating about the possibilities of using electricity to spark life into a corpse on the night Mary had her nightmare.

In fact, if there is a 'real' Victor Frankenstein, it is probably Mary's highly strung and excitable husband, the radical poet Percy Bysshe Shelley.

As for the creature, he is not a shuffling mute, but a huge and powerful Romantic anti-hero – more Byron than zombie. He is articulate and complex – more complex than any other character in the novel. He is tall with long black hair. The horror of his appearance comes from its lifelessness, his pale, shrivelled skin, his watery eyes, his white teeth set between thin black lips.

It is almost possible to read *Frankenstein* as a doppelgänger story. They are seldom seen together (by anyone but the reader). The creature does have something of the demonic double about him as he pursues Frankenstein across the frozen wastes. Robert Louis Stevenson would take this idea further with Dr Jekyll and Mr Hyde.

Shelley claimed to have seen his doppelgänger shortly before he drowned at sea. He met his double on the terrace of their villa in Tuscany, and reported that it asked him 'How long do you mean to be content?'

And the creature and Shelley shared the same end. The creature promises to construct a funeral pyre for his own destruction at the novel's climax, and Shelley was burned on an Italian beach on a pyre constructed by friends, including Lord Byron and Edward John Trelawney.

Frankenstein begins his obsessive quest to create life in response to the death of his mother. Mary never knew her mother – the feminist radical Mary Wollstonecraft – who died giving birth to her. Mary Shelley also suffered the deaths of three of her children. One was a prematurely born daughter named Clara. A second daughter, also named Clara, died on the same ill-fated Italian adventure that claimed her father's life.

Most horribly, Mary gave the name William to the boy the creature kills in *Frankenstein*. This was the name of her own son (and of her father,

William Godwin). William Shelley was to die of malaria in Rome, aged three.

By the time the 1831 edition of *Frankenstein* was published, Byron and Keats would also be dead. Tragedy seemed to loom large in Mary's life. Perhaps she, more than anyone, could relate to Frankenstein's dangerous urge to conquer Death.

CHRIS PRIESTLEY'S TOP FIVE MONSTER MOVIES

Cinema and television played a huge part in my development as a writer. In the case of horror fiction, I was encouraged to read the books because of the movies they had inspired, whether it was *Dracula* or *Dr Jekyll and Mr Hyde* or *The Masque of the Red Death*. Here is a list of my top five *Frankenstein*-inspired movies:

FRANKENSTEIN The 1931 James Whale directed movie is an extraordinary creation by any measure. It does owe a debt to Fritz Lang's *Metropolis* from five years earlier, and even to *The Golem* of 1920, but they are cold in comparison. It is Karloff's performance that makes this movie unforgettable and that has made Frankenstein's monster part of our modern mythology.

BRIDE OF FRANKENSTEIN James Whale's second visit to Mary Shelley's novel was a lot stranger than his first and all the better for it. It also features a wonderful double performance by Elsa Lanchester as both Mary Shelley in the prelude and the bride. Now of course, if she was betrothed to anyone, it was the creature not his creator, and in the novel Frankenstein destroys his work before he brings it to life, but as with his first movie, James Whale's lack of respect for his source material produces something a little bit wonderful.

BLADE RUNNER Frankenstein is the godfather of all rebel robot and android movies. Mary Shelley was playing with the issues around what it means to be human a long time before Philip K Dick wrote his novel *Do Androids Dream of Electric Sheep?* (filmed as *Blade Runner* by Ridley Scott). It also owes a debt to *Metropolis* (by way of Film Noir), but the famous dying speech by Rutger Hauer's android before his death seems to have something of the pathos and Romantic grandeur of Mary Shelley's creature.

TERMINATOR 2 The *Terminator* franchise also owes a debt to *Frankenstein*, of course, (and what a great creature Arnold Schwarzenegger would have made) but *Terminator 2* deals more directly with some of the issues in Mary Shelley's novel: about the arrogance of scientists and the unseen and potentially catastrophic consequences of invention. This James Cameron movie – teaming a teenager with the Terminator – was very much in my mind when I wrote *Mister Creecher*.

EDWARD SCISSORHANDS Edward is a composite creature – as is the creature in the movies of *Frankenstein* (although Mary was vague about how the creature was created in her novel). Tim Burton is always fascinated by the bizarre and the freakish and this fascination, as it is here, is usually sympathetic. Edward's scissor-hands change from a disability to the means of creating beauty. A monster movie with a happy ending.

READING GUIDE

THEMES

Nature and Nurture

Is Billy bad by nature? Or is he a criminal because he has no other option, because he has no family, no positive influence? Is the Bill Sikes of the book's end a monster because of the terrible things that have happened to him during the story? Is Creecher murderous and violent because he was made that way or because Frankenstein abandoned him and the world looks at him in horror?

Town and Country, and Modernity

London is unnatural, foggy, suffocating. Billy has no option but to steal. Out in the country, he finds labour. He grows strong. He feels fresh. What is the impact of town? Is modern civilisation unhealthy? Is modern science part of that?

Crime and Punishment, and Responsibility

Billy and Creecher steal to live. Creecher murders when it suits his purpose. They do these things with little regret. Are any crimes justified? How important is it that they pay for their crimes?

They feel responsibility towards each other at various points. Does this redeem their characters at all?

WRITING STYLE

By using characters the reader will recognise – all readers will know who Creecher and Frankenstein are, and the quicker will see Fagin, Bill Sikes, Shelley and others – Priestley draws the reader into a world which is half new and half familiar.

This is echoed by his language – he does not shy away from the horror of his subject, and he has chosen to use a rich vocabulary and colourful metaphors to evoke his Victorian setting. There is nothing parodic about it, and nothing unclear to the modern reader, but it nods to his story's Dickensian and Gothic roots.

The slow emergence of the truth, the frequent cliffhangers have twin roots – they are what one might expect from Young Adult fiction, but they also draw on the Dickensian tradition of stories serialised in separate, thrilling episodes.

QUESTIONS TO DISCUSS

Crime

'Amber light seeped like honey from upstairs windows, glowing between the heavy curtains and solid shutters that formed a barrier to the cold and to the fear-filled world beyond.' (p.4)

'He looked at it with the cynical detachment that years on the street had gifted him. He did not know this man and did not care how he had lived or how he came to die. Only the rich could afford to be sentimental. He cared for no one but himself. He was alone. Everyone was.' (p.5)

• Do you sympathise at all with Billy's attitude? How does it make you think about present-day crime?

Murder

'All those thousands of people and yet it was *his* mother who had to die. Billy wondered how many of the people milling around the cathedral were there that day. Why did they live and not her? He would have killed any one of them with his bare hands if it would have brought her back to life.

The image of Creecher's mighty hands around

Fletcher's head came fleetingly into his mind's eye again, but he was able to waft it away. He would not feel remorse for that animal. Creecher had done the world a favour.' (p.101)

• Is it OK to think like this about your mother? Would killing someone random be justified to save her? Or is it understandable but not justified? What is the difference between thinking such a thing and acting on the thought?
• Did Creecher really do the world a favour by killing Fletcher?
• What about the other murders? The grave-robbers? Frankenstein's brother?
• How does the talk of murder during the book change how you feel and sympathise with the protagonists?

Heaven and Hell
'*Maybe I've died,* he thought. *Maybe this is what the world is like when you die.* But if he was dead, then where was this? He was fairly sure he wouldn't gain entry through heaven's pearly gates, but it didn't look much like hell either.

Maybe he was in that other place: the place where you waited to have your fate decided. He tried to remember its name but could not recall it. Perhaps this was all there was.' (p.15/16)

• Billy has this thought early in the book, and soon after dreams of being a sweep, stuck between letting go and dropping into the fire and climbing up into the light. How important is this image? Where does language of heaven, hell, devils and angels recur?

• What other images recur? How about city versus country? The fog? When is the last time Billy goes into the fog? What does it mean?

Novels
'"Shut up," said Billy, smiling. "You're reading too many of these novels of yours. You're beginning to sound like a woman."' (p.323)

• Billy says several times that reading, especially novels, is womanish. Is it? Was it then? What has changed? Think of the female characters in the book. What is their role?

Pretence
'"We were never friends!" yelled Billy. "We were just two freaks walking in the same direction!"' (p.360)

'Billy had wanted to visit Jane, but the giant's words still rankled with him. *She doesn't love you. She loves the boy you pretend to be.*' (p.361)

• Is Billy right? Were they ever truly friends? Could either of them ever fit in, be normal? Victor Frankenstein said they could never be friends. What more is there to friendship beyond walking in the same direction?
• Is Creecher right? Do you blame Billy for pretending to be a poet?
• What is the difference between being something and pretending to be something? Is Creecher pretending to be a person or is he a person? Is Billy always a thief, but pretends for a short while that he might be something else?

Nature or Nurture?
'"And whose fault is that?" said Billy. "Who built him? It's your blood in his veins!"

"Can a father be responsible for every action of his son? How could I know that I would make a monster?"' (p.352)

'But Billy was incapable of being a bad thief. It was like asking a falcon to slow its flight. It just wasn't in his nature. *You are what you are,* thought Billy. *That's all there is. That's all there ever is.'* (p.45)

'That weaker, whining Billy was dead. The new Billy was never going to be beaten or bullied or bossed about by anyone ever again.' (p.384)

• What made Creecher a monster? Was it his father's blood? Or was it his father's lack of love?
• What made Billy a monster? Was he really born to be a thief, and nothing could have changed his nature? Or was it because he was beaten and bullied? Or was it bad luck and the death of Jane?
• What do you think made Fletcher a monster? Think of some monsters from the news. What made them?

Structure and Storytelling
• How do you feel about the characters at different points in the story? When do you sympathise with them and why? Why do you lose sympathy? When does the author give you clues and when does he do things you don't expect?

These notes are available to download at: www.bloomsbury.com/readingguides